The Heart of Denise

and Other Tales

BY

S. LEVETT YEATS

Author of "The Chevalier d'Aunac,"
"The Honour of Savelli," etc.

NEW YORK

LONGMANS, GREEN, AND CO.

LONDON AND BOMBAY

1899

ROBERT DRUMMOND, PRINTER, NEW YORK.

CONTENTS.

THE HEART OF DENISE.

PAGE

I. M. DE LORGNAC'S PRICE...................... 1

II. THE ORATORY.............................. 13

III. THE SPUR OF LES ESCHELLES............... 22

IV. AT AMBAZAC.............................. 33

V. M. LE MARQUIS LEADS HIS HIGHEST TRUMP..... 45

VI. AT THE SIGN OF THE GOLDEN FROG........... 55

VII. UNMASKED 65

VIII. BLAISE DE LORGNAC...................... 75

IX. LA COQUILLE'S MESSAGE................... 88

X. MONSIEUR LE CHEVALIER IS PAID IN FULL..... 98

THE CAPTAIN MORATTI'S LAST AFFAIR.

I. "ARCADES AMBO"........................... 107

II. AT "THE DEVIL ON TWO STICKS"............. 117

III. FELICITÀ 125

IV. CONCLUSION—THE TORRE DOLOROSA........... 134

THE TREASURE OF SHAGUL..................... 143

THE FOOT OF GAUTAMA........................ 165

v

THE DEVIL'S MANUSCRIPT.

PAGE

I. THE BLACK PACKET............................ 191

II. THE RED TRIDENT............................. 201

III. "THE MARK OF THE BEAST".................... 208

UNDER THE ACHILLES............................ 217

THE MADNESS OF SHERE BAHADUR.............. 229

REGINE'S APE...................................... 239

A SHADOW OF THE PAST.......................... 253

THE HEART OF DENISE

CHAPTER I.

ONE afternoon I sat alone in the little anteroom before the Queen Mother's cabinet. In front of me was an open door. The curtains of violet velvet, spangled with golden lilies, were half drawn, and beyond extended a long, narrow, and gloomy corridor, leading into the main salon of the Hôtel de Soissons, from which the sound of music and occasional laughter came to me. My sister maids of honour were there, doubtless making merry as was their wont with the cavaliers of the court, and I longed to be with them, instead of watching away the hours in the little prison, I can call it no less, that led to the Queen's closet.

In the corridor were two sentries standing as motionless as statues. They were in shadow, except where here and there a straggling gleam of light caught their armour with dazzling effect, and M. de Lorgnac, the

lieutenant of the guard, paced slowly up and down the
full length of the passage, twisting his dark moustache,
and turning abruptly when he came within a few feet
of the entrance to the anteroom.

I was so dull and wearied that it would have been
something even to talk to M. de Lorgnac, bear though
he was, but he took no more notice of me than if I
were a stick or a stone, and yet there were, I do not
know how many, who would have given their ears for a
tête-à-tête with Denise de Mieux.

I ought not to have been surprised, for the lieutenant
showed no more favour to any one else than he did to
me, and during the year or more I had been here, enjoying for the first time in my life the gaieties of the
Court, after my days in apron-strings at Lespaille, my
uncle de Tavannes' seat, I had not, nor had a soul as
far as I knew, seen M. de Lorgnac exchange more than
a formal bow and a half-dozen words with any woman.
He was poor as a homeless cat, his patrimony, as we
heard, being but a sword and a ruined tower somewhere
in the Corrèze.   So, as he had nothing to recommend
him except a tall, straight figure, and a reputation for
bravery—qualities that were shared by a hundred others
with more agreeable manners, we left Monsieur L'Ours,
as we nicknamed him, to himself, and, to say the truth,
he did not seem much discomposed by our neglect.

As for me I hardly noticed his existence, sometimes
barely returning his bow; but often have I caught him
observing me gravely with a troubled look in his grey
eyes, and as ill-luck would have it, this was ever when
I was engaged in some foolish diversion, and I used to
feel furious, as I thought he was playing the spy on

me, and press on to other folly, over which, in the solitude of my room, I would stamp my foot with vexation, and sometimes shed tears of anger.

This afternoon, when I thought of the long hours I had to spend waiting the Queen's pleasure, of the mellow sunlight which I could see through the glazing of the dormer window that lit the room, of the gaiety and brightness outside, I felt dull and wearied beyond description. I had foolishly neglected to bring a book or my embroidery, so that even my fingers had to be still, and in my utter boredom I believe I should have actually welcomed the company of Catherine's hideous dwarf, Majosky.

It had come to me that perhaps M. de Lorgnac, who had, no doubt, a weary enough watch in the corridor, might feel disposed to beguile a little of his tedium, and to amuse me for a few minutes, and I had purposely drawn the curtains and opened the door of the anteroom so that he might see I was there, and alone, and that the door of the Queen Mother's cabinet was shut. I then, I confess it, put myself in the most becoming attitude I could think of, but, as I have said before, he took not the slightest notice of me, and walked up and down, *tramp, tramp,* backwards and forwards as if he were a piece of clockwork—like that which Messer Cosmo, the Italian, made for Monsieur, the King's brother.

I began to feel furious at the slight—it was no less I considered—that he was putting on me, and wished I had the tongue and the spirit of Mademoiselle de Chateauneuf, so that I could make my gentleman smart as she did M. de Luxembourg. For a moment or so I

pulled at the silken fringe of my *tourette-de-nez,* and
then made up my mind to show M. de Lorgnac that the
very sight of him was unpleasant to me. So I waited
until in his march he came to a yard or so from the spot
where he regularly turned on his heel, and then, springing up, attempted to draw the curtains across the door.
Somehow or other they would not move, and de Lorgnac stepped forward quietly and pulled them together.
As he did this our eyes met, and there was the twinkle
of a smile in his glance, as if he had seen through my
artifices and was laughing at them. I felt my face grow
warm, and was grateful that the light was behind me;
but I thanked him icily, and with his usual stiff bow
he turned off without a word.

I came back to my seat, my face crimson, my
eyes swimming with tears, and feeling if there was a
man on earth that I hated it was the lieutenant of the
guard.

It had a good two hours or so to run before my time
of waiting would be over, and I may take the plunge
now, and confess that the lengthened period of attendance to which I was subjected, was in a measure a punishment, for my having ridden out alone with M. de
Clermont, and, owing to an accident that befell my
horse, had not been able to return until very late. The
ill-chance which followed all my girlish escapades was
not wanting on this occasion, with the result, that
whereas ten others might have escaped, I was observed
in what was after all but a harmless frolic, and my
conduct reported on—and Madame, who had a weak
enough eye for follies, and sometimes sins, that were
committed by rule—she loved to direct our ill-doings—

rated me soundly and imposed this penance, and perhaps the worse punishment that was to follow, on me.

In the anteroom there was but a cushioned stool for the lady in waiting, and this was placed close to the door, so that one could hear Queen Catherine calling, for she never rang for us, as did the Lorrainer for even such ladies as the Duchesse de Nemours, the mother of Guise.

I pushed the seat closer towards the door and, hardly thinking what I was doing, leaned my head against the woodwork and dropped off into a sort of troubled doze. How long I slept in this manner I cannot say; but I was suddenly aroused by the distinct mention of my name, followed by a laugh from within the cabinet. I looked up in affright, for the laugh was the King's, and for the moment I wondered how he had passed in, then recollecting the private passage I knew that he must have come in thence. I would have withdrawn, but the mention of my name coupled with the King's laughter aroused my curiosity, and I remained in my position, making, however, a bargain with my conscience by removing my head from the carved oak of the door. It was my duty to be where I was, and although I would make no effort to listen, yet if those within were talking of me, and loud enough for me to hear, I thought it no harm to stay, especially as it was Henri who was speaking, for I knew enough to be aware that no one was safe from his scandalous tongue. I may have been wrong in acting as I did, but I do not think there is one woman in a thousand who would have done otherwise, supposing her to be as I was—but one-and-twenty years of age.

So thick, however, was the door, that, my head once removed, I could hear but snatches of the converse within.

"It is his price, Madame," I heard the King say, "and, after all, it is a cheap one, considering her escapade with de Clermont. *Morbleu!* But he is a sad dog!"

And then came another surprise, for the gruff voice of my uncle, the Marshal de Tavannes, added:

"Cheap or dear! I for one am willing that it should be paid, and at once. She has brought disgrace enough on our house already. As for the man; if poor he is noble and as brave as his sword. He is well able to look after her."

"If he keeps his head," put in the King, whilst my ears burned at the uncomplimentary speech of my guardian, and my heart began to sink. Then came something I did not catch from Catherine, and after that a murmur of indistinct voices. At last the King's high-pitched tones rose again. It was a voice that seemed to drill its way through the door.

"Enough! It is agreed that we pay in advance—eh, Tavannes? Send for the little baggage, if she is, as you say, here, and we will tell her at once. The matter does not admit of any delay. St. Blaise! I should say that after thirty a man must be mad to peril his neck for any woman!"

I rose from my seat trembling all over with anger and apprehension, and as I did so the Queen Mother's voice rang out sharply:

"Mademoiselle de Mieux!"

The next moment the door opened, and the dwarf Majosky put out his leering face.

"Enter, mademoiselle!" he said, with a grotesque bow, adding in a rapid, malignant whisper as I passed him, "You are going to be married—to me."

At any other time I would have spared no pains to get him punished for his insolence; but now, so taken aback was I at what I had heard, that I scarcely noticed him, and entered the room as if in a dream. Indeed, it was only with an effort that I recollected myself sufficiently to make my reverence to the King. He called out as I did so, "*Mordieu!* I retract, Tavannes! I retract! Faith! I almost feel as if I could take the adventure on myself!"

A slight exclamation of annoyance escaped the Queen, and Tavannes said coldly:

"Perhaps your Majesty had better inform my niece of your good pleasure," adding grimly, "and I guarantee mademoiselle's obedience."

There was a minute or so of silence, during which the King was, as it were, picking his words, whilst I stood before him. Majosky shuffled down at Catherine's feet, and watched me with his wicked, blinking eyes. I do not remember to have looked around me, and yet every little detail of that scene will remain stamped on my memory until the day I die.

Madame, the Queen Mother, was at her secretary, her fingers toying with a jewelled paper-knife, and her white face and glittering eyes fixed steadily on me, eyes with that pitiless look in them which we all knew so well, and which made the most daring of us tremble. A little to my right stood de Tavannes, one hand on the back of a chair, and stroking his grizzled beard with the other. Before me, on a coffer, whereon he had negligently thrown himself, was the King, and he surveyed me without speaking, with a half-approving, half-sarcastic look that made my blood tingle, and almost gave me back my courage.

In sharp contrast to the solemn black of Catherine's robes and the stern soldierly marshal was the figure of the King. Henri was dressed in his favourite colours, orange, green, and tan, with a short cloak of the same three hues hanging from his left shoulder. His pourpoint was open at the throat, around which was clasped a necklet of pearls, and he wore three ruffs, one such as we women wear, of lace that fell over the shoulders, and two smaller ones as stiff as starch could make them. He wore earrings, there were rings on his embroidered gloves, and all over his person, from his sleeves to the aigrette he wore on the little turban over his peruke, a multitude of gems glittered. On his left side, near his sword hilt, was a bunch of medallions of ladies who had smiled on him, and this was balanced on the other hand by an equally large cluster of charms and relics. As he sat there he kept tapping the end of one of his shoes with a little cane, whilst he surveyed me with an almost insulting glance in the mocking eyes that looked out from his painted cheeks.

The silence was like to have become embarrassing had not Catherine, impatient of delay, put in with that even voice of hers :

" Perhaps I had better explain your Majesty's commands ; " and then without waiting for an answer she went on, looking me straight in the face—

' " Mademoiselle. In his thought for your welfare—a kindness you have not deserved—the King has been

pleased to decide on your marriage. Circumstances
necessitate the ceremony being performed at once, and
I have to tell you that it will take place three hours
hence. His Majesty will do you the honour of being
himself present on the occasion."

This was beyond my worst fears. I was speechless,
and glanced from one to the other in supplication; but
I saw no ray of pity in their faces. Alas! These were
the three iron hearts that had sat and planned the
Massacre.

The Queen's face was as stone. The King half closed
his eyes, and his lips curled into a smile as if he enjoyed the situation; but my uncle, within whose bluff
exterior was a subtle, cruel heart, spoke out harshly :

"You hear, mademoiselle! Thank the King, and
get you gone to make ready. I am sick of your endless flirtations, and there must be an end to them—
there must be no more talk of your frivolities."

Anger brought back my courage, and half turning
away from Tavannes, I said to the Queen :

"I thank the King, madame, for his kindness. Perhaps you will add to it by telling me the name of the
gentleman who intends to honour me by making me his
wife."

"*Arnidieu!* She makes a point," laughed the King.

"She shall marry a stick if I will it," said de Tavannes ; but Madame the Queen Mother lifted her hand
in deprecation.

"It is M. de Lorgnac," she said.

"De Lorgnac! De Lorgnac!" I gasped, hardly believing my ears. "Oh, madame! It is impossible. ▸ I
hate him. What have I done to be forced into this ?

Your Majesty," and I turned to the King, " I will not marry that man."

" Well, would you prefer de Clermont ? " he asked, with a little laugh ; but de Tavannes burst out :

" Sire ! This matter admits of no delay. She shall marry de Lorgnac, if I have to drag her to the altar."

" Thank you, monsieur," I said with a courtesy ; " it is kindness itself that you, the Count de Tavannes, peer and marshal of France, show to your sister's child."

He winced at my words; but Catherine again interposed.

" Mademoiselle ! you do not understand ; and if I hurt you now it is your own fault. Let me tell you that for a tithe of your follies Mademoiselle de Torigny was banished from court to a nunnery. You may not be aware of it, but the whole world, at least our world, and that is enough for us, is talking of your affair with de Clermont, who, as you well know, is an affianced man. It is for the sake of your house, for your own good name, and because you will do the King a great service by obeying, that this has been decided on, and you must—do you hear ?—must do as we bid you."

She dropped her words out one by one, cool, passionless, and brutal in their clearness. My face was hot with shame and anger, and yet I knew that the ribald tongues that spared not the King's sister would not spare me. I, the heiress of Mieux, to be a by-word in the court ! I to be married out of hand like a laundress of the *coulisse !* It was too much ! It was unbearable ! And to be bound to de Lorgnac above all others ! Was ever woman wooed and wed as I ?

I burst into a passion of angry tears. I went so far as to humble myself on my knees; but Henri only laughed and slipped out by the secret door, and de Tavannes followed him with a rough oath.

"Say this is a jest, madame!" I sobbed out to the Queen. "I am punished enough. Say it is a jest. It must be so. You do not mean it. It is too cruel!"

"No more is happening to you than what the daughters of France have to bear sometimes."

"That should make you the more pitiful, madame, for such as I. Let me go, madame, to a nunnery—even to that of Our Lady of Lespaille—but spare me this!"

"It is impossible," she said sharply. "See, here is Madame de Martigny come, and she will conduct you to your room. Tush! It is nothing after all, girl. And it will be better than a convent and a lost name. Do not make a scene."

I rose to my feet stunned and bewildered, and Madame de Martigny put her arm through mine, and dried my eyes with her kerchief.

"Come, mademoiselle," she said, "we have to pass through the corridor to gain your apartment. Keep up your heart!"

"I offer my escort," mocked the dwarf, "and will go so far as to take M. de Lorgnac's place, if your royal pleasure will allow—ah! ah!"—and he broke into a shriek, for Catherine had swiftly and silently raised a dog-whip, and brought it across his shoulders as he sat crouching at her feet.

"Begone!" she said. "Another speech like that and I break you on the wheel!" Then she turned to Madame de Martigny.

"Take her away by the private door. She is not fit
to see or be seen now. Tell Parè to give her a cordial
if she needs it, and see that she is ready in time. Go,
mademoiselle, and be a brave girl!"

CHAPTER II.

You who read this will please remember that I was
but a girl, and that my powers of resistance were limited. Some of you, perhaps, may have gone through the
same ordeal, not in the rough-and-ready way that I had
to make the passage, but through a slower if not less
certain mill. The result being the same in both cases,
to wit, that you have stood, as I did, at the altar with
vows on your lips that you felt in your heart were false.

A thought had struck me when I was led back to my
room, and that was to throw myself on the mercy of de
Lorgnac. But means of communication with him were
denied to me by the foresight of my persecutors. Even
my maid, Mousette, was not allowed to see me, and
Madame de Martigny, though kindness itself in every
other way, absolutely refused to lend herself to my sug-
gestion that she should aid me, if only to the extent
of bearing a note from me to my future husband, in
which I meant to implore him, as a man of honour and
a gentleman, not to force this marriage upon me. I
then tried Parè, who, by the Queen's command, had
been sent to me. He brought me a cordial with his own
hands, and to him I made my request, notwithstanding

13

all Madame de Martigny's protests, to carry my note to
de Lorgnac. He listened with that acute attention
peculiar to him, and answered :

"Mademoiselle ! I have not yet discovered the
balsam that will heal a severed neck—you must excuse
me."

When he left, Madame de Martigny tried to comfort
me in her kindly way.

"My dear," she said, "after all it is not so very terrible. I myself never saw M. de Martigny more than
twice before we were married, and yet I have learned
to love him, and we are very happy. Believe me ! Love
before marriage does not always mean happiness. In
five years it will become a friendship—that is all. It
is best to start as I did, so that there will be no
awakenings. As for de Lorgnac—rest you assured that
monsieur is well aware of the state of your mind towards
him, else he would never have taken the course he has
adopted. Be certain, therefore, that all appeal to him
will be in vain ! "

I felt the force of the last words and was silent, and
then de Clermont's face came before me, very clear and
distinct, and with a sob I broke down once again and
gave way to tears.

I will pass over the rest of the time until I found
myself ready for the ceremony, noting only with surprise, that I was to be married in a riding-habit, as if
the wedding was to be instantly followed by a journey.
Unhinged though I was, I asked the reason for this, but
Madame de Martigny could only say it was the Queen's
order, and I honestly believe she had no further explanation to offer.

At the door of the oratory the marshal met me, and led me into the chapel, which was but dimly lighted, and where my husband that was to be, was already standing booted and spurred, ready, like myself, to take to horse. There were a dozen or so of people grouped around, and one seated figure which I felt was that of the King. I made a half-glance towards him, but dared not look again, for behind Henri's chair was de Clermont, gay and brilliant, in marked contrast to the sombre, if stately, figure of de Lorgnac.

At last the time came when I placed a hand as cold as stone in that of my husband, and the words were spoken which made us man and wife. When it was all over, and we had turned to bow to the King, de Clermont stepped forward and clasped a jewelled collar round my neck, saying in a loud voice, " In the King's name," and then, aided by the dim light, and with unexampled daring, he swiftly snatched away one of my gloves, which I held in my hand, with a whisper of " This for me."

Henri spoke a few jesting words, and then rising, left the chapel abruptly, followed by de Clermont; but those who remained, came round us with congratulations that sounded idle and hollow to me. It was then that I noticed for the first time that Catherine was not present, although I saw Queen Margot, and Madame de Canillac there. The marshal, however, cut the buzz of voices short.

" The horses are ready, de Lorgnac, and, as arranged, you start to-night. And now, my good niece, adieu, and good fortune be with you and your husband."

With that he bent, and touching my forehead with

his stiff moustache, stepped back a pace to let us pass.

As I walked by my husband's side, dazed and giddy, with a humming in my ears, there came back to me with a swift and insistent force, the words of the vows, which, if I had not spoken, I had given a tacit assent to. They were none the less binding on this account. Two of them I could not keep. One cannot control one's soul, and I felt that in this respect my life would be henceforth a living lie; but one I thought I might observe, and that was the oath to obey ; yet even in the short passage leading from the oratory to the entrance to the chapel, my heart flamed up in rebellion, and, with a sudden movement, I withdrew my hand from my husband's arm, and biting my lips till the blood came, forced myself to keep by his side. He made no effort to restrain me, spoke never a word, until we came to the door where the horses were waiting, with half-a-dozen armed and mounted men. Here de Lorgnac turned to me, saying, almost in a whisper, " May I help you to mount ? "

I made a movement of my hand in the negative, and he stepped back ; but the animal was restive, and at last I was forced to accept his aid. As we passed out of the gateway, riding side by side, I spoke for the first time.

" May I ask where you are going to take me, Monsieur de Lorgnac ? "

He answered, speaking as before, in low tones, " I thought you knew—you should have been told. We go first to the house of Madame de Termes."

Like lightning it came to me that the man was afraid of me. I cannot say how I knew it. I felt it, and made up my mind to use my advantage, with a vengeful

joy at being able to make my bear dance to my tune.
I therefore broke in upon his speech.

"Enough, monsieur! I should not have asked the
question. It is a wife's duty to obey without inquiry."

I looked him full in the face as I said this coldly, and
he touched his horse with the spur and rode a yard or
two in front of me, muttering something indistinctly.
But my heart was leaping at the discovery, and I inwardly thanked God that it was to Madame de Termes
we were to go, for apart from the fact that both she and
her husband, whose lands of Termes marched with
mine, had been life-long friends of our house, she was
one whom I knew to be the noblest and best of women.
I was not aware that she was known to de Lorgnac; but
I hid my curiosity and asked no questions, and there
was no further speech between my husband and myself
until we came to our destination. As we entered the
courtyard of the Hôtel de Termes all appeared to be
bustle and confusion within, and the flare of torches
fell on moving figures hurrying to and fro, on saddled
horses and packed mules, and on the flash and gleam
of arms. My surprise overcame my resolve of silence,
and I asked aloud, "Surely Madame de Termes is not
leaving Paris?"

"News has come that the Vicomte is grievously ill
in his government of Perigueux, and Madame is hastening there."

"And we travel with her? There! It is impossible,
monsieur, that I can face so long a journey without
some preparation. It is cruel to expect this of me."

"It is the King's order that we leave Paris to-night,
and I have done my best."

"Say your worst, monsieur ; it will be more correct," and then we came to the door. We appeared to be expected, for we were at once ushered up the stairway into a large reception room, where Madame stood almost ready to start, for her cloak was lying on a chair, and she held her mask in her hand. She came forward to meet us, but as the light fell on my face, she started back with a little cry :

"You, Denise—you ! My dear, I did not know it was you who were to travel with me. You are thrice welcome," and she took me in her arms and kissed my cold cheek. "I was but told," she went on, "that a lady travelling to Guyenne would join my party, which would be escorted by M. de Lorgnac. But what is the matter, child ? You are white as a sheet, and shiver all over. You are not fit for a long journey."

"M. de Lorgnac thinks otherwise, madame."

"Blaise de Lorgnac ! What has he to do with it ? " and the spirited old lady, one arm round my waist, turned and faced my husband, who stood a little way off, fumbling with the hat he held in his hand.

"It is a wife's duty to obey, madame, not to question."

I felt her arm tighten round my waist, and I too turned and faced de Lorgnac, who looked like a great dog caught in some fault.

"A wife's duty to obey ! " exclaimed Madame ; "but that does not concern you. Stay ! What do you mean, child ? "

"I mean, madame, that I was married to M. de Lorgnac scarce an hour ago."

Her hand dropped from my side, and she looked from one to the other of us in amazement.

" I cannot understand," she said.

" It is for my husband to explain," I said bitterly. " It is for the gentleman, to whom we are to trust our lives on this journey, to say in how knightly a manner he can treat a woman."

And there de Lorgnac stood, both of us looking at him, his forehead burning and his eyes cast down. Even then a little pang of pity went through me to see him thus humbled, so strangely does God fashion the hearts of us women. But I hardened myself. I was determined to spare him nothing, and to measure out in full to him a cup of bitterness for the draught he had made me drink.

" Speak, man," exclaimed Madame. " Have you no voice ? "

" He works in silence, madame," I burst in with an uncontrollable gust of anger; " he lies in silence. Shall I tell you what has happened ? I, Denise de Mieux, am neither more nor less than M. de Lorgnac's price—the hire he has received for a business he has to perform for the King. What it is I know not—perhaps something that no other gentleman would undertake. All that I know is that I, and my estates of Mieux, have become the property of this man, who stands before us, and is, God help me, my husband. Madame, five hours ago, I had not spoken ten words to him in my life, and now I am here, as much his property, as the valise his lackey bears behind his saddle."

" Hush, dear—be still—you forget yourself," and

Madame drew me once more to her side and turned to my husband.

"Is this true, Blaise de Lorgnac? Or is the child ill and raving? Answer, man!"

"It is," he answered hoarsely, "every word."

In the silence that ensued I might have heard my glove fall, and then Madame, with a stiff little bow to my husband, said, "Pray excuse me for a moment," and stepped out of the room. He would have held the door for her, but she waved him aside, and he moved back and faced me, and for the first time we were alone together.

In the meanwhile I had made up my mind. I had repeated parrot-like the words that it was my duty to obey. I had vowed to follow my husband whithersoever he went; but vow or no vow I felt it was impossible, and I spoke out.

"Monsieur, you stand self-convicted. You have pleaded guilty to every charge I have made. Now hear me before Madame comes back, for I wish to spare you as much as possible. I have been forced into this marriage; but I am as dead to you as though we had never met. I decline to accept the position you have prepared for me, and our paths separate now. Would to God they had never crossed! I shall throw myself on the protection of Madame de Termes, and at the first opportunity shall seek the refuge of a convent. You will have to do your work without your hire, M. de Lorgnac."

He made a step forward, and laid his hand on my cloak.

"Denise—hear me—I love you."

"You mean my château and lands of Mieux. Why add a lie to what you have already done ? It is hardly necessary," and I moved out of his reach.

His hand dropped to his side as he turned from me, and at the same time Madame re-entered the room.

"Monsieur," she said, "I fear the honour of your escort is too great for such as I, and I have arranged to travel with such protection as my own people can give me. As for this poor girl here, if she is willing to go with me, I will take the risk of the King's anger—and yours. She shall go with us, I say, and if there is a spark of honour left in you, you will leave her alone."

"She is free as air," he answered.

"Then, monsieur, you will excuse me ; but time is pressing."

CHAPTER III.

THE SPUR OF LES ESCHELLES.

DE LORGNAC was gone. Through the open window overlooking the courtyard, that let in the warm summer evening, we heard him give an order to his men in a quick, resolute voice, far different from the low tones in which he had spoken before, and then he and his troop rode off at a rapid trot in the direction, as it seemed, of the Porte St. Honoré. I could hardly realize that I was free and that de Lorgnac had resigned me without a struggle. All that I could think of was that he was gone, and with a quick gasp of relief I turned to my friend.

"Oh, madame ! How can I thank you ? What shall I say ? "

"Say nothing to me, my child, but rather thank the good God that there was a little of honour left in that man. And now, before we start, you must have some refreshment."

"I cannot—indeed, no. I am ready to go at once. I want to put leagues between me and Paris."

"You must be guided by me now, Denise," and as she spoke a servant brought in some soup and a flask of wine. Despite my protests I was forced to swallow something, though I felt that I was choking ; yet the little Frontignac I drank, I not being used to wine, seemed to steady my shaking limbs and restore my scattered faculties.

As we put on our cloaks and demi-masks preparatory to starting, Madame de Termes kept saying to herself, " I cannot understand—Blaise de Lorgnac to lend himself to a thing like this ! I would have staked my life on him. There is something behind this, child," and she put a hand on each of my shoulders and looked me full in the eyes. " Have you told me all—have you withheld nothing ? "

" Has he not himself admitted what I said, madame ? If that is not enough I will add every word of what I know ; " and as we stood there I detailed what I have already told, forcing myself to go on with the story once or twice when I felt myself being unnerved, and finishing with a quick, " And, madame, I was taken by storm. Indeed, I hardly know even if this is not some frightful dream."

" Would it were so," she said, and added, " Denise, I believe every word you say ; and yet there is something behind de Lorgnac's action. I know him well. He would never lend himself to be the tool of others. Once, however, at Perigueux you will be safe with the Vicomte and myself, and it will be a long arm that would drag you thence—nothing short of that of the Medicis. But Catherine owes much to de Termes ; and now let us start."

What was my surprise when we reached the court-yard, to hear my maid Mousette's voice, and I saw her perched on a little nag, already engaged in a flirtation with one of the men. When I spoke to her she pressed her horse forward and began hurriedly :

"I was sent here with Madame's things," she said. "I am afraid the valises are but hastily packed, and much has had to be left behind ; but Madame will excuse me, I know ; it was all so quick, and I had so little time."

"Thank you, Mousette," and I turned to my horse, her address of Madame ringing strangely in my ears.

We were, including Madame de Termes' servants, who were well armed, a party of about twelve, small enough to face the danger of the road in those unsettled days, but no thought of this struck me, and as for Madame de Termes, she would, I do believe, have braved the journey alone, so anxious was she to be by the Vicomte's side, for between herself and the stout old soldier, who held the lieutenancy of Périgord, there existed the deepest affection.

As we rode down the Bourdonnais, I could not help thinking to myself how noble a spirit it was that animated my friend. Not for one moment had she allowed her own trouble to stand in the way of her helping me. Her husband, whom, as I have said, she dearly loved, was ill, perhaps dying, and yet in her sympathy and pity for me, she had let no word drop about him, except the cheery assurance of his protection. Nevertheless, as we rode on, she ever kept turning towards Lalande, her equerry, and bade him urge the lagging baggage animals on. Passing the Grand Chatelet, we crossed the arms of the river by the Pont au Change, and the Pont St. Michel, and kept steadily down the Rue de la Harpe towards the Porte St. Martin. We gained this not a moment too soon, for as the last of the baggage animals passed it, we heard the officer give the word to lower

the drawbridge and close the gates. The clanking of
the chains, and the creaking of the huge doors came to
me with something of relief in them, for it seemed to
me that I was safe from further tyranny from the Hôtel
do Soissons, at any rate for this night.

As we passed the huge silhouette of the Hôtel de
Luxembourg, we heard the bells of St. Sulpice sounding
Compline, and then, from behind us, the solemn notes
rang out from the spires of the city churches. Yield-
ing to an impulse I could not resist, I turned in my saddle and looked back, letting my eyes run over the vast,
dim outlines of the city, so softened by the moonlight
that it was as if some opaque, fantastic cloud was resting on the earth. Above curved the profound blue of
the night, with here and there a star struggling to force
its way past the splendour of the moon. All was quiet
and still, and the church bells ringing out were as a
message from His creatures to the Most High. I let
my heart go after the voices of the bells as they travelled
heavenward, and had it not been for Mousette's shrill
tones, that cut through the quiet night and recalled me
to myself, I might have let the party go onwards, I do
not know how far. As it was, I had to bustle my little
horse to gain the side of Madame de Termes once more.
It was not, of course, our intention to travel all night.
That would have been impossible, for it would have en-
tailed weary horses, and a long halt the next day ; but
it was proposed that we should make for a small château
belonging to Monsieur de Bouchage, the brother of the
Duc de Joyeuse, which he had placed at Madame de
Termes' disposal, and there rest for the remainder of
the night, making a start early the next morning, and

then pressing on daily, as fast as our strength would allow. Lalande had sent a courier on in advance to announce our sudden coming. We did not expect to reach de Bouchage's house until about midnight, and the equerry was fussing up and down the line of march, urging a packhorse on here, checking a restive animal there, and ever and again warning the lackeys to keep their arms in readiness, for the times were such that no man's teeth were safe in his head, unless he wore a good blade by his side.

We were, in short, on the eve of that tremendous struggle which, beginning with the Day of the Barricades, went on to the murder of the Princes of Lorraine on that terrible Christmastide at Blois, and culminated with the dagger of Clement and the death of the miscreant whom God in His anger had given to us for a king.

Already the Huguenots were arming again, and it was afloat that the Palatine had sent twenty thousand men, under Dhona, to emulate the march of the Duc de Deux Ponts from the Rhine to Guyenne. It was said that the Montpensier had gone so far as to attempt to seize the person of the King, swearing that once in her hands, he would never see the outside of four walls again, and rumours were flitting here and there, crediting the Bearnnois with the same, if not deeper, resolves.

Things being so, the land was as full of angry murmurs as a nest of disturbed bees ; the result being that the writ of the King was almost as waste paper, and bands of cut-throat soldiery committed every excess, now under the white, then under the red scarf, as it suited their convenience.

It was for this reason that Lalande urged us on, and we were nothing loath ourselves to hasten, but our pace had to be regulated by that of the laden animals, and do what we would our progress was slow.

Madame and I rode in the rear of the troop, a couple of armed men immediately behind us. Lalande was in front, and exercised the greatest caution whenever we came to a place that was at all likely to be used for an ambuscade.

Nothing, however, happened, and finally we set down to a jogging motion, speaking no word, for we were wearied, and with no sound to break the silence of the night except the shuffling of our horses, the straining of their harness, and the clink of sword sheath and chain bit.

Suddenly we were startled by the rapid beat of hoofs, and in a moment, a white horse and its rider emerged from the moonlit haze to our right, coming as it were straight upon us. Lalande gave a quick order to halt, and I saw the barrel of his pistol flashing in his hand ; but the horseman, with a cry of "For the King ! Way ! Way !" dashed over the road at full gallop, and sped off like a sprite over the open plain to our left.

" Did you hear the voice, Denise ? " asked Madame.

" Yes."

" It is stranger than ever," she said, and I could make no answer.

There was no doubt about it. It was de Lorgnac ; and instead of going to the Porte St. Honoré as I thought when he left us, he must have crossed by the Meunniers and come out by the St. Germains Gate. He had evidently, too, separated himself from his men.

"I shall be glad when we reach de Bouchage's house," I said with a shiver, for the apparition of my husband had sent a chill through me.

"It is not far now," replied Madame ; and then we both became silent, absorbed in our own thoughts. She, no doubt, thinking of the Vicomte, and I with my mind full of forebodings as to what other evil fate had in store for me ; and with this there came thoughts of de Clermont, whose presence I seemed absolutely to feel about me. I could not say I loved him, but it was as if he had a power over me that sapped my strength, and I felt that I was being dragged towards him. I cannot explain what it was, but others have told me the same, that when his clear blue eyes were fixed on them, they seemed to lose themselves, and that his glance had a power, the force of which no one could put into words, nor indeed, can I.

It was only by an effort and a prayer that I succeeded in collecting myself ; and it was with no little joy that I saw the grey outlines of the Château de Bouchage, and knew that for the remainder of the night there was rest.

I will pass over our journey till we reached the Limousin. Going at our utmost strength, we found we could barely cover more than six leagues a day; and as day after day passed, and no news of the Vicomte came, Madame's face grew paler, and she became feverishly impatient for us to hurry onward ; yet never for one moment did she lose the sweetness of her temper or falter in her kindness towards me. No mishap of any kind befell us ; but at the ford of the Gartempe, there at last came good news that brought the glad tears to Madame's eyes, and the colour once more to her cheeks, for here a courier met us, riding with a red spur, to say that the Vicomte was out of danger, and striding hour by hour towards recovery. The courier further said, in answer to our questions, that the messenger whom Madame de Termes had sent on in advance, to announce her coming, had never arrived, and he himself was more than surprised at meeting us, believing Madame to be yet at Paris. No doubt the poor man who had been sent on in advance had met with ill, and we thanked God for the lucky chance that had put us in the way of the Vicomte's messenger, and also that it was not with us as with our man, for he had doubtless been killed, and indeed he was never seen again. Back we sent the courier with a spare horse to announce our speedy coming, and it was a gay and joyous party that splashed through the sparkling waters of the Gartempe. Even I, for the moment, forgot everything with the glad tidings that had come like the lark's song in the morning to cheer my friend's heart, and for a brief space I forgot de Lorgnac and my bonds, and was once more Denise de Mieux, as heedless and light-hearted as youth, high spirits, and health could make me. It was decided to push on to Ambazac at any cost by that evening. The news we had heard seemed to lighten even the loads of the pack animals, and we soon left the silver thread of the river behind us, and entered the outskirts of the Viennois. As for me, I do not know how it was, but I was, as I have said, in the wildest of spirits, and nothing could content me but the most rapid motion. At one

time I urged my horse far in advance of the party, at
another I circled round and round them, or lagged behind, till they were all but out of sight, and then caught
them up at the full speed of my beast, and all this despite Lalande's grumbling that the horse would be worn
out. He spoke truly enough, but I was in one of those
moods that can brook no control, and went my own way.
I was destined, however, to be brought back sharply to
the past, from which for the moment I had escaped.
As we reached the wooded hills of Les Eschelles, I had
allowed the party to go well in advance of me, and, stopping for a moment, dismounted near a spring from
which a little brook, hedged in on each side with ferns,
babbled noisily off along the hillside. To me, who after
all, loved the fresh sweet country, the scene was en-
chanting. The road wound half-way up the side of the
spur, and the rough hillside with its beech forests,
amongst the leaves of which twined the enchanter's
nightshade, swept downwards in bold curves into a wild
moorland, covered with purple heather and golden
broom. The sheer rock above me was gay with pink
mallow, and the crimson of the cranesbill flashed here
and there, whilst the swish of the bracken in the breeze
was pleasant to my ears. Overhead, between me and the
absolute blue of the sky, was a yellow lacework of birch
leaves, and a wild rose, thick with its snowy bloom,
scrambled along the face of the rock just above the
spring. It was to gather a bouquet of these flowers for
Madame that I had halted and dismounted. The task
was more difficult than I imagined, and whilst I was
wrestling with it, I heard the full rich baritone of a
man's voice singing out into the morning, and the next

moment, the singer turned the corner of a bluff a few yards from me, and Raoul de Clermont was before me. He stopped short in his song with an exclamation, and, lifting his plumed hat, said in astonishment:

"You, mademoiselle! Pardon—Madame de Lorgnac! Where in the world have you dropped from? Or, stay—are you the genius of this spot?" and his laughing eyes looked me full in the face.

I stood with my flowers in my hands, inwardly trembling, but outwardly calm.

"It is rather for me to ask where in the world you have sprung from, monsieur. It is not fair to startle people like this."

"I ask your pardon once more. As it happens, I am travelling on business and pleasure combined. My estates of Clermont-Ferrand lie but a short way from here, as you perhaps know; but let me help you to add to those flowers you have gathered," and he sprang from his horse.

"No, thank you, Monsieur de Clermont," I answered hastily. "I must hurry on lest Madame de Termes, with whom I am travelling, should think I am lost."

"So it is Monsieur de Clermont now, is it? It will be a stiff Monsieur le Marquis soon," and my heart began to beat, though I said nothing, and he went on: "For old sake's sake let me gather that cluster yonder for you, and then Monsieur de Clermont will take you to Madame."

With a touch of his poniard he cut the flowers, and handed them to me, breaking one as he did and fastening it into the flap of his pourpoint. So quiet and masterful was his manner that I did nothing to resist, and then, putting me on my horse, he mounted himself, saying with that joyous laugh of his :

" Now, fair lady, let us hasten onward to Madame de Termes. I need protection, too—I fear my knaves have lagged far behind."

CHAPTER IV.

AT AMBAZAO.

THE road swept onward with gentle curves, at one time hanging to the edge of the hillside, at another walled in on either hand by rocks covered with fern and bracken, to whose jagged and broken surface—whereon purples, greens, and browns seemed to absorb themselves into each other—there clung the yellow agrimony, and climbing rose, with its sweet bloom full of restless, murmuring bees.

Sometimes the path lost itself in some cool arcade of trees, where the sunlight fell in oblique golden shafts through the leaves that interlaced overhead, and then suddenly, without warning, we would come to a level stretch on which the marguerites lay thick as snowflakes, and across which the wind bustled riotously.

As we cantered along side by side, my companion again broke forth into a joyous song, that sprang fullthroated and clear, from a heart that never seemed to have known a moment of pain. His was a lithe, leopard-like strength, and as I looked at him, my thoughts ran back to the time when we first met, on his return from the Venetian Embassy, whither he had gone when M. de Bruslart made a mess of things. I do not know why it was, but he singled me out for his particular notice; and though it was openly known that he was betrothed to the second daughter of M. D'Ayen, I, like a fool, was flattered by the attentions of this gay and brilliant cavalier, and day by day we were thrown together more and more, and a sort of confidence was established between us that was almost more than friendship. There was, as I have said, that in his masterful way, that had the effect of leaving me powerless ; and though he could put all its light in his eyes, and all its tones in his voice, I felt instinctively that he did not love me, but was merely playing with me to exercise his strength, and dragging me towards him with a resistless force. In short, the influence of de Clermont on me was never for my good, and our intercourse always left me with the conviction that I had sunk a little lower than before ; and it was at times like these, when I met de Lorgnac's grave eyes, that I felt the unspoken reproach in their glance, and would struggle to rise again, and then, in the consciousness of my own folly, I felt I fairly hated him for seeing my weakness. What right had de Lorgnac even to think of me ? What did it matter to him what I did or said ? So I used to argue with myself ; yet in my heart of hearts, I felt that my standard of right and wrong, was being measured by what I imagined a man, to whom I had hardly ever spoken, might think.

When I make this confession, and say that the influence of de Clermont over me was never for my good, I do not mean to imply that I was guilty of anything more than foolishness ; but the effect of it was to sap my high ideas, and I now know that this man, aided by his surroundings—and they were all to his advantage —took the pleasure of a devil in lowering my moral nature, and in moulding me to become " of the world," as he would put it. God be thanked that the world is not as he would have made it. At that time, however, I was dazzled—all but overpowered by him, and day by day my struggles were growing weaker, like those of some poor fly caught in a pitiless web. The knowledge of all this was to come to me later, when, by God's help, I escaped ; but then I was blind, and foolish, and mad.

My companion's song was interrupted by Lalande, who came galloping back in hot haste, and in no good temper, to say that the whole party had halted to wait for me ; and quickening our pace we hurried onward, and found them about a mile further on. To say that Madame de Termes was surprised at seeing de Clermont is to say little, and I could see, too, that she was not very well pleased ; but he spoke to her so fairly and gracefully that, in spite of herself, she thawed ; and half an hour later he was riding at her bridle hand, bringing smiles that had long been absent to her face. He was overjoyed to hear of the Vicomte's recovery, and said many flattering things about him, for he knew him well, having served under him in the campaign of Languedoc, and then he went on to become more communicative about himself, saying that he was the bearer of a despatch to the King of Navarre, adding, with a laugh, " a duplicate, you know—the original being carried by M. Norreys, the English freelance. *Ma foi !* But I should not be surprised if I reached the Bearnnois before the sluggish islander."

" Hardly, if you loiter here, Monsieur le Marquis," I said.

"You must bear the blame for that, Madame ; but I will add that my orders are to pass through Périgueux as well, and so, Madame," and he turned to my friend, "if you will permit Raoul de Clermont to be your escort there, he will look upon it as the most sacred trust of his life."

He bowed to his saddle-bow, and looked so winning and handsome that Madame replied most graciously in the affirmative. A little beyond La Jonchère something very like an adventure befell us—the first on this hitherto uneventful journey. At the cross road leading to Bourganeuf, we met with a party of six or eight men, who did not require a second glance to make us see that they were capable of any mischief. They had halted to bait their horses, and, flung about in picturesque attitudes, were resting under the trees—as ill-looking a set of fellows as the pleasant shade of the planes had ever fallen upon. Had they known beforehand that we were travelling this way, they would very probably have arranged an attack on us; but as it was we came upon them rather suddenly, and as our party—which had been added to by de Clermont's two lackeys—was somewhat too strong to assault openly, without the risk of broken heads and hard knocks—things which gentry of this kind do not much affect—they let us alone, contenting themselves with gathering into a group to watch us as we went by ; and this we did slowly, our men with their arms ready. As we approached, however, and saw their truculent faces, I had doubts as to whether we should pass them without bloodshed, and begged de Clermont in a low voice to prevent any such thing. He had drawn a light rapier that he wore, but

as I spoke he put it back with a snap, and holding out
his hand, asked for the loan of my riding-whip—a little
delicate, agate-handled thing.

" It will be enough," he said as I gave it to him, and
he began to swing it backwards and forwards, as if
using it to flick off flies from his horse. To my joy
they made no attempt to molest us, though at one time
a quarrel hung on a cobweb. For as we passed, the
leader of the troop, a big burly man, with a very long
sword trailing at his side, and a face as red as the constant dipping of his nose into a wine cup could make it,
advanced a step into the wood, and, wishing us the day,
tried deliberately to get a better look at me, with an
unspeakable expression in his eyes. I saw de Clermont's
face grow cold and hard, he quietly put his horse
between me and the man, and checking it slightly,
stretched out the whip, and touched a not very clean
white scarf the creature wore over his shoulder, saying :

" You are a trifle too near Limoges to wear this, my
man—take my advice and fling it away."

" That is my affair," answered the man insolently.

" Precisely, Captain la Coquille. I spoke but for your
good. Ah ! take care ! " and de Clermont's horse, no
doubt secretly touched by the spur, lashed out suddenly, causing the man to spring back with an oath and
an exclamation of

" You know me ! Who the devil are you ? "

To this, however, de Clermont made no answer, but
as we passed on he returned my whip to me, saying,
" I am glad I did not have to use it. It would have de-
prived you of a pretty toy had I done so."

"Thank you. Who is that horrible man ? You called him by name."

"Yes, la Coquille. I know him by sight, though he does not know me. He was very near being crucified once, and escaped but by a fluke. He is robber, thief, and perhaps a murderer, and——"

" And what ! "

De Clermont reached forward and brushed off an imaginary fly from his horse's ears.

" And has something of a history. I believe he was a gentleman once, and then went under—found his way to the galleys. After that he was anything, and perhaps I ought not to tell you, but in time he became de Lorgnac's sergeant—his confidential man—and it was only his master's influence that saved him from a well-deserved death. It was foolish of de Lorgnac, for the man knew too many of his secrets, and was getting dangerous. I hope I have not pained you," he added gently.

" Not in the least," I replied, and rode on looking straight before me. So this vile criminal was once my husband's confidential servant, was perhaps still connected with him in his dark designs. And then I said a bitter thing, " Like master, like man. Is not that the adage, monsieur ? " But as the words escaped me, I felt a keen regret.

" God help you, Denise," I heard de Clermont murmur as if to himself, and then he turned abruptly from me, and joined Madame de Termes, leaving me with a beating heart, for his words had come to me with a sense of undying, hopeless love in them, and he was so brave, he seemed so true, and looked so handsome, that

my heart went out in pity for him.   How the mind can
move !   In a moment there rose before me thoughts of
a life far different from the one to which I was doomed,
and with them came the grim spectres of the vows that
bound me forever, and which I would have to keep.
God help me !   Yes, I needed help—de Clermont was
right.

We passed on, leaving the gang still under the plane-
trees, and soon came in view of Ambazac, lying amidst
its setting of waving cornfields.   Here for a little time
we suddenly missed de Clermont and one of his lackeys,
and both Madame and I were much concerned, for the
same thought struck us both, that he had lagged behind
and then gone off hot-foot to punish la Coquille.   We
were about to turn after him when he came in sight,
followed by his man, and caught us up, riding with a
free rein.   He perhaps saw the inquiry in my look, for
he said softly to me, " I went back to pick up a souvenir
I had dropped," and his eye fell on the lapel of his coat
where my rose was, a little, however, the worse for wear.
After that he did not speak to me, but kept by Madame
and devoted himself to her with a delicacy for which I
was grateful, for I felt I wanted all my thoughts for
myself.   At Ambazac, which we reached in a little,
we found good accommodation at a large inn, although
the town was full, it being the *fête* of St. Etienne de
Muret ;   and after taking some light refreshment Madame and I retired to our apartments, to rest until the
supper hour, for we were wearied.   We supped in the
common hall, but at a small table a little apart from the
others, and de Clermont, who sat next to me, gave
Madame an interesting account of the defence of Am-

bazac, made by her husband against the Prince of Condé.
It was whilst he was detailing the incidents of this
adventure that, with a great clattering and much loud
talking, la Coquille and his men entered the dining-
room, and began to shout for food and drink. Most of
the people in the inn being common country folk and
unarmed, made way for the crew with haste, and even
an expression of alarm appeared on Lalande's face, for
our own servants were but six in number, including the
baggage drivers, and Madame's maid and my own, who,
of course, were useless, and two of our men-servants
were at the moment attending to the horses ; so that we
were at a decided disadvantage, and la Coquille was not
slow to perceive this.

"*Dame*," he exclaimed, looking towards us, " here is
my popinjay and his sugar-plum. Look you, my good
fellow, join those boys there, whilst I bask in beauty's
smiles."

His men crowded round our servants with rough jok-
ing, and he, picking up a stool, placed it at our table,
and held out an immense greasy paw to me.

" Shake hands, *ma mignonne !* Never mind the old
lady and the silk mercer. There is no lover like a
brave soldier."

Madame was white with anger. I had sprung to my
feet, meditating flight, and the villain's followers raised
a hoarse shout, " Courage, captain ! None but the
brave deserve the fair."

Then de Clermont's hand was on the man's neck, and
with a swing of his arm he sent him staggering back
almost across the room. He recovered himself on the
instant, however, for he was a powerful man, and rushed

forward ; but stopped when he saw de Clermont's rapier
in his hand, and began to tug at his fathom of a sword.
His men, however, offered no assistance to him, contenting themselves with breaking into loud laughter.
As for de Clermont, he was as cool and self-possessed
as if he were at a Court function.

" Out of this," he said. " Begone—else I shall have
you flogged and you shall taste the *carcan*. Be
off."

" The *carcan* ! You silkworm, you cream-faced danc-
ing-master ! " yelled the man, who had now drawn his
sword. " Who the devil are you to threaten *me*—la
Coquille—with the *carcan* ? Blood of a Jew ! Who are
you ? "

" The Marquis de Clermont-Ferrand," was the answer, " and these ladies are of the household of M. de
Termes, and now I will give you and your men two
minutes to go. If not I shall have them stoned out of
the place ; and you—you know what to expect. If you
are wise you will put a hundred leagues between yourself and Périgord after this ; and now be off—fool."

The man dropped his sword into its sheath and stammered out, " Your pardon, monseigneur ! I did not
know. Come, boys," he said with an affectation of unconcern, " these ladies complain that the place is too
crowded; we will go elsewhere. At your service, mes-
dames," and making a bow that had a sort of faded
grace about it, he swaggered off followed by his men,
who took his lead with surprising alacrity. The people
in the inn and our servants raised a cheer, and were for
going after them, doubtless to administer the stoning ;
but de Clermont put a stop to this, saying in a per-

emptory tone, "Let them go ; I will see that they are dealt with."

As may be imagined we were in no mood for much supper after this. My knees felt very weak under me, and Madame de Termes was trembling all over ; but she thanked de Clermont very gracefully, and he made some modest answer with his eyes fixed on me, and I— I could say nothing. We would have retired at once, but de Clermont pressed us to stay, and Madame, with a little smile, agreed, saying, "I am afraid even after all these years I am not quite a soldier's wife." So we lingered yet a little longer and found our nerves come back to us. After that we sat in the garden where the moonlight was full and bright, and the breeze brought us the scent of the roses. Then de Clermont bringing out his lute sang to us. He had a voice such as neither I, nor any one else I knew who had listened to it, had ever heard equalled. So, perhaps, sang his old troubadour ancestors, and the sweet notes had died with the days of chivalry to be born in Raoul de Clermont. The song he chose was one that was perchance written by one of his minstrel forbears, and described in that old tongue that we no longer use, a lover's agony at being separated forever from his mistress. The words were, perhaps, poor, but there was genuine feeling in them, and sung by de Clermont, it might have been the wail of an angel shut out from Paradise. Never did I hear the like—never would I care to hear the like again, and as the last of the glorious notes died away in a liquid stream of ineffable melody, I saw Madame's face buried in her hands, and there was a great sob behind me that came from the broad chest of Lalande, who had stolen

up to hear, and was blubbering like a child. Then
Madame de Termes rose, and hurried off followed by
Lalande, and we were alone, I sitting still with my
whole soul full of that wondrous song, and every nerve
strung to its highest pitch, whilst de Clermont remained
standing, his lute, slung by its silken sash, in the loop
of his arm.

" Denise ! " he said, " you understand, dear ? "

" Yes." I could barely whisper the word ; and then
he bent down and kissed me softly on the forehead,
and the touch of his lips seemed to burn into me like
a red-hot seal. With a little cry I rose to my feet, and
hardly knowing what I was doing, ran past him, never
stopping until I reached my room. Here I remained
as if lost in a dream, with a hundred mad thoughts dancing in my brain. I tried to pray, but my lips could only
frame words, for there was nothing in my heart ; and
then I thought I would seek forgetfulness in sleep. But
sleep would not come, and I lay awake watching the
broad banner of moonlight that came in through the
open window, and all the memories of the past awake
within me. De Clermont's kiss still burned hotly on
my face, and I shivered with the shame and the sin
of it, for I was another's wife—and Heaven help me !
I thought then that I loved de Clermont. Oh ! the
misery of those hours, when I tossed from side to side
with dry, burning eyes and bitter shame in my heart.
At last, as the moon was paling, I could endure it no
longer, and, rising from my bed, began to pace the
room. I felt that what I needed was motion, movement
—I could not be still. If I could only pray ! and as the
thought came to me once more I heard a little *clink*,

and stooping, picked up a small locket containing a miniature of my mother which I wore round my neck, the gold chain by which it was suspended having broken in my restless movements. I opened the locket, and standing near the window looked at the picture, and as I live it seemed to lighten so that I could see each feature, with the soft eyes bent on me in pity ; and then a voice—it was her voice—said :

"Denise, pray ! "

And then my eyes were blinded with tears, and flinging myself on my knees with my hands clasped on the mullions of the window I sobbed out, "God ! Dear God ! Have pity on me ! "

I could say no more, but my whole soul went out with these words and I knelt there, still and motionless, with the sense of a great peace falling upon me. Then it was as if the very heavens grew bright as day, and the light filled my room so that my eyes were dazzled and I could not see. And I covered my face with my hands to shield my eyes from the splendour.

*   *   *   *   *

When I looked up again the glory was gone, but my soul was at rest. I stood at the window and let the cool breeze fan me, whilst I peered out into the darkness, for the moon had sunk and it was now the black hour that touches the dawn. As I watched I heard the bells of St. Etienne calling the Lauds across the grave of the night, and I knew that in two hours it would be daylight, and felt that the Unseen God had heard my prayer.

CHAPTER V.

M. LE MARQUIS LEADS HIS HIGHEST TRUMP.

WHEN I came down in the morning I found we were all ready to start. Madame was mounted, and de Clermont was standing to assist me to my horse. It all seemed so strange after the crisis of last night. I had not schooled myself. I had not had time to meet de Clermont with unconcern, and overcome by a sudden shyness I declined his aid, and he said in his cool, level voice :

" You are very proud this morning."

The touch of proprietorship in his tone, which he so often used towards me, and to which I had hitherto submitted, jarred on me now, and in a moment my courage had come back. I looked him full in the face and answered :

" It is necessary to be proud sometimes, monsieur."

Our eyes held each other for an instant, and for the first time I saw in his clear blue glance an expression of hesitation and surprise, and I felt that the compelling power of his look was gone, and then—he dropped his gaze, and stepping back lifted his hat without a word ; but I saw the white line of his teeth close on his nether lip.

Then we started, and de Clermont dropped away to

the rear of the party, leaving Madame de Termes and
myself alone. She was full of the strange song of last
night.

"I had heard of his voice before," she said, "but
never thought it was anything like that. St. Siege!"
and she gave a little shudder. "I am an old woman;
but it was maddening. I forgot everything. I could
think of nothing except that sorrow in that last verse—
the poor man, the poor man!" And the dear old lady's
eyes filled once more with tears at the recollection.
"But it was not a good song," she went on in a moment, "it was a beautiful evil thing, and he shall sing
it no more. I will speak to him. It is wrong. It is
wicked to touch the heart as that song can. He is very
silent and grave to-day. I wonder if it affected him as
it did me?"

But I made no answer, for my mind was full of other
things, of the hopeless love in the heart that I thought
so strong and brave, and of the wondrous power that
had come over me and enabled me to be victor over
myself, and I cast up an unspoken prayer that this
strength should be continued to me, and then I found
de Clermont once more by my side.

Madame kept her word about the song, and he said
gravely:

"I promise. I will never sing it again. It hurts me,
too," and, changing the subject, other matters were
spoken about. In a little I found myself separated
from Madame, and de Clermont, bending forward, said:

"I have news I should have given before that will
interest you, madame—something you ought to know
—of M. de Lorgnac."

" Is it really of importance ? "

" I think so. It will remain for you to decide."

" Then what is it, monsieur ? "

" I cannot well tell you here. We will let them go onward, and ride slowly behind."

I agreed silently, and we soon found ourselves at a little distance from the party. We were descending the wooded valley of the Briance, and a turn in the forest road left us alone. Then de Clermont, who had up to now remained silent, began abruptly :

" Madame, it has been given to me to find out the business on which M. de Lorgnac is engaged, and over which you have been sacrificed. You are a brave woman—the bravest I have ever met—and I know you will bear with the bluntness of my speech, for this is no time to beat about the bush."

" Monsieur, it does not concern me on what business M. de Lorgnac is engaged. I only ask and pray God to give me some refuge where I may never see him again."

" Hear me a moment. I think it does concern you, and vitally too."

" Then what is it ? "

" Now call to mind your race, and all that can give you strength. Denise de Mieux, your husband is nothing more than an assassin. He has been hired by the King and that she-devil the Queen Mother to murder Navarre. It is a political necessity for them, and they have found an instrument in Blaise de Lorgnac base enough for their purpose. His price was high, though—it was you, Denise, and de Tavannes, who is in the secret, has paid it. How he came to persuade

himself to do so, I know not. He is your uncle, and I
will not say anything against him."

I felt as if I had received a blow. There was truth in
every line of de Clermont's face, in every tone of his
voice ; but I struggled against it, and said faintly :

" This does not concern me—I am but a wife in name.
I shall never see de Lorgnac. He is dead to
me."

" Would to God he were dead indeed ! " he burst out.
" But there is more. Catherine is tyrant to her finger
nails. She has heard that you have refused to remain
with your husband, and at his request an order has been
sent to de Termes to deliver you up to him at Périgueux.
Norreys has taken that order, and it has already reached
him. If you doubt me here is the duplicate. You may
read it for yourself."

He placed a letter in my hands. I knew the seal well.
The red shield with the *palle* of the Medici—Catherine's
private signet. But I could not read it. My mind became a chaos. " Oh ! what shall I do ? What shall I
do ? " I exclaimed aloud in my despair.

" Denise ! " he said, " there is one way of escape and
only one, for de Lorgnac has already made his claim at
Périgueux, and you go straight into the lion's jaws."

" What is it ? Tell me."

He laid his hand on my rein. " Denise—put your
trust in me and come. My dear, I love you—I love you.
This marriage is an infamy. Vows such as they made
you swear are not binding. Come with me, my dear,
and under the banner of the Emperor, with you by my
side to help me, I will work out a new life, and the
name of Clermont-Ferrand is already known. Denise !

Last night I saw the love-light in your eyes. Let it burn
there again for me. Come."

He made as if to turn my horse's head, and it was
only with an effort that I restrained him. God knows
I was sorry for the man. I know, too, that it was in
my heart to take the great love I thought he was giving
me, and, forgetting everything, to follow him to the
world's end. In the few seconds that passed, I went
through a frightful struggle, and then the strength of
last night came back to me.

"De Clermont! It is impossible; and now go—go.
If you say you love me, go in pity!"

"Denise, you know not what you say! Think, dear!
In two hours we will be safe. In two hours the world
itself could not part us. I will not let you sacrifice
yourself. You love me, dear, and you know it, and
when love like ours exists there is no right and no wrong
—only our love."

"It cannot be—it cannot be. De Clermont, you are
tempting the woman you say you love, to dishonour. Let
me tell you plainly, I do not love you. For one moment
I thought I did; but I am sure of myself now; and
even did I love you, as I feel sure you deserve to be
loved, I would never consent to—to what you propose."

"*Mordieu!*" he exclaimed hoarsely, "you are not
yourself. Come, Denise. I hear Lalande riding back,
and in a moment it will be too late."

"Let go my reins, monsieur, else I shall call out. I
hear Lalande, too. Go, monsieur, whilst I can still
think of you as I always have. Go and forget me."

His hand dropped to his side, and taking the occasion
I struck my horse smartly with the whip and he sprang

forward. De Clermont made no attempt to follow, but at the bend of the road, as I glanced across my shoulder, I saw him turn his horse's head and plunge into the forest, and a moment later I met Lalande.

I could only realize that I had escaped a great danger; beyond that my mind could not go ; but I was conscious that, despite the terrible earnestness of his words, there was something that was not convincing in de Clermont. The narrow escape that I had drove all other things out of my mind, and it was only when I came in sight of our party again that I recollected de Clermont's warning that by going to Périgueux I was going straight into the lion's mouth, and an absolute despair fell upon me.

When I rode up to Madame's side she glanced at me narrowly and asked for de Clermont.

I answered truly enough that I did not know, and she looked at me again with her clear, searching eyes. " It is odd, Denise, but do you know that his lackeys have gone, too ? They left us an hour ago—and now it seems he has gone, too, without a word of good-bye."

" Monsieur made too sure of the success of his plans," I said bitterly, and Madame's answer was sharp and swift :

" Denise, there is something wrong—what is it ? "

And as we rode close together, side by side, I told her every word, hiding nothing. My voice sounded hard and dry to my own ears, my eyes were burning, and when I had finished, she said, " Denise, I cannot believe M. de Clermont's story. I *feel* it is untrue. Even if it were true de Termes would never carry out the order about you. He is incapable of such baseness."

"There is always one way of escape, madame, and I am my father's daughter."

"And there is a God above, girl. Your father's daughter should never talk like that."

"Then why does He not hear my prayers?" I said, in impious forgetfulness. "Is heaven so far that our voices cannot reach there?"

And my dear old friend sighed deeply in answer.

We were to halt at Chalusset for the night, and here confirmation was received of the truth of de Clermont's story, for an equerry of the Vicomte's met us here with a letter to his wife in his own hand, in which he said that our message, the one we had sent from the Gartempe, had reached him, and that he was hastening forward himself to meet us. Then he went on to other matters, and his letter concluded with a postscript:

"M. Norreys is here with an order from the King, or, rather, from the Queen Mother. It is very unfortunate, but must be obeyed."

She first read the letter herself—we were sitting together in her apartment, in the one inn at Chalusset—and then she handed it to me with a request to read it aloud to her. I did so; but on coming to the postscript my voice faltered in spite of myself, and then she bent forward and kissed me.

"Denise, it will never be. Are you strong enough to do a brave thing?"

"I will try."

"It is clear to me that de Termes' postscript is a warning for you not to go to Périgueux. I knew that he

would be incapable of carrying out such orders as he has
received—and I can read his meaning between the lines
of his message. Denise, you must not be with me when
my husband and I meet."

"God Himself seems to have abandoned me. What
can I do—where shall I hide ?"

"I will tell you. My sister Louise is Abbess of Our
Lady of Meymac. I will send you to her. The convent
has special rights of sanctuary that even Catherine herself would not dare to violate—but she will never know
you are there. Yet it is a long journey, and you will
have to cross the mountains. Will you risk it to-
night ?"

"I am ready now, madame."

"Very well," and, calling to her maid, she asked for
Lalande, and when the equerry came she turned to
him :

"Lalande, how long is it that you have followed
Monsieur le Vicomte ?"

"Thirty years, madame, from the days when Monsieur was a simple cavalier of the guard."

"And you would do anything for Monsieur ?"

"Madame, I have been his man in lean times and in
fat—in famine and in full harvest. He saved my life
at Cerisolles, and it was I who got him out of the Bas-
tille ; I have been by his side from the time he was a
simple gentleman to the present day, when Monsieur
is a marshal and a peer of France. You ask if I would
do anything for Monsieur. If Monsieur le Vicomte
were to ask me to lay down my life to-morrow I would
do so willingly."

"I believe you, Lalande. Now listen. Madame de

Lorgnac here is in great danger. It is Monsieur le Vicomte's wish that she should be conveyed to the Convent of Our Lady of Meymac, and we trust her to you. No one is to know where she is placed. You must protect her with your life—do you understand ? And you must start now—and alone—for Madame's hiding-place is a secret."

"We could start in a few minutes, madame, and I will do what you say."

"Then be ready in half an hour."

"Madame," and he was gone.

"Do not let Mousette know whither you are bound, Denise. She is a chattering ape, and, though she loves you, can never keep a secret. As for de Termes, I will arrange to manage him—and, dear, keep a brave heart. I would go with you myself ; but you know it is impossible."

*   *   *   *   *

The moon was just rising when, after taking an affectionate farewell of Madame de Termes, who had been to me as a mother, we started—Mousette, Lalande, and myself. Our horses had been brought to a little gate at the back of the straggling garden attached to the inn, by the equerry himself, so that we might get away unobserved. Hither Madame accompanied us, and after giving some further instructions in a low tone to Lalande, embraced me again and again, and I am afraid we both wept, whilst Mousette joined in to keep us company. Finally we started, and I turned once or twice to look back, and saw the slender grey-clad figure still at the gate, growing fainter and fainter in outline at each step we took, and seeming at last to slip away into

the silver haze of the moonlight, until when I turned
for the last time, I could see nothing but the winding
road, the ghostly outline of the trees, and the pointed
roof of the inn. I have often wondered if the girls of the
present day would endure and act as we women had to
do then. All women have to endure passively. This
will be so for all time unless the world be made anew,
but with us there were times and seasons when we had
to act like men.

Last year, when I was in Paris, where I had taken
my daughter for her presentation, a great lady called on
me, the wife and daughter of a soldier, and she reached
our house almost in hysterics, because one of the wheels
of her coach had come off, and she had to walk a hundred paces or so. She was in fear of her life at the
accident. And when we had made much of her and
she was gone, my husband's eyes met mine, and the
same thought struck us both, for he came up and kissed
me, saying :

"*Mordieu !* I thank God I am not thirty years
younger ! "

CHAPTER VI.

AT first we managed to get along at a fair pace, as
the road was good and we were well able to see our way
by the moonlight ; but after crossing the Taurion by
a frail wooden bridge, which creaked and groaned
ominously as we passed over it, Lalande took a turn
to the right and followed a narrow track whereon we
had to ride nose to tail. Womanlike, I began to think
he was taking the wrong road, and asked him whither
he was leading us.

" St. Priest-Taurion lies on the main road, madame,
and it would be well to avoid it. Let not madame have
any fear. I could make my way to Meymac blind-
fold."

" And want to show off by picking the most horrible
paths," shrilled out Mousette, whose temper, never of
the best, had gone to ribbons, and little wonder, too,
poor thing !

" It would be well if we speak in lower tones—better
still not to speak at all," said the equerry, and silencing
Mousette with a reprimand, I asked Lalande to lead on.

Whilst the motion was fast it was not possible to
think, but now that we were going at something like a
snail's pace, I unconsciously gave myself over to my re-
flections, though I had by this time reached a state of

mind when it seemed impossible for me to distinguish
between right and wrong, or to think coherently. The
proof of the truth of de Clermont's story had accentu-
ated the bitterness in my heart against my husband, and
this was not lessened when I remembered the infamy
of the enterprise which he had undertaken, and of which
I was the price. I had it once or twice in my mind to
try and prevent the crime he contemplated by attempting to warn the Bearnnois ; but it was impossible to
do so from here, and I should have to make the attempt
from Meymac. Then that thought gave place to de
Clermont, and with the memory of him regrets that I
had not taken his offer, and by one desperate stroke
freed myself forever from de Lorgnac, even at the cost
of that good opinion of the world, we pretend to despise
and yet value so much, even against what I felt to be
the teachings of my conscience. After all I was merely
holding to vows that I had never really made. The
priest's benediction surely could not bind me forever
to a hateful life. I had my dreams as all young women
and young men have—of a life that I could share with
one whom I could trust and honour and love. One
whose joys would be my joys, whose sorrows would be
my sorrows, whose ambitions and hopes would be my
ambitions and hopes, and so to pass hand in hand with
him until one or both of us were called away to fulfil
the mystery of life by death. And de Clermont ? Could
he have been the one to have so travelled with me ?
Did I love him ? For the life of me I could not tell at
that moment. At one time I seemed dragged towards
him, at another there was a positive repulsion, and
through it all there was an ever-warning voice within

me, like the tolling of a bell hung over a sunken rock
to warn mariners of danger, telling me, "Beware ! Beware !" I felt in my heart that he did not ring true
metal—why, I could not tell—nor can I tell now. But
I suppose that God, who has limited the capacity of us
women to reason as compared with man, has given to
us this faculty of intuition by which we can know.
Would that it were followed more often ; would that its
warnings were ever heeded ! Such were the thoughts
that chased each other through my brain as the long
hours passed, and then they seemed to twine themselves
together into a network that left me powerless to follow
them and unravel the tangle. Oh, it was a weary ride !
Overhead hung the moon now light, then darkened by
flitting clouds, with a few stars showing here and there
in the sky. On all sides of us floated a dim silvery haze
that made it appear as if we were going through Dreamland ; dark shadows of trees, fantastic rocks that might
have been thrown here and there by giants at play, and
a road that turned and twisted like a serpent's track,
full of stones and boulders, on which our horses continually stumbled, but, mercifully, did not come down
and bring us with them. There was one advantage we
derived from these boulders. They kept the horses and
ourselves from sleeping, for after a stumble and a jerk,
both beast and rider began to see the folly of nodding,
and bravely strove to keep awake. At last we came
to something that looked like level ground, and Lalande
suggested that we should increase our pace to a canter,
adding truly enough that it would rouse us all up. We
followed his advice, nothing loath, and kept at this pace
with occasional halts to rest the horses, for the best part

of the night. At last, however, neither Mousette nor
myself could endure going on longer, and indeed our
horses were as much, if not more worn out than we were.
In short, we were so fatigued that I had got into a frame
of mind in which I did not care what happened to me,
one way or the other, and Mousette, poor girl, was crying softly to herself, though she kept her way with the
greatest courage. This being the case, I called to Lalande that we could not go on any further ; but at his
intercession we made yet another effort, and at last we
halted near a clump of beeches, close to which a small
brook purled by. I do not think I shall ever forget the
kindness and attention of the honest fellow. He made
us as comfortable a resting-place as he could contrive
with the aid of saddles and rugs, and then, giving us
some wine to drink, bade us sleep, whilst he retired a
little distance—not to rest, but to attend to the horses
and keep a watch. So utterly tired out were we that
we must have fallen asleep at once, and the sun was already rising when Lalande aroused us.

"If madame does not mind," he said, " it will be
well if we move further up into that wood yonder and
rest there, whilst I go to a village hard at hand, and
procure some food, and take news of the state of the
road."

To this I assented readily, and after walking for about
a quarter of a mile we found a spot which exactly suited
our purpose, where both we and the horses could be
concealed for the remainder of the day, if it was so
necessary, without any fear of discovery. Lalande then
started off for the village, and we waited his coming
with a hungry impatience, taking, however, the oppor-

tunity of his absence to make a forest toilet. It was
some time before the equerry came back, and we were
just beginning to be alarmed at his absence when
he appeared, bearing with him the things he went to
procure, and whilst Mousette and I were eating, he told
us what he had found out, adding :

"I regret that madame will not be able to travel by
daylight—that *croquemort* la Coquille and his gang
passed through St. Bathilde yesterday, and are in the
neighbourhood, and not they alone, but one or two
others of like kidney. We shall have to make our way
as best we can by night."

But this was too much—not for anything was I going
to endure the misery of last night over again, and I
argued and expostulated with Lalande, Mousette join-
ing with me with shrill objurgations, and at last the
poor fellow gave in, but I confess with a very bad grace,
grumbling a good deal to himself and declaring he
would be no longer responsible for our safety. I own
now that we were wrong in persisting as we did, but I
put it to any one if they would have endured what we
had to endure without protest ; and then we were women,
and I am afraid possessed some of that contrariness of
disposition which I have heard the opposite sex credit
us with—though for pure, mulish obstinacy, give me
a man who thinks he has made up his mind.

Lalande was, however, determined upon one thing,
and that was to avoid the main road, and as I had so far
successfully opposed his plan of forcing a night journey, I did not feel justified in making further objections,
and allowed him to follow the by-paths he chose without
further protest, though indeed, it was as if there was

some truth in Mousette's remark of last night, that he
was choosing the most difficult tracks to show how well
he knew the way. We now entered the mountains of
the Limousin, and what would have been a mile elsewhere, became three here with the ups and downs, the
turns and twists. For miles we passed never a human
habitation, except now and again a few woodcutters'
huts, and sometimes a small outlying farm, and I felt
the justice of Lalande's remark, when he defended himself from a sharp attack by Mousette, by saying he had
chosen this road because it was safe from gentlemen like
la Coquille, who never found any bones worth the picking on it, and therefore left it and its difficulties severely
alone—though, of course, there was the odd chance of
our meeting them, and so again to the old argument of
travelling by night. As we went on the scenery became
wilder and more savage, and once a large grey wolf,
with two cubs by her side, appeared on the track about
, fifty paces or so in front of us, and after giving our
party a quiet survey, and showing us a line of great
strong teeth as she snarled on us, trotted calmly off with
her family down the hillside. Both Mousette and myself were not unnaturally alarmed ; but Lalande, with
a " Never fear, madame, there is no danger," kept
quietly along, though I saw that he had pulled a pistol
from his holster. As the day advanced we became
aware that the sun was being obscured by clouds more
often than it should be at this time of year, and
every now and again gusts of wind would race down the
ravines, and lose themselves with ominous warnings
through the forest. Still, however, the horizon was
clear, and high above all others we could make out the

crest of Mount Odouze. I asked Lalande if he thought
there was likely to be a storm.

"It is hard to tell, madame ; storms come on very
suddenly in these hills, but if there is one it will not be
very bad, for we can see the Cradle, as that dip between the two peaks of Mount Odouze is called, quite
distinctly."

But though he spoke thus reassuringly, I saw that
he increased the pace, and that ever and again he would
scan the horizon, and look up at the sky. Once when he
thought I had caught him, he explained as he pointed
upwards :

" 'Tis a red eagle, madame, that must have flown here
from the Pyrenees—a long journey. See—there it is—
that speck in the sky."

I followed his glance, but could make out nothing.
"You have sharp eyesight, Lalande," I said with a smile,
and then the matter dropped. I could not, however, but
think how good a heart was beneath that rough exterior,
and not the finest gentleman I have ever met could
have behaved to us with more chivalrous courtesy than
did that simple under officer of horse. A little past mid-
day we rested for an hour or so, more for the sake of
the animals than ourselves, and then continued our
journey.

"We should make St. Yriarte by about three o'clock,
madame," said Lalande, "and there is a small inn there
kept by my sister and her husband, for we are of the
Limousin. It is called ' The Golden Frog.' We will
stay there for the night, and a long march to-morrow
will bring us to Meymac by nightfall."

" Thank goodness ! " exclaimed Mousette, " for every

bone in my body aches as if some one had beaten me."

As the time passed, bringing with it no storm, I began to think we were safe from that annoyance, and at last from the crest of a hill over which we were riding we suddenly came in sight of St. Yriarte, lying below us in a little valley. As we did so Lalande called out, "We will be there in half an hour, madame—and save all chance of a wetting for to-night."

It took us a little time to descend the slope of the hill, but after that we came to more or less level ground, and in a few moments reached the gates of the inn, which stood in a large garden some way apart from the hamlet, for St. Yriarte could be called by no other name.

As we rode in a dog commenced to bark ; Lalande called out "Jeanne! Jeanne!" and, on our halting near the entrance, gay with honeysuckle, in full bloom, Lalande's sister and her husband came out to meet us, and seeing him, fell to embracing him, and there was an animated converse carried on by all three at once, whilst Mousette and I were kept waiting. Whilst we did this patiently, I began to look around me, and for the first time became aware of the presence of a stranger. He had been sitting on a garden seat, half-hidden by the falling honeysuckle, but, as my eyes fell on him, he rose politely, and stood as if in doubt, whether he should offer to assist me to dismount, or not. He was a tall well-built man, with aquiline features, fair hair, and blue eyes, and wore a short pointed beard slightly tinged with grey. His dress was simple though rich, and it was easy to see that, whoever he was, he was a person of some consequence. The position was getting just a little absurd when Jeanne's voice rang out sharply :

" Of course ! Of course ! Madame de Lorgnac shall have the best we can provide."

I saw the stranger start perceptibly, and an odd, curious look came into his eyes. Then as if with an effort he stepped forward, and lifting his hat said with a foreign accent :

" Will Madame de Lorgnac permit me to assist her to alight ? I have the honour to be known to Monsieur le Chevalier de Lorgnac. My name is Norreys—Colonel Norreys, of whom, perhaps, you may have heard."

I became almost sick with fear and apprehension, for this was the very man whom I least wished to meet. It was he who had borne the order concerning me to de Termes. He must therefore be aware that my presence there meant that I was in flight. He acknowledged himself to be a friend of my husband, and I felt that all was lost. Mustering up as much courage as I could I thanked him for his offer, and he helped me to dismount, saying as he did so :

" Madame will find the inn more than comfortable. I have been here for two days awaiting a friend. If he comes this evening I shall have to leave to-morrow with the greatest regret. It has been so quiet and peaceful here."

I glanced at him again. It was a strong, good face. The eyes looked at me honestly, and in their clear depths I could see no deceit. That woman's instinct of which I have spoken, told me at once that here was a man to be trusted, that he was incapable of treachery. But the same feeling used to come over me whenever I saw de Lorgnac, and yet—who was more base than he ?

Nevertheless, I was now moved by an impulse I could not resist.

" Monsieur de Norreys, will you see me in an hour ? I have a favour to ask of you."

He looked a little surprised, but bowed. " If there is anything I can do for you, madame, command me." His tone was cold and formal, and chilled me. Then he stepped to one side to let me pass, and I entered the inn.

I had made up my mind. I felt sure that he was here to prevent my going further. What else could have brought him to this out-of-the-way place ? But he looked a gentleman and a man of honour, and I would follow the dictates of my heart, and throw myself on his mercy.

CHAPTER VII.

UNMASKED.

Now do I reverently thank God that by His mercy I was strong enough to take the course I adopted. For had I not done so, I know not what had been my fate. On the surface, the impulse on which I had acted seemed foolish and ill-advised, yet when I think over all calmly now, and especially of the circumstances that led to my meeting with Monsieur de Norreys, and the events which followed, I am sure and confident that the Merciful Power which had so far watched over me had heard my prayers and answered them. At the moment, however, I did not know or think of this ; my one idea was to try, if possible, to enlist the Englishman on my side, and if this was not to be, then I knew not what I should do, though the most desperate resolves were rioting in my brain. I was too excited to rest, but a bath, a change of toilet, and a little food, refreshed me and steadied my nerves, and then I sat for a space by the open window of my small room to try and collect myself for my interview with M. de Norreys. The clouds seemed to have passed away, though far behind over the mountains there was a grey bank that showed that the storm was hovering over us, and the wind still blew in fitful, uncertain gusts. Below me Lalande was attend-

ing to the horses, and a bow-shot or so beyond the garden of the inn, under some walnut trees I saw what I had
not noticed before, and that was a small encampment
of lances. This did not tend to reassure me, and if I
had any doubts as to whom the troops belonged, they
were set at rest by the sight of Norreys, mounted on a
powerful black horse, riding slowly towards the inn,
evidently with a view of keeping his appointment with
me. I had tried to set out in my mind what I would
say to him, but each effort seemed to be worse than the
other, and at last I determined to simply throw myself
on his chivalry, and stand the hazard of the result. At
one time I thought that we might perhaps make a dash
for it and escape ; but even I could see that our wearied
horses would not have a chance against fresh ones, and
if it came to a struggle we had but one sword to de-
pend upon—a brave one, it is true—but what could one
poor man do against ten ? No, there was no way but
the one way, the idea of which had come so suddenly
to me. Now I heard Norreys dismounting at the door
of the inn, and after a moment's hesitation, I took my
courage in both hands, and stepped down to meet him.
He was standing in the little parlour, his back to the
light, as I entered, so that I could not see the expression of his face, but he bowed, I thought stiffly, on my
coming in, and handed me one of the rough chairs in
the room, saying as he did so, " I trust I have not kept
you waiting, madame ; I was delayed a little longer than
I expected with my men, as I have much to arrange
for." The last words, measured out in his prim, formal
speech, appeared to me to convey a hint to be quick
with my business, and as a natural result all but took

away from me the power of saying anything. Mustering up courage, however, I took the chair he offered,
saying, as I did so, "Will you not be seated, monsieur ? "

" Thank you," came the answer in the same set tone,
and then he fixed his eyes on me with a grave attention,
in which, however, there was mingled, as I thought,
much repressed curiosity.

"Monsieur de Norreys," I began desperately, "you
cannot but be aware that I fully understand why you are
here."

He started slightly, but recovered himself at once,
though he said nothing.

" And, monsieur," I went on, " I have come to throw
myself on your mercy. Monsieur, you look a gentleman. What object can you gain by carrying out your
orders against a poor weak woman, whose only end is to
hide herself from the world ? I have done no wrong,
monsieur, and if you knew my story you would pity me
—I ask you as a gentleman—as a man of honour."

" Madame," he interrupted, genuine amaze in his
voice, " I do not understand. As far as I am concerned
you are as free as air. I know you to be the wife of
my friend de Lorgnac, and my only regret is that I am
unable to offer you my escort——"

" Say that again, monsieur. Do you mean your
business here has nothing to do with me ? "

" Absolutely nothing, madame. I am afraid you have
alarmed yourself needlessly."

" But M. de Clermont told me ; he said you had gone
to Périgueux to have me delivered over to my husband."

" Madame, I know of no necessity for doing so, and

if I was not certain that you must be mistaken I would
say that M. de Clermont deceived you."

"I tell you he did not. He showed me the despatch
with the Queen's cipher on it—asked me to read it.
Monsieur, listen ; he did not lie, and I shall tell you
why. It is you who deceive me and are playing with
me. Wait, monsieur."

A flicker of a smile passed over his face and shone in
his eyes, but he answered simply :

"I am attention ; but, madame, think before you
tell me things which perhaps I ought not to know."

"Let me be the judge of that, and I will show you,
monsieur, that it is useless, even in kindness, to hide
your orders from me."

Then I told him briefly of my marriage, and of the
circumstances attending it, whilst he leaned back in
his chair and listened without a word, and with so little
sympathy in his look, that he might have been cut out
of a block of wood. The result was that as I spoke I
grew somewhat excited, and my tongue was bitter
against de Lorgnac, whom, to my sorrow, I upbraided
with the infamy of this enterprise ; and then I spoke of
de Clermont, of his bravery and kindness, forgetting
other things that had happened, and how he had warned
me of my danger, and especially about Norreys himself,
finishing with a rapid "and, monsieur, surely you will
let me go. I put myself on your chivalry."

He stopped me with a movement of his hand, and,
rising from his seat, faced me. "Madame de Lorgnac,
I tell you again that you are utterly mistaken. I have
nothing to do with your movements. Yet I am glad you
have spoken, for de Lorgnac is my friend, and I now see

what the other man is. It is not my habit to meddle
with other people's affairs ; but, because de Lorgnac is
my friend, I will tell you something that will give you
pain, but will open your eyes, and you must forgive the
plain speech of my country, for we have no mincing
turns of the tongue. On the authority of the Marquis
de Clermont you have accused me of playing catch-
pole. This is not a matter that troubles me, my honour
is in safe keeping ; but you have also accused your husband and my friend, and believe Blaise de Lorgnac
to be an assassin, and capable of forcing a marriage on
you for the sake of your wealth. For your own sake,
for the sake of de Lorgnac, you shall know the truth."

"I listen, monsieur."

"I'll tell you. At a supper party given by that
croquemitaine of a King of yours, a certain matter was
discussed, there was no assassination in it ; but the exe-
cution of it had to be dropped, as no one of those present who was offered the enterprise would accept it.
Later on the wine passed, and a fool, after the fashion
of your Court, began to boast openly of his conquests
and spoke openly of your favour."

"Monsieur, how dare you ! "

"Madame, it is the fashion amongst your fine gentlemen to lie like this. I will do de Clermont the justice
to say that it was not he, for he was not there, and the
man who spoke is dead, so let his name pass. But
Tavannes was there, and had to be reckoned with. The
King offered to have you married, and the marshal
burst out that he would give you to the first man who
asked."

"Oh ! "

"Blaise de Lorgnac was on guard at the door. He had heard every word, and now stepped forward and claimed your hand, offering at the same time to undertake the affair for which an agent could not be found. His offer was accepted, and in the early morning, madame, in the yard of la Boucherie, where I had the honour to be your husband's second, your traducer met with his death, and with his last breath confessed that he had lied. That was the very day, madame, that you foolishly rode out with de Clermont. Stay, there is yet a little more, and that concerns the despatch. My business at Périgueux was to give an order to de Termes to receive at St. Priest-Taurion a prisoner of state, who was to be handed over to him by myself and de Clermont. I am here to receive that prisoner, and it is Blaise de Lorgnac who is entrusted with the duty of taking him alive. The duplicate despatch, if there is such a one—and you say you have seen the cover—does not refer to you, and de Clermont has lied. I will settle with him for using my name ; but, madame, you are as free as air, and may go where you like, and for Blaise de Lorgnac's sake I will help you all I can—and this is all."

"Oh ! I don't know what to think."

"You are free to go, I say ; and as de Clermont will be here soon, and not alone, I would advise an immediate departure. I will detach a brace of lances to act as further escort, and let me give the order now. I will be back in a moment."

He did not wait for my reply, but turning on his heel stepped out of the room, and I sat with my brain burning, and my head between my hands. I could not doubt

this story, and if ever woman passed through a furnace
of shame and anger I did so in those few minutes. I
now knew what de Lorgnac was. I now for the first
time saw de Clermont in his true colours, with his mask
off ; and yet and yet—perhaps Norreys was mistaken
about him. I had proved myself to be so utterly wrong,
to have jumped to conclusions so rashly, that I dared
not sit in judgment any more on a soul, and whilst I
floundered on in this way Norreys came back.

"I have arranged everything, madame ; the orders
have been given to your people. They will be ready
to start in a half hour. About midnight you should
reach Millevranches, and I should halt there and go on
with the morning."

"Monsieur, how can I thank you ? I have no
words."

"Let the matter rest, Madame de Lorgnac," and then
his voice took a gentler tone. "I would not urge your
going at once except that we are on de Clermont's own
estates, and he has a hundred lances with him at his
Château of Ferrand. It is shut out from view by the
hills, but it lies yonder." He pointed to the west
through the open window, and as he did so an exclamation of surprise burst from him, and he crossed himself.

I followed his glance and saw, high in the heavens,
hanging over the mountainous pile of reddening clouds
that lay in the west, the grim outline of a vast fortress.
The huge walls reflected back with a coppery lustre the
red light of the sun, and it was as if we could see figures
moving on the ramparts and the flash of arms from the
battlements. From the flag-staff on the donjon a broad

banner flaunted itself proudly, and so clear and distinct
was the light that we made out with ease the blazon on
the standard, and the straining leashed ounces of the
house of Clermont-Ferrand. And then the clouds took
a duskier red, and the solid mass of castle faded away
into nothing. I stood still and speechless, and Norreys
burst forth, " Sorcery, as I live. Madame, that was the
Château de Ferrand."

I had never seen the like before, never again did I see
it, nor do I wish to, and it left me so chilled and faint,
that Norreys noticed it at once and called for wine. As
he did so, I fancied that I heard the beat of a horse's
hoof, but paid no attention to it ; and then the wine
came and I drank, he standing over me. I was just
setting down the glass when there was a grating at the
entrance, a long shadow fell through the doorway, and
de Clermont stepped in with a cheery " Good-day,
Monsieur de Norreys. I see you have not been neglect-
ing your time here. *Arnidieu !* Denise ! Is it you ?
You seem to be forever dropping from the clouds across
my path," and he held out his hand ; but I took no
notice, though I rose from my chair, and Norreys merely
bowed frigidly in return to his greeting. De Clermont
seemed in nowise disconcerted, but there was an angry
flash in his eyes, and for a second he stood tapping the
end of his boot with his riding-whip, and looking from
one to another of us with a half smile on his lips. Then
putting his plumed hat on the table, and drawing off his
gloves, he drawled out with a veiled insolence in·every
tone of his voice, " Upon my word, M. de Norreys, I
congratulate you, and if it were not for our business I
would leave you in peace, for madame seems to have

learned the lesson that 'It is well to be off with the old love before you are on with the new.' "

He had grasped the weakness of the situation at a glance, and took full advantage of it, but though outwardly cool and self-possessed there was death in his eyes. I could bear it no longer, and turned to leave the room. He rose from his seat, saying, "Pray do not leave us, madame—you look pale, though, and perhaps need rest. I trust, however, your indisposition has nothing to do with the sight I observed you watching from the window. Do you know what it means ? " and he turned to Norreys.

In spite of myself I stopped for an instant ; but Norreys ignored him, and de Clermont went on :

"It means, monsieur, that this apparition is always seen when a man dies by the hand of de Clermont-Ferrand."

Norreys simply bowed, though I thought I heard the word "boaster" muttered between his teeth, and, turning to me, said, "Permit me, madame," and gave me his arm to take me from the room.

Outside, in the narrow passage that led to my chamber, he stopped and held out his hand.

"Let me say adieu, madame. I would accompany you if I could, but it is impossible. I would advise you to leave at once before any of M. le Marquis's men come up. I can see he is ripe for mischief."

"Monsieur de Norreys, I am no fool—I can understand. For mercy's sake avoid a quarrel with de Clermont. He is a deadly swordsman, and if anything happens to you, I shall feel all my life that I was the cause of it. God knows I owe you much, for you have

opened my eyes. Promise me, monsieur, promise
me ! ”

"Madame, the use of the sword is not confined to your
country nor to de Clermont alone,” and then he saw
the tears that sprang to my eyes. " Ah ! madame, not
that ; you will unman me ! See, there is your equerry.
Commend me to de Lorgnac when you meet, and
adieu ! ”

He dropped my hand and turned on his heel, but I
could not let him go like that.

"Monsieur, not that way. Promise me what I ask.”

" I promise to avoid a quarrel if possible ; I can say
no more.” With that he went, erect and stately. Of
what followed I never knew ; but, alas ! There is one
sorrow that ever haunts me ; and in the quiet church-
yard of St. Yriarte is a tomb which I visit yearly with
my husband, and it covers the heart of as brave and
gallant a gentleman as ever lived—poor Norreys !

CHAPTER VIII.

BLAISE DE LORGNAC.

WE lost no time in setting forth from The Golden Frog, and as Lalande had apparently been warned by Norreys of the danger of our meeting any of de Clermont's following, we once more left, what by a stretch I might call the direct road, and again took to the hill tracks, where our wearied beasts, whom from my heart I pitied, stumbled slowly and painfully along.

But if the beasts were wearied, how was it with myself and my maid ? I was able to keep up, no doubt because of the mental excitement under which I laboured ; but I have never understood how my faithful Mousette endured that journey ; it was in truth a road of suffering.

I simply went on mechanically, my mind a prey to a thousand conflicting emotions, and to thoughts that chased one another across it like dry and fallen leaves in a forest glade, blown hither and thither by an autumn wind. It had struck me, as there was nothing to be feared from de Termes, that I should order Lalande to turn and guide me back to Madame and Périgueux ; but de Clermont barred the way, and it was better after all to push on to Meymac, and there with a cooler head than I now possessed, decide what to do. What had I not passed through within the last few hours ? I had made trouble enough for myself by jumping womanlike

to conclusions, and imagining that the postscript of de
Termes' letter to his wife referred to me, whereas it
clearly concerned some one else. That was perhaps a
pardonable error considering the circumstances ; but
there were other things, and even now my face grows
hot when I think of them.

My nature is proud ! That can never alter, though
sorrow and many a bitter lesson has brought me good
sense ; but it cut like a knife to realize how I had been
fooled by de Clermont, and how near I had been to fall
a victim to a pitiless libertine. It is a bad and cruel
lesson for any woman to learn that she has been the
sport of a man, ten times bad and cruel if the woman be
proud and high-spirited. And as for de Lorgnac I did
not know what to think. My mind concerning him was
a chaos. I had misjudged him, wronged him utterly ;
but it was gall to me to know that he had stood forth
as my champion. It was bitterness untold to think that
I must humble myself in my heart before him ; I could
never do so in words to his face, if ever we met, a
daughter of Mieux could not do that. It was awful to
think that his hands were red with blood for my sake,
and I shuddered as I reflected that I had been as it were
the immediate cause of a frightful death ; de Lorgnac
had no business to kill that man whoever he was ; he
had no right to make me feel almost a murderess ; and
withal there rose in my heart a kind of fierce pride in
the man who could do this for my sake, and a joy I
could not make out because he was other than I took
him to be—because, in short, he was a gallant gentleman, and not—oh ! I need say no more.

When we had travelled for about the space of two

hours the horse of one of the two troopers, whom M.
Norreys in his kindness had lent to me, fell whilst crossing a water-cut, and on examination it was found to be
so hurt that it was impossible for it to continue the
journey to Millevranches. It was decided that the two
men should be left behind to return to their camp—they
had not far to go—and that we should press on as before.
I gave the good fellows a brace of crowns apiece, and
commending myself to M. de Norreys, we went on, the
sheep track—I can call it by no better name—now passing through all the wildest scenery surrounding the Puy
de Meymac.

"If luck befriends us, madame, and the storm which
has kept off so long does not come, we should reach
Millevranches in a little over two hours," said Lalande
to me as we rode down a narrow and steep descent.

"Why should the storm come on now? There is no
breath of air stirring, and the moon is clear."

The equerry did not reply until reaching the more
level ground at the foot of the incline down which we
had ridden, and then, pointing behind me, said simply,
"Look, madame!"

Turning, I saw that half the arc of the heavens was
obscured as it were by a thick curtain, that hung heavily
and sullenly over it, and as we looked a chain of fire ran
across the blackness, the distant roar of thunder came
to us, and then a low, deep moaning vibrated through
the air.

"The storm is afoot, I fear, madame. We must press
on and cross the Luxège, which though narrow enough
to jump over now, may in an hour be impassable, and
with the darkness it will be impossible to tell the way."

At this speech Mousette gave a little cry of alarm, and then, her fears overcoming her, began to declare that she could go no further, and begged us to leave her there to die, to be killed by the storm or eaten up by the wolves, it did not matter which, either alternative was preferable to going on. I tried all I could to pacify the poor girl, but she was getting into a state of hysterical excitement, and absolutely refused to move, though every moment was precious, and the dead stillness formerly around us was now awake with the voice of the coming storm. At last I began to despair of moving her, when Lalande said grimly, " Leave her to me, madame. I am an old married man." Then bending forward he seized my bridle and with a cool " Adieu, mademoiselle ! I hope you will not disagree with the wolves," to Mousette, began to urge our beasts forward, notwithstanding my protests. But the issue showed he was right, though I confess I was surprised to see the way in which my maid recovered her strength under this rough-and-ready treatment, for in two minutes she was bustling along at our heels. But the lost time never came to our hands again, and as we began to descend the wooded slope towards the Luxège, which we could hear humming angrily below us, the stream burst with a shriek of the winds, and an absolute darkness, that was rendered more intense and horrible by the vivid flashes of lightning, and the continuous roar of thunder. In a trice Lalande had dismounted and taken us from our horses, and the poor animals seemed so overcome by fear or fatigue, or both combined, that they stood perfectly still.

" It is death, madame, attempting to ride now. We

must get to the river on foot." Saying this, Lalande managed somehow to get the horses in front of us, and then, holding on to each other and guided by the incessant flashes of lightning, we began a slow and painful progress. I soon began to feel the fatigue and exhaustion so much that I, in my turn, begged Lalande to stop.

" Courage, madame, 'tis but a few yards more to the river bank," he answered, " there we can stop and rest," and I took my heart up and strove onwards once again. At last, when within a few yards of the river, I sank down utterly exhausted and unable to move further, and Mousette alternately sobbed and prayed over me, whilst now and again I could see the tall figure of Lalande standing grim and motionless, and once I fancied I heard a deep oath.

He gave us some cognac from a flask he carried, and then there was nothing for it but to wait and meet death, if it was so to be. Now there came a series of lightning flashes that lit up the terrific scene, and I almost gasped, for right before me on a butting crag I made out a small castle. Lalande saw it too, for he blew long and shrilly on his horn, and then we watched and waited for a time that seemed interminable, when all at once the flare of a huge beacon rose bright and red against the darkness, and an answering bugle reached our ears. Lalande blew again, and to our joy there was a reply. Strength came back to me with the prospect of safety, and rising to my feet I called to Lalande: " On ! On ! "

He answered, " The river, madame——"

I looked, and saw below me a white lashing flood that swung and swirled past with a savage roar. The lightning showed us the angry water, and the wicked dancing foam, that seemed to leap up in delight at the prospect of the black swirl below it dragging us down to death. Then again we heard the bugle notes, and saw the lights of torches, and heard the shouting of men from the opposite bank.

"Let us go on to meet them—we are saved!" screamed Mousette, and holding on to each other we staggered forward past the horses, who stood all huddled together, only to be stopped here by the utter darkness, and Lalande.

" For the love of heaven, madame, do not move," he cried, " rescue is coming."

And it did come.

All that I can remember was seeing the light of many sputtering torches around us. Some one lifted me in his arms like a child, and I heard a voice say, " Be careful with the horses over the bridge, Pierre," and then my strength gave way.

*   *   *   *   *

I had been asleep, asleep for ages it seemed, and all the past was a dream, thank God ! This was the thought that struck me as I opened my eyes ; but as I looked around, I saw the room in which I lay was strange to me, and inch by inch everything came back—all except the events of the last moments by the river, where my recollection became confused. It was daylight, but still the remains of the storm of last night were in evidence, and I could hear the water dripping from the eaves, and through the half-open dormer window, the murmur of the Luxège, still angry and unappeased, reached my ears.

Where was I ? I looked about me, and found that I
was in a large room, warm from the effects of a huge
wood fire that danced cheerily in the fireplace. Leaning
on one elbow, I glanced still further about me, and saw
that the furniture was of the same old and heavily
antique make that we had at Mieux. The curtains of
the bed were, however, worn and faded, the tapestry
on the walls was older and more faded still ; and then
my eyes were arrested by the coat-of-arms carved on
the stonework of the fireplace—two wolves' heads, with
a motto so chipped and defaced that I could not read
it. Whose was the device ? I lay back and thought,
but could not make it out. Certainly not that of any
of the great houses—no doubt my kind preserver belonged to the lesser nobility—but I could soon find out.
Then I closed my eyes once more and would have slept,
but was aroused by some one entering the room, and,
looking up, saw Mousette.

"Ah ! madem—madame, I mean," she said eagerly,
"thank God, you are looking none the worse for that
terrible night. I little thought we would ever live to see
daylight again."

"Where are we, Mousette ? And who are the kind
people who saved us ? "

"I do not know, madame," she answered quickly,
"but we are the only women here. But," she ran on,
"it is mid-day and touching the dinner hour. Will
madame rise or be served here ? "

"I will rise, of course, Mousette ; " and during the
course of my toilet I asked if the people of the house
knew who we were.

"I have not mentioned anything, madame," replied

Mousette, with her face slightly turned away, "and Lalande is discreet."

I felt that Mousette knew more than she cared to tell; but it is not my way to converse with servants; and finishing my dressing in silence, I asked her to show me the way to the salon, and as I spoke I heard a gong go.

"Monsieur will be served at once," said Mousette. "This way, madame," and opening the curtains of the door, she led me down a series of winding steps worn with the feet that had passed up and down there for perhaps a couple of centuries, and then, past a long passage hung with suits of rusty armour and musty trophies of the chase, to a large door. I gathered that Mousette had been making good use of her time whilst in the house, but kept silent. The door was open, and as I passed in Mousette left me. I found I was in a room that was apparently used as a dining-room and salon as well. There was trace of recent occupation, for a man's hat and a pair of leathern gloves somewhat soiled with use were lying on a table, and a great hound rose slowly from the rushes on the floor, and, after eyeing me a moment, came up in a most friendly manner to be patted and made much of. A small table near the fireplace was laid for one, and as I was looking towards it a grey-haired and sober servant brought in the dinner, and then, bowing gravely, announced that I was served.

"Is not monsieur—monsieur— ?" I stammered.

"Monsieur le Chevalier has had to go out on urgent business. He has ordered me to present his compliments to madame——"

"I see ; monsieur does not dine here."

The man bowed, and I sat down to a solitary meal with the big dog at my feet, and the silent, grave attendant to wait on me. I amused myself with the hound, and with taking note of the room. Like everything else I had seen, its furniture and fittings seemed a century old, and spoke of wealth that had passed away. There was a sadness about this, and a gloom that saddened me in spite of myself, so that it was with an effort I managed to eat, and then, when dinner was over, I told the servant to inform his master that I desired to thank him for the great kindness shown to me.

"I will deliver madame's message," and with this reply he went.

Left to myself, I went to the window and looked out through the glazing. The landscape was obscured by a rolling mist ; but the sun was dissipating this bravely. It was a wild and desolate scene, and, despite the sunlight, oppressed me almost as much as my solitary meal, so I turned back into the room, and, seating myself in a great chair, stared into the fireplace, the hound stretching himself beside me. I was still wearied, and my thoughts ran slowly on until I caught myself wondering who my unknown host was, and getting a trifle impatient, too, because he did not come, for I was anxious to set forward to Meymac.

Suddenly I heard a steady measured step in the passage, the hound leaped up with a bay of welcome, and as I rose from my seat the curtain was lifted, and I stood face to face with my husband.

"You ! De Lorgnac !" I gasped.

"Even I," he said. "I thought you knew. Are you none the worse for your adventure of last night ? "

"I am quite well, thanks to God." "And thanks to you," I was about to add, but my lips could not frame the words, and I felt myself beginning to tremble. Monsieur noticed this.

"I am afraid you underrate your strength ; do sit down," he said kindly.

"I prefer to stand, thank you, Monsieur le Chevalier," and then there was a silence, during which I know not what passed through de Lorgnac's mind ; but I, I was fighting with myself to prevent my heart getting the better of me, for if so I would have to humble myself —I, a daugher of Mieux ! Monsieur broke the silence himself.

"Denise, I give you my word of honour that I would not have intruded on you, but that you asked to see me, and I thought you knew whom you wished to see. Besides, I felt that I owed a little to myself. You have accused me of being a dishonoured gentleman, of being little less than a common bravo, of wedding you to your misery for your estates." He came forward a step and looked me full in the face with his clear strong eyes. "As God is my witness," he went on, "you are utterly mistaken. I am going to-day on an affair the issue of which no one can foresee. Think ! Would I go with a lie on my lips ? Answer me—tell me. Whatever else you may think, you do not believe this."

I was fumbling with one of his gloves, and could not meet his look.

"You put me in a difficult position, monsieur—this is your own house."

He looked about him with a bitter smile. "Yes—it is my house—hardly the house to which one would bring the heiress of Mieux—but is that your answer to me ?"

And still I was silent. I could not bring myself to say what he wanted. And now too it was not only pride that was holding me back. I felt that if I gave him the answer he wished, manlike he would begin to press his love on me, and I was not prepared for this. I did not know my own feelings towards him; but of one thing I was sure—I would not be bound by hollow vows that were forced upon me, and so I fenced.

"This adventure of yours, monsieur—is it so very dangerous ?"

"It is not the danger I am thinking of. It is your faith in my honour. No man is blameless, and least of all I. I own I was wrong—that I sinned grievously in marrying you as I have. My excuse is that I love you —that is a thing I cannot control. But I will do all I can to make reparation. I will never see you again, and the times are such that you may soon be as free as air. All that I ask is this one thing."

"But, monsieur, have you no proof—nothing to bring forward ?"

"I have nothing to offer but my word."

"Your word—your word—is that all you can say ?"

He bowed slightly in reply, but his look was hungry for his answer. Still I could not give it, and played with time.

"You say you love me. Does love resign its object as you do—without a struggle ? If I believe one thing I must believe all, monsieur. I cannot believe a profes-

sion of love like yours "—how false I knew this to be—
" and the rest must follow."

He twisted at his moustache in the old way, and I saw
his sunburnt face grow, as it were on a sudden, wan and
haggard, and the pity that lies in all women's hearts
rose within me.

" Monsieur le Chevalier, if you were to get the answer
that you wanted, would you still adhere to your promise
and never see me again ? "

" I have said so," he said hoarsely.

" Then, monsieur, let me tell you that I have found I
was wrong, and that I do believe your word—nay, more,
monsieur, I have found de Lorgnac to be a gallant
gentleman—whom Denise de Mieux has to thank for
her honour and her life——"

" Denise ! "   There was a glad note in his voice, and
in a moment he had stepped up to me, and I had
yielded, but that I wanted this king amongst men to be
king over himself.

" A moment, monsieur.   You have given me your
word, be strong enough to keep it.   I have learned to
respect and honour you; but I do not love you.   You
must keep your word, de Lorgnac, and go—until I ask
you to come back."

Without a word he turned on his heel and walked towards the door ; but I could not let him go like that
and I called to him.   He stopped and turned towards
me, but made no further advance, and then I went up
to him with my hand outstretched.

" Monsieur, there is one thing more.   I have the
honour to be the wife of de Lorgnac, and for the present
I crave your permission to make Lorgnac my home.

Will you not grant me this request ? And will you not shake hands before you go ? "

I thought I had tried him too far, and that the man would break down ; but no, the metal was true. Yet the haggard look in his face went out as he answered :

" Denise, Lorgnac is yours to its smallest stone, and I thank you for this." Then he bent down and touched my fingers with his lips, and was gone.

CHAPTER IX.

LA COQUILLE'S MESSAGE.

"UNTIL I ask you to come back."

These were my own words to de Lorgnac, and they rang in my ears as I listened to his footsteps dying away along the passage. Would I ever call him back? It was on my tongue to do so as he went; but I held myself in, and began restlessly to pace the room, the dog watching my movements with his grave eyes. I could not bear to have them fixed upon me—those eyes that seemed to have a soul imprisoned behind them, and that were so like, in their honest glance, to those of my husband. I bent down and stroked the great shaggy head.

"If I but knew myself! If I but knew myself!" I called out aloud, and then moved aimlessly towards the window. Here I looked out, but saw nothing of the view, for I was looking into my own heart, and there all was mist and fog. The more I tried to think the more hopeless it all seemed, and it came to me to abandon my position, and, accepting my fate, make the best of circumstances as other women had done. I could give respect and trust; and as long as my husband knew this, and I looked after his comforts, he would never know that I did not love him. I had seen enough of the

world to know how selfishly blind men are in this respect. But de Lorgnac was not as other men. I felt
that his keen eye would take in the part I was playing,
that his great love for me would penetrate and grasp
all my devices, and that he would feel that he had only
a wife—not a lover as well. What was this love that I
was in doubt about ? If it meant absolute sacrifice of
myself, then I could give it to no man. If it meant
respect, and honour, and a desire for a constant guiding
presence about me, then I felt I could give that to
Blaise de Lorgnac ; but I felt, too, that more was due
to him, and it was well to wait—to wait until my heart
told me undeniably that I had found its king.

The neigh of a horse, and the clatter of hoofs on
stony ground, aroused me. Bending forward over the
window, I looked out and saw de Lorgnac and a half
dozen mounted men riding out of the courtyard. My
husband rode a little in advance, square and erect, his
plumeless helmet glittering in the sunlight ; but he
never gave one backward glance to the window. Even
if he thought I was not there, he might have done so ;
he might have given me the chance. The men who
rode behind him seemed stout, strong fellows, though
their casques were battered and their cuirasses rusty ;
and as the last of them went out I recognised la Coquille. I know I had no right to pick and choose for
de Lorgnac, but I would have given my right hand not
to have seen that swashbuckler riding behind my husband. Such men as he were never employed on honest
deeds ! With a stamp of my foot I turned from the
window and saw Pierre, the old servant, waiting patiently near the door, with a huge bunch of keys on a

salver in his hand. As our eyes met he bowed to the
ground.

"I did not know it was Madame de Lorgnac who was
here until an hour ago," he said. "Monsieur le
Chevalier has directed that these should be given over
to you, and the household is outside awaiting madame's
orders."

Half amused, half embarrassed, I took the keys. I
felt sure de Lorgnac had given no such order, but that
this was the spontaneous outcome of old Pierre's polite-
ness. Fastening them in my girdle, I said, with as
gracious, yet dignified an air as I could assume, "Call
in the people, please."

Pierre bowed once more to the ground and vanished
to reappear in two minutes with a well-grown youth,
and the two stood bolt upright before me. This was
the household of de Lorgnac, then. The smile died
away from my lips as I thought of the straits to which
a gallant gentleman was reduced. "Pierre," I said,
"you must add Mousette, my maid, to the household,
and see that the good Lalande is well treated," and I
placed a small purse containing a half dozen or so of
gold crowns that I happened to have with me in
the old man's hands. He held the little silken bag for
a moment, and then his face began to flush.

"There is no need, madame ; we have enough."

"You forget, Pierre, what I am giving you is Monsieur le Chevalier's, to whom God grant a safe return."

He took the money, though I saw a suspicious swimming of his eyes, and I hastily asked :

"And do those men who rode out with Monsieur
belong to the household, too, Pierre ? "

" St. Blaise—no, madame ! They came here but yesterday morning, and with their leader have drunk and sworn about the place ever since. They filled the lower hall with disorder ; but they are stout fellows, and we had hardly been able to help you so well last night but for them ; they follow Monsieur le Chevalier for a little time only."

I well knew for what purpose, but kept silent on that point, saying, " And how far is Lorgnac from here ? "

" The town you mean, madame ? "

" Precisely."

" At the foot of the hill to the right of the château ; we cannot see it from here. Ah ! it was a fine place until Monsieur de Ganache, and his bandits of Huguenots, came over from La Roche Canillac one fine day and put the place to fire and sword. Monsieur le Chevalier has vowed his death at the shrine of Our Lady of Lorgnac. Ah ! he is a devil, is Monsieur de Ganache ; he is with the Bearnnois now."

" And is there any news of the Huguenots moving now ? "

" None, madame ; but Antoine the peddler of Argentat says that a great lady from Paris is at the Château de Canillac, and that Monsieur de Turenne, and many a high lord from the south have been visiting her. They will be tired of dancing and singing soon, those hot bloods, and we may have to look to the castle walls."

" This evening, then, you must take me to Lorgnac," I said with a view to end the conversation.

" It is madame's order, but——" and he stopped short for a second, and then continued, " Antoine, the peddler's daughter, who married Gribot, the wood-

man of Lorgnac, has a cow and calf for sale, and there
is none in the château."

" Then buy it of her, Pierre," and with another low
bow the old man withdrew with the " household," who
had evidently been trained in a severe school by Pierre,
for he had stood bolt upright like a soldier at attention,
and never moved muscle during the whole of the interview.

So my business as mistress of Lorgnac had begun ;
but there were one or two things that required immediate attention from me before I began my household
duties.   I called Mousette, and going over the money
we had, found that it reached to about a hundred
crowns.   This was enough for all present requirements,
though I would want much more soon, if all the designs
that were flitting through my brain, in shadow as it
were, were carried out; but that could be easily arranged
hereafter.   Then I saw Lalande, and informing him
that my journey was over, asked if there would be any
difficulty in his remaining at Lorgnac for at least a few
days, as I wanted his help.   He answered that he was
at my service, and this being settled, I set about ex-
ploring the quaint old mansion, and as I did so all kinds
of dreams of changing its cheerless aspect possessed me,
and the time passed on wings.

In the afternoon we visited the town.   Alas !   It
had been for a century but a hamlet, and all traces of
town, if ever there was any, had long gone.   But small and
poor and obscure as Lorgnac was, the hand of war had
not spared it, and blackened rafter and fallen roof still
bore witness to Monsieur de Ganache's pitiless visit.
Privation and want had left their marks on the faces of

the score or so of inhabitants of the village ; but when they found out who I was, they came forward eagerly, and a small child, no doubt prompted by her elders, gave me a bouquet of wild flowers, and I went back, vowing in my heart that ere many weeks were over all this would be changed.

That night as I sat before the huge log fire in the hall with Moro the hound—I found out his name from Pierre—for the first time for many days my mind was at rest, and I began to feel also, for the first time, the glow that comes to the heart when one is able to help one's fellow creatures. I knew I was young and inexperienced, that my life, especially within the last year in the poisonous air of the Court, had been made up of frivolities and follies that had brought their own sharp punishment with them, yet I had always in my mind the desire for a nobler life, where my wealth could be used to help the distressed, and as far as it could go to add to the happiness of others. So far so good ; but there was my own happiness and that of de Lorgnac to think of. There was a great pity in my heart for him ; but was it right to mistake pity for love, and give myself wholly to a man to make him happy, to my own sorrow ? For the life of me I could not see this. I felt that a man who would accept such a sacrifice would be unworthy of it. But Blaise de Lorgnac was not of those who would do this. He was true metal. Was there another man who would have acted as he did— whose love was so generous and yet so strong ? I doubt it. I well knew the profession of a man's love, that swore it was ready to die for its object ; but was unable to abandon or to forego anything in its selfishness. But

the love that was, as it were, in the hollow of my hand
was not as this ; and then I began to see the hidden
secret of my own heart, and called out aloud, " Come
back, de Lorgnac. Come back ! " But the echo of
the vaulted roof was my only answer. Yet that night
I slept a happy woman, for I knew what it was now to
love.

The days passed, and notwithstanding that I threw
myself heart and soul into my plans about Lorgnac,
there was an ever-eating care in my heart, for no tidings
came of my husband, and it was not pride now, but a
shyness that I could not overcome, do what I would,
that absolutely prevented me from making any inquiry,
though no doubt inquiry would have been fruitless and
vain. Listless and tired, I sat one day towards the afternoon at the window by the hall, my favourite seat, and
looked down the winding road, that clung to the side of
the steep rocks, hoping against hope that I should see
the great white horse, when suddenly I .spied a horseman riding towards the castle with a loose rein, and at
times he swayed from side to side like a drunken man.
In a moment I felt the worst tidings, and knew that the
rider was bringing me sorrow. With an effort I roused
myself, and with shaking limbs went down to the courtyard, and there, calling Lalande and Pierre, waited for
his coming, who was bringing me the evil message I
felt I already knew. We had not long to wait. With
a thunder of hoofs, the horseman passed the lower drawbridge, and reining in sharply, slid rather than dismounted from his saddle. It was la Coquille, covered
with blood and dust, and the red gone out of his
cheeks.

"Madame—Madame de Lorgnac!" he called out in a cracked voice.

"I am here, monsieur."

"I can stay but a moment. Fly! Fly! The blood-hounds are even now on my track, and they will be here in an hour."

"Is that all?" How my heart beat, though my voice was cool!

"All? No. But give me to drink, and I will speak. My throat is parched and I have lost much blood."

Pierre handed him a flagon of wine, which he drained at a draught, and then went on.

"It will not take long to tell. *Mordieu!* It was the best plan ever laid, and to think it was spoiled by a traitor. Madame, if we had succeeded, France would have been at peace, and your husband a marshal and peer. We watched the Bearnnois for days, and then laid out to seize him, on the day of a hunting party. We got all details of movements from that double-dyed traitor, de Clermont; but he played the right hand for Navarre, and the left for us. We laid out as I said, and the King came: but not alone—our ambuscade was surprised, and five as good fellows as ever drew sword now swing to the branches of the beech trees of Canillac. I got off somehow, but alas! they have taken de Lorgnac, though not easily, for Monsieur de Ganache fell to his sword, and I think another too."

"Taken de Lorgnac!"

"Yes, madame—*Mordieu!* It is the fortune of war! They are coming straight here, for what purpose I know not; but, *mille diables!* I have wasted enough time already, and the skin of la Coquille is the skin of

la Coquille. There is not a moment to spare. Fly if you
value your lives ! " And with this he put his foot in his
stirrup, and made as if he would mount his panting
horse again.

" Save your skin, Monsieur la Coquille," I said. " As
for me and mine, we stay here. Would to God my husband had true swords at his back ! "

He stopped and put down his foot.

" You can say what you please, madame, but we did
our best ; but as God is my witness the Huguenots
mean death, and I advise you to go. In a half-hour it
will be too late."

" Monsieur, I have asked you to save the skin of la
Coquille."

His broad face became dark and red with the blood
that rushed to it. " I know I deserve nothing at your
hands, madame," he said. "You think me a cur, and one
I am. *Mordieu !* For a bribe of twenty crowns—so
fallen am I—I once played the craven for de Clermont
before you. It was at Ambazac not so many days ago.
Did I know you were de Lorgnac's wife, I had cut off
my sword arm rather than do what I did then. Let me
make some recompense. I implore you to go. Fools,"
and he turned to Lalande and Pierre, " do you wish
to swing from the rafters here ? Take her away, by
force if necessary."

" Enough, monsieur. You have said too much ! I
am sorry for you. I would help you if I could, but my
place is here. Save yourself whilst there is yet time.
As for me, I and mine will defend Lorgnac to the last
stone."

He flung the reins he held in his hand from him, and

over the sin-marked features of the man there came somehow an expression of nobleness.

"Then, by God, madame, I stay! And I thank you for teaching me how to die. Twenty-five years— twenty-five years ago I was a gentleman, and to-day I bridge over the past. I will stay, madame, and the sword of la Coquille will help to hold the castle for you. Hasten, men. Up with the drawbridge. *Ah! sacre nom d'un chien!* We are too late!"

CHAPTER X.

IT was too late. Before I realized it, the courtyard was full of armed men. La Coquille, who had flung himself to the front with his sword drawn, was ridden down and secured ere he could strike a blow, whilst Lalande and Pierre, who bore no weapons but their poniards, and were utterly surprised, shared the like fate. So suddenly and quickly was this done that— for the courage had gone out of my finger-tips—I had no time to flee, and I stood like a stone, whilst a sea of savage faces surged around me. I gave myself for dead, and one, a trooper—more brute than man—raised his sword to slay me, but was struck from his horse in the act. Then some one seemed to come from nowhere to my side—a tall, straight figure, with a shining blade in his hand, and he called out, " Back ! back ! Or I run the first man through ! "

The men were called to order in a moment at that tone of command, though a voice I well knew and now hated called out :

" Well done, de Rosny, my squire of dames. *Pardieu !* We have the whole hive—Queen-Bee and all."

" By God ! " said another, " they will hang from the rafters in a half-hour, then—my poor Ganache ! "

And the speaker, whose rough, harsh voice was as piti-

less as his speech, swore a bitter oath. " Gently,
Tremblecourt," replied the one who had been called de
Rosny; "our poor de Ganache's soul has not flown so far
but that the others can overtake it in time." And then
de Clermont came up to me, but as he passed la Coquille
in so doing, the latter strained at his cords, and hissed
rather than spoke out the word " Traitor ! " as he spat
at him.

" You hang in a little time head downwards at de
Lorgnac's feet for that," said de Clermont calmly, and
then turning to me, " 'Tis a sad business this, madame ;
but war is war, and after all things are going as you
would have them, are they not ? "

I could not bear to meet that sneering, beautiful face,
which, now that its mask was snatched away, cared not
in how evil an aspect it showed itself. Words would
not come to me, and as I stood there before de Clermont,
quivering in every limb at the awful threat conveyed
in his speech to la Coquille, de Tremblecourt's voice
rang out again, mad and broken with rage :

" Away with them ! Sling them from the parapet—
now ! "

The men around rushed with a yell at la Coquille and
his fellow-prisoners—God pardon those who cause the
horrors of war—but my defender, de Rosny, again interposed, and drove them back, despite de Tremblecourt's
angry protests, whilst de Clermont stayed his rage with
a quiet :

" Be still, Tremblecourt. The King will be here in
ten minutes with our other prisoner, and we will deal
with Messieurs—in a bunch," and he glanced at me
with a meaning in his eyes that I read as an open page.

"Come, madame," said de Rosny, who saw my pallor,
"let me take you out of this. I pledge the word of
Bethune that no harm will touch you ; but that is to
happen, I fear, which is not fit for you to see." With
these words he took my arm kindly and led me inside,
unresisting and as in a dream. In the hall where we
stopped I forced myself to regain some courage. It
was no time for a faint heart.

"Monsieur ! What does this all mean ? What is to
happen to de Lorgnac ? Tell me—I am his wife, monsieur.".

He bowed gravely yet sadly. "The King of Navarre
is generous, madame. Henri will be here soon, and all
may yet be well. In the meantime rest you here, and
compose yourself—you are safe from harm."

With this, he, who was in after years to be the first
man in France, left me almost stunned and broken by
what I had heard. Now that I was about to lose him—
nay, had already lost him, for nothing, I felt sure,
would move these pitiless hearts—I realized to the end
what de Lorgnac was to me, and with this came the
dreadful conviction that it was I, and I alone, who had
brought this on my husband. I, a fool in my folly, who
did not know my own heart, I who with a word might
have stayed and kept him who was all in all to me, had
driven him forth with my senseless pride to death. I
could do nothing to save him. What could a woman
do against these men ? And then it was as if the whole
horror that was to be pictured itself before my eyes,
and a mocking fiend gibed in whispers in my ears, "You,
you have done this ! " Almost with a cry I sprang from
my seat, my hand on my forehead and an unspoken

prayer on my lips. I felt that my brain was giving way, and that I must do something to regain myself and think. This was no time for aught but action, and here I was giving way utterly. I might do something—surely my woman's wit could suggest some means of saving my husband? Then what happens to those who are face to face with an awful terror happened to me, and, as once before, I fell on my knees before God's Throne, and prayed in a mortal agony. " God help me in my distress ! " I called out aloud, and a quiet voice answered :

" Perhaps He has sent the help, Denise."

I sprang up with a start, a wild hope rushing through my heart, and saw Raoul de Clermont before me, with the sneering hardness out of his face and all the old soft light in his eyes. If it was so—if he but bore me the glad tidings his words hinted at—I could forgive him all, and be his friend forever.

" Say that again, monsieur," I gasped ; " say it again and I will bless you to my last breath." And as I spoke the heavy folds of the curtain that covered the doorway moved as if stirred by a wind.

" I said that perhaps God "—and he bowed reverently —ah ! devil and traitor !—" that perhaps God has answered your prayer. You have asked for help, and it has come. I am here to offer it. I, and I alone, can save de Lorgnac, by force if necessary, for I have fifty lances at my heels, and it rests with you to say the word. I have been mad, Denise ; then I came to my senses ; and now I am mad again. I love you—do you hear ? Love you as man never loved woman. You beautiful thing of ice ! Come with me, and de Lorgnac is free. Come ! "

In his eagerness he put forth his hand towards me, but with a shudder I drew back and his face darkened. Then nerving myself, I made one last appeal.

"Raoul de Clermont, I believed you once to be a man of honour. Let me think so again ; give me the chance. Be merciful for once. Save my husband as you say you can. See, it is a wife who pleads. Man ! There must be some spark of knighthood in you to fire your soul ! You are brave, I know. Can you not be generous and pitiful ? You have tried to kill my soul. Monsieur, I will forget that—I will forget the past, and thank you forever if you do this. Save him, for I love him ! "

" Love him ! "

" Yes, love him as he deserves to be loved, and by a better woman. De Clermont, be true to yourself."

His breath came thick and fast, and then he spoke with an effort :

" You ask too much, Denise. I have offered you my terms. I give you five minutes to say yes or no, and I will take your answer as final. God is answering your prayer in His own way," he went on, with the shadow of a sneer once more across his lips.

" He mostly does," came the reply, as the curtain was lifted and de Rosny stepped in, calling out as he entered, " Madame, the King ! "

Then there was a tramp of spurred boots, the clashing of steel scabbards, the waving of plumes, and ere I knew it I was at the feet of the Bourbon, sobbing out my prayer for mercy.

He raised me gently—there was no more knightly heart than his. " Madame ! It is not enemies that Henri

de Bourbon needs, but friends. It is not sorrow his
presence would cause, but joy. There has been enough
blood shed already in this miserable affair, and—I think
it is my good de Rosny here who anticipated me—all
our prisoners are free, but there is some one here who
will tell you the rest himself better than the Bearnnois
can." And, putting a kind hand on my shoulder, he
faced me round to meet the eyes of de Lorgnac.

"I have come back unasked, Denise," he said ; but
I could make no answer, and then he took me in his
arms and kissed me before them all.

"A wedding present to the happy pair !" and something struck me lightly on the shoulder and fell at my
feet. It was the glove that de Clermont had snatched
from me on the day of my marriage. "I return a present from madame, given to me on her wedding day. It
is no longer of use to me—Monsieur le Chevalier, will
you not take it ?" and de Clermont was before us, the
same awful look in his eyes that I had seen there when
he played with death before de Norreys.

De Lorgnac's arm dropped from my waist, and his
bronzed face paled as he stood as if petrified, looking
at the soft white glove at my feet. Then with a voice
as hard and stern as his look he turned to me, and
pointing to the glove, said :

"Is this true, madame ?"

"It is my glove," was all I could say.

"And permit me to restore it to you," cut in the
King, and with a movement he lifted the glove and
placed it in my husband's hand. "Give it to her back,
man ! Madame de Canillac was at your wedding, and
my good Margot who writes me such clever letters, and

they have both told me the story of your marriage, and
the incident of the glove. They both saw it snatched
from your wife's hand by M. le Marquis—Ventre St.
Gris ! For once I think a woman's gossip has done
some good—and on the word of Navarre what I say is
true. As for you, monsieur," and Henri turned to de
Clermont, " Monsieur de Rosny here has my commands
for you, and your further presence is excused."

My husband's arm was round my waist once more ;
but de Clermont made no movement to go, standing
quietly twisting his short blonde moustache.

" Monsieur, you have heard his Majesty," put in de
Rosny.

" Yes—I thought, however, that Monsieur de Lorgnac might have a word to say ere I went."

" That will be in another place, and over our crossed
swords, Monsieur le Marquis," replied my husband,
heedless of my entreating look and gesture, and in as
cold and measured a voice as de Clermont's.

" I am at your service, monsieur, when and wherever
you please," and with this, and a formal bow to the
King, he passed from the room—a man under God's
right arm of justice.

What happened I never was able to find out exactly ;
but as far as I could gather it was this. As already
mentioned, la Coquille, Lalande, and Pierre, had been
released by Navarre on his coming, and the former being
faint from his wounds was resting on a wooden bench
in the courtyard. As de Clermont passed, the sight of la
Coquille and the memory of the insult he had put on
him roused the haughty noble, already in a white heat
with rage, to madness, and he struck the freelance once,

twice, across the face with a light cane he bore in his hand, and fell a moment after stabbed to the heart, his murderer being cut down by the men-at-arms.

At once all was hurry and confusion. The dying man was borne in as gently as he could be, and placed on a settle. There was no leech in hand, and long before the priest of Lorgnac came it was all over. We did what we could, and in the horror of the fate that had overtaken this man in the pride of strength I forgot the past utterly. I could only see a terrible suffering for which there was no relief. We gathered, an awestruck group, around him, and he spoke no word at first, but suddenly called out, " Hold me up—I choke ! "

Some one—I afterwards found it was Tremblecourt —raised him slightly and he spoke again, " De Lorgnac ! Say what you have to say now, I'm going."

And Blaise de Lorgnac knelt by the couch, saying as he did so :

" I have no message now—forget my words, de Clermont."

" Would to God I had died by your hand," came the answer, " but to go like this—struck down like a dog. Your hand, de Lorgnac—yours, Denise—quick—I am going. Forgive."

De Tremblecourt laid him softly back on the cushion, and my tears fell fast on the cold hand I held in mine. Who could remember wrongs at such a moment ?

The King bent over him and whispered in his ear. I thought I heard the word " pray," and a wan smile played on the lips of the dying man.

" Too late—I cannot cringe now. Ah ! Norreys ! I will join you soon. Denise—pardon," and he was gone.

    *   *   *   *   *

Late that night when all had gone to rest I walked on the ramparts of Lorgnac, and leaning against the parapet, looked out into the moonlight. So lost was I in thought that it was not until his hand was on my shoulder that I knew my husband had joined me.

"Denise," he said, "the King goes to-morrow, and—I—do I go or stay?"

And Monsieur le Chevalier—he is Monsieur le Maréchal Duc now—got the answer he wanted.

THE END.

THE CAPTAIN MORATTI'S LAST AFFAIR

CHAPTER I.

"ARCADES AMBO."

"HALT!" The word, which seemed to come from nowhere, rang out into the crisp winter moonlight so sharply, so suddenly, so absolutely without warning, that the Cavaliere Michele di Lippo, who was ambling comfortably along, reined in his horse with a jerk; and with a start, looked into the night. He had not to fret his curiosity above a moment, for a figure gliding out from the black shadows of the pines, fencing in each side of the lonely road, stepped full into the white band of light, stretching between the darkness on either hand and stood in front of the horse. As the two faced each other, it was not the fact that there was a man in his path that made the rider keep a restraining hand on his bridle. It was the persuasive force, the voiceless command, in the round muzzle of an arquebuse pointed at his heart, and along the barrel of which di Lippo could see the glint of the moonlight, a thin bright streak ending in the wicked blinking star of the lighted fuse. The

107

cavaliere took in the position at a glance, and being a
man of resolution, hurriedly cast up his chances of
escape by spurring his horse, and suddenly riding down
the thief. In a flash the thought came and was dis-
missed. It was impossible ; for the night-hawk had
taken his stand at a distance of about six feet off, space
enough to enable him to blow his quarry's heart out,
well before the end of any sudden rush to disarm him.
The mind moves like lightning in matters of this kind,
and di Lippo surrendered without condition. Though
his heart was burning within him, he was outwardly
cool and collected. He had yielded to force he could
not resist. Could he have seen ever so small a chance,
the positions might have been reversed. As it was,
Messer the bandit might still have to look to himself,
and his voice was icy as the night as he said : " Well !
I have halted. What more ? It is chill, and I care not
to be kept waiting."

The robber was not without humour, and a line of
teeth showed, for an instant, behind the burning match
of the weapon he held steadily before him. He did not,
however, waste words. " Throw down your purse."

The cavaliere hesitated. Ducats were scarce with
him, but the bandit had a short patience. " *Diavolo !*
Don't you hear, signore ? "

It was useless to resist. The fingers of the cavaliere
fumbled under his cloak, and a fat purse fell squab into
the snow, where it lay, a dark spot in the whiteness
around, for all the world like a sleeping toad. The
bandit chuckled as he heard the plump thud of the
purse, and di Lippo's muttered curse was lost in the
sharp order : " Get off the horse."

"But——"

"I am in a hurry, signore." The robber blew on the match of his arquebuse, and the match in its glow cast a momentary light on his face, showing the outlines of high aquiline features, and the black curve of a pair of long moustaches.

"*Maledetto !*" and the disgusted cavaliere dismounted, the scabbard of his useless sword striking with a clink against the stirrup iron, and he unwillingly swung from the saddle and stood in the snow—a tall figure, lean and gaunt.

As he did this, the bandit stepped back a pace, so as to give him the road. "Your excellency," he said mockingly, "is now free to pass—on foot. A walk will doubtless remove the chill your excellency finds so unpleasant."

But di Lippo made no advance. In fact, as his feet touched the snow, he recovered the composure he had so nearly lost, and saw his way to gain some advantage from defeat. It struck him that here was the very man he wanted for an affair of the utmost importance. Indeed, it was for just such an instrument that he had been racking his brains, as he rode on that winter night through the Gonfolina defile, which separates the middle and the lower valleys of the Arno. And now—a hand turn—and he had found his man. True, an expensive find ; but cheap if all turned out well—that is, well from di Lippo's point of view. This thing the cavaliere wanted done he could not take into his own hands. Not from fear—it was no question of that ; but because it was not convenient; and Michele di Lippo never gave himself any inconvenience, although it was sometimes thrust upon him in an unpleasant manner by others. If he could but induce the man before him to undertake the task, what might not be ? But the knight of the road was evidently very impatient.

" Blood of a king ! " he swore, " are you going, signore ? Think you I am to stand here all night ? "

" Certainly not," answered di Lippo in his even voice, " nor am I. But to come to the point. I want a little business managed, and will pay for it. You appear to be a man of courage—will you undertake the matter ? "

" *Cospetto !* But you are a cool hand ! Who are you ? "

" Is it necessary to know ? I offer a hundred crowns, fifty to be paid to you if you agrée, and fifty on the completion of the affair."

" A matter of the dagger ? "

" That is for you to decide."

The bandit almost saw the snarl on di Lippo's lips as he dropped out slowly : " You are too cautious, my friend—you think to the skin. The rack will come whether you do my business or not." The words were not exactly calculated to soothe, and called up an unpleasant vision before the robber's eyes. A sudden access of wrath shook him. " Begone, signore ! " he burst out, " lest my patience exhausts itself, and I give you a bed in the snow. Why I have spared your life, I know not. Begone ; warm yourself with a walk——"

" I will pay a hundred crowns," interrupted di Lippo.

" A hundred devils—begone ! "

" As you please. Remember, it is a hundred crowns, and, on the faith of a noble, I say nothing about to-night. Where can I find you, in case you change your mind ? A hundred crowns is a comfortable sum of money, mind you."

There was no excitement about di Lippo. He spoke slowly and distinctly. His cool voice neither rose nor dropped, but he spoke in a steady, chill monotone. A hundred crowns *was* a comfortable sum of money. It was a sum not to be despised. For a tithe of that—nay, for two pistoles—the Captain Guido Moratti would have risked his life twice over, things had come to such a pass with him. Highway robbery was not exactly his line, although sometimes, as on this occasion, he had been driven to it by the straits of the times. But suppose this offer was a blind ? Suppose the man before him merely wanted to know where to get at him, to hand him over to the tender mercies of the thumbscrew and the rack ? On the other hand, the man might be in earnest—and a hundred crowns ! He hesitated.

"A—hun—dred—crowns." The cavaliere repeated these words, and there was a silence. Finally the bandit spoke :

"I frankly confess, signore, that stealing purses, even as I have done to-day, is not my way ; but a man must live. If you mean what you say, there must be no half-confidences. Tell me who you are, and I will tell you where to find me."

"I am the Cavaliere Michele di Lippo of Castel Lippo on the Greve."

"Where is Castel Lippo ? "

"At the junction of the Arno and the Greve—on the left bank."

"Very well. In a week you will hear from me again."

" It is enough. You will allow me to ransom the horse. I will send you the sum. On my word of honour, I have nothing to pay it at once."

" The signore's word of honour is doubtless very white. But a can in the hand is a can in the hand, and I need a horse—Good-night ! "

" Good-night ! But a can in the hand is not always wine to the lips, though a hundred crowns is ever a hundred crowns ; " and saying this, di Lippo drew his cloak over the lower part of his face, and turned sharply to the right into the darkness, without so much as giving a look behind him. His horse would have followed; but quick as thought, Moratti's hand was on the trailing reins, and holding them firmly, he stooped and picked up the purse, poising it at arm's-length in front of him.

" Silver," he muttered, as his fingers felt the coins through the soft leather—" thirty crowns at the most, perhaps an odd gold piece or so—and now to be off. *Hola !* Steady ! " and mounting the horse, he turned his head round, still talking to himself : " I am in luck. Cheese falls on my macaroni—thirty broad pieces and a horse, and a hundred crowns more in prospect. Captain Guido Moratti, the devil smiles on you—you will end a Count. *Animo !* " He touched the horse with his heels, and went forward at a smart gallop ; and as he galloped, he threw his head back and laughed loudly and mirthlessly into the night.

In the meantime it was with a sore heart that the cavaliere made his way through the forest to the banks of the Arno, and then plodded along the river-side, through the wood, by a track scarcely discernible to any but one who had seen it many times. On his right hand the river hummed drearily ; on his left, the trees sighed in the night-wind ; and before him the narrow track wound, now up, then down, now twisting amongst the pines in darkness, then stretching in front, straight as a plumb-line. It was gall to di Lippo to think of the loss of the crowns and the good horse ; it was bitterness to trudge it in the cold along the weary path that led to the ferry across the Arno, which he would have to cross before reaching his own home ; and he swore deeply, under the muffling of his cloak, as he pressed on at his roundest pace. He soon covered the two miles that lay between him and the ferry ; but it was past midnight ere he did this, and reaching the ferryman's hut, battered at the door with the hilt of his sword. Eventually he aroused the ferryman, who came forth grumbling. Had it been any one else, honest Giuseppe would have told him to go hang before he would have risen from his warm bed ; but the Cavaliere Michele was a noble, and, although poor, had a lance or two, and Castel Lippo, which bore an ill name, was only a mangonel shot from the opposite bank. So Giuseppe punted his excellency across ; and his excellency vented his spleen with a curse at everything in general, and the bandit in particular, as he stepped ashore and hurried to his dwelling. It was a steep climb that led up by a bridle-path to his half-ruined tower, and di Lippo stood at the postern, and whistled on his silver whistle, and knocked for many a time, before he heard the chains clanking, and the bar put back. At last the door opened, and a figure stood before him, a lantern in one hand.

"St. John ! But it is your worship ! We did not expect you until sunrise. And the horse, excellency ? "

"Stand aside, fool. I have been robbed, that is all.
Yes—let the matter drop ; and light me up quick. Will
you gape all night there ? "

The porter, shutting the gate hastily, turned, and
walking before his master, led him across the courtyard.
Even by the moonlight, it could be seen that the flag-
stones were old and worn with age. In many places
they had come apart, and with the spring, sprouts of
green grass and white serpyllum would shoot up from
the cracks. At present, these fissures were choked with
snow. Entering the tower by an arched door at the end
of the courtyard, they ascended a winding stair, which
led into a large but only partially furnished room.
Here the man lit two candles, and di Lippo, dropping
his cloak, sank down into a chair, saying : " Make up
a fire, will you—and bring me some wine ; after that,
you may go."

The man threw a log or two into the fireplace, where
there was already the remains of a fire, and the pine-
wood soon blazed up cheerfully. Then he placed a flask
of Orvieto and a glass at his master's elbow, and wishing
him good-night, left him.

Michele di Lippo poured himself out a full measure
and drained it at a draught. Drawing his chair close to
the blazing wood, he stretched out his feet, cased in long
boots of Spanish leather, and stared into the flames.
He sat thus for an hour or so without motion. The
candles burned out, and the fire alone lit the room,
casting strange shadows on the moth-eaten tapestry of
the hangings, alternately lighting and leaving in dark-

ness the corners of the room, and throwing its fitful
glow on the pallid features of the brooding man, who sat
as if cut out of stone. At last the cavaliere moved, but
it was only to fling another log on the flames. Then he
resumed his former attitude, and watched the fire. As
he looked, he saw a picture. He saw wide lands, lands
rich with olive and vine, that climbed the green hills
between which the Aulella babbles. He saw the grey
towers of the castle of Pieve. Above the donjon, a
broad flag flapped lazily in the air, and the blazon on it
—three wasps on a green field—was his own. He was
no longer the ruined noble, confined to his few acres,
living like a goat amongst the rocks of the Greve ; but
my lord count, ruffling it again in Rome, and calling the
mains with Riario, as in the good old times ten years
ago. Diavolo ! But those were times when the Borgia
was Pope ! What nights those were in the Torre
Borgia ! He had one of Giulia Bella's gloves still, and
there were dark stains on its whiteness—stains that were
red once with the blood of Monreale, who wore it over
his heart the day he ran him through on the Ripetta.
Basta ! That was twelve years ago ! Twelve years !
Twelve hundred years it seemed. And he was forty now.
Still young enough to run another man through, however. *Cospetto !* If the bravo would only undertake
the job, everything might be his ! He would live again
—or perhaps ! And another picture came before the
dreamer. It had much to do with death—a bell was
tolling dismally, and a chained man was walking to his
end, with a priest muttering prayers into his ears. In
the background was a gallows, and a sea of heads, an
endless swaying crowd of heads, with faces that looked

on the man with hate, and tongues that jeered and shouted curses at him. And the voices of the crowd seemed to merge into one tremendous roar of hatred as the condemned wretch ascended the steps of the platform on which he was to find a disgraceful death.

Michele di Lippo rose suddenly with a shiver and an oath : "*Maledetto !* I must sleep. It touches the morning, and I have been dreaming too long."

CHAPTER II.

AT "THE DEVIL ON TWO STICKS."

It was mid-day, and the Captain Guido Moratti was at home in his lodging in "The Devil on Two Sticks." Not an attractive address; but then this particular hostel was not frequented by persons who were squeamish about names, or—any other thing. The house itself lay in the Santo Spirito ward of Florence, filling up the end of a *chiassolino* or blind alley in a back street behind the church of Santa Felicita, and was well known to all who had "business" to transact. It had also drawn towards it the attention of the *Magnifici Signori*, and the long arm of the law would have reached it ere this but for the remark made by the Secretary Machiavelli, "One does not purify a city by stopping the sewers," he said; and added with a grim sarcasm, "and any one of us might have an urgent affair to-morrow, and need an agent—let the devil rest on his two sticks." And it was so.

Occasionally, the talons of Messer the Gonfaloniere would close on some unfortunate gentleman who had at the time no "friends," and then he was never seen again. But arrests were never made in the house, and it was consequently looked upon as a secure place by its customers. The room occupied by Moratti was on the second floor, and was lighted by a small window which faced a high dead wall, affording no view beyond that of the blackened stonework. The captain, being a single man, could afford to live at his ease, and though it was mid-day, and past the dinner hour, had only just risen, and was fortifying himself with a measure of Chianti. He was seated in a solid-looking chair, his goblet in his hand, and his long legs clothed in black and white trunks, the Siena colours, resting on the table. The upper part of his dress consisted of a closely fitting pied surcoat, of the same hues as his trunks ; and round his waist he wore a webbed chain belt, to which was attached a plain, but useful-looking poniard. The black hair on his head was allowed to grow long, and fell in natural curls to his broad shoulders. He had no beard ; but under the severe arch of his nose was a pair of long dark moustaches that completely hid the mouth, and these he wore in a twist that almost reached his ears. On the table where his feet rested was his cap, from which a frayed feather stuck out stiffly ; likewise his cloak, and a very long sword in a velvet and wood scabbard. The other articles on the table were a half-empty flask of wine, a few dice, a pack of cards, a mask, a wisp of lace, and a broken fan. The walls were bare of all ornament, except over the entrance door, whence a crucified Christ looked down in His agony over the musty room. A spare chair or two, a couple of valises and a saddle, together with a bed, hidden behind some old and shabby curtains, completed the furniture of the chamber ; but such as it was, it was better accommodation than the captain had enjoyed for many a day. For be it known that " The Devil on Two Sticks " was meant for the aristocrats of the " profession." The charges

were accordingly high, and there was no credit allowed.
No ! No ! The *padrone* knew better than to trust his
longest-sworded clients for even so small a matter as
a brown *paolo*. But at present Moratti was in funds, for
thirty broad crowns in one's pocket, and a horse worth
full thirty more, went a long way in those days, and
besides, he had not a little luck at the cards last night.
He thrust a sinewy hand into his pocket, and jingled
the coins there, with a comfortable sense of proprietorship, and for the moment his face was actually pleasant to look upon. The face was an eminently handsome one. It was difficult to conceive that those clear,
bold features were those of a thief. They were rather
those of a soldier, brave, resolute, and hasty perhaps,
though hardened, and marked by excess. There was
that in them which seemed to point to a past very different from the present. And it had been so. But that
story is a secret, and we must take the captain as we find
him, nothing more or less than a bravo. Let it be remembered, however, that this hideous profession, although looked upon with fear by all, was not in those
days deemed so dishonourable as to utterly cast a man
out of the pale of his fellows. Troches, the bravo of
Alexander VI., was very nearly made a cardinal ; Don
Michele, the strangler of Cesare Borgia, became com-
mander-in-chief of the Florentine army, and had the
honour of a conspiracy being formed against him—he
was killed whilst leaving the house of Chaumont.
Finally, there was that romantic scoundrel " Il
Medighino," who advanced from valet to bravo, from
bravo to be a pirate chief and the brother of a pontiff,
ending his days as Marquis of Marignano and Viceroy

of Bohemia. So that, roundly speaking, if the profession of the dagger did lead to the galleys or the scaffold, it as often led to wealth, and sometimes, as in the case of Giangiacomo Medici, to a coronet. Perhaps some such thoughts as these flitted in the captain's mind as he jingled his crowns and slowly sipped his wine. His fellow-men had made him a wolf, and a wolf he was now to the end of his spurs, as pitiless to his victims as they had been to him. He was no longer young ; but a man between two ages, with all the strength and vitality of youth and the experience of five-and-thirty, so that with a stroke of luck he might any day do what the son of Bernardino had done. He had failed in everything up to now, although he had had his chances. His long sword had helped to stir the times when the Duke of Bari upset all Italy, and the people used to sing :

> Cristo in cielo è il Moro in terra,
> Solo sa il fine di questa guerra.

He had fought at Fornovo and at Mertara ; and in the breach at Santa Croce had even crossed swords with the Count di Savelli, the most redoubted knight, with the exception of Bayard, of the age. He had been run through the ribs for his temerity ; but it was an honour he never forgot. Then other things had happened, and he had sunk, sunk to be what he was, as many a better man had done before him. A knock at the door disturbed his meditations. He set down his empty glass and called out, " Enter ! "

The door opened, and the Cavaliere Michele di Lippo entered the room. Moratti showed no surprise, although the visit was a little unexpected ; but beyond pointing to a chair, gave di Lippo no other greeting, saying simply : " Take a seat, signore—and shut the door behind you. I did not expect you until to-morrow."

" True, captain ; but you see I was impatient. I got your letter yesterday, and, the matter being pressing, came here at once."

" Well—what is the business ? "

The cavaliere's steel-grey eyes contracted like those of a cat when a sudden light is cast upon them, and he glanced cautiously around him. " This place is safe— no eavesdroppers ? " he asked.

" None," answered Moratti ; and slowly putting his feet down from the table, pushed the wine towards di Lippo. " Help yourself, signore—No ! Well, as you wish. And now, your business ? "

There was a silence in the room, and each man watched the other narrowly. Moratti looked at the cavaliere's long hatchet face, at the cruel close-set eyes, at the thin red hair showing under his velvet cap, and at the straight line of the mouth, partly hidden by a moustache, and short peaked beard of a slightly darker red than the hair on di Lippo's head. Michele di Lippo, in his turn, keenly scanned the seamed and haughty features of the bravo, and each man recognised in the other the qualities he respected, if such a word may be used. At last the cavaliere spoke: " As I mentioned, captain, my business is one of the highest importance, and——"

" You are prepared to pay in proportion—eh ? " and Moratti twirled his moustache between his fingers.

" Exactly. I have made you my offer."

" But have not told me what you want done."

"I am coming to that. Permit me ; I think I will change my mind ; " and as Moratti nodded assent, di Lippo poured himself out a glass of wine and drained it slowly. When he had done this, he set the glass down with extreme care, and continued : " I am, as you see, captain, no longer a young man, and it is inconvenient to have to wait for an inheritance "—and he grinned horribly.

"I see, cavaliere—you want me to anticipate matters a little—Well, I am willing to help you if I can."

"It is a hundred crowns, captain, and the case lies thus. There is but one life between me and the County of Pieve in the Val di Magra, and you know how uncertain life is."

He paused ; but as Guido Moratti said nothing, continued with his even voice : " Should the old Count of Pieve die—and he is on the edge of the grave—the estate will pass to his daughter. In the event of *her* death——"

"*Whew !*" Moratti emitted a low whistle, and sat bolt upright. " So it is the lady," he cried. " That is not my line, cavaliere. It is more a matter of the poison-cup, and I don't deal in such things. Carry your offer elsewhere."

" It will be a new experience, captain—and a hundred crowns."

" Blood of a king, man ! do you think I hesitate over a paltry hundred crowns ? Had it been a man, it would have been different—but a woman ! No ! No ! It is not my way ; " and he rose and paced the room.

" Tush, man ! It is but a touch of your dagger, and you have done much the same before."

Moratti faced di Lippo. "As you say, I have exe-
cuted commissions before, but never on a woman, and
never on a man without giving him a chance."

"You are too tender-hearted for your profession, captain. Have you never been wronged by a
woman? They can be more pitiless than men, I assure
you."

The bronze on Moratti's cheek paled to ashes, and his
face hardened with a sudden memory. He turned his
back upon di Lippo, and stared out of the window at
the dead wall which was the only view. It was a chance
shot, but it had told. The cavaliere rose slowly and
flung a purse on the table. "Better give him the whole
at once," he muttered. "Come, captain," he added,
raising his voice. "It will be over in a moment; and
after all, neither you nor I will ever see heaven. We
might as well burn for something; and if I mistake
not, both you and I are like those Eastern tigers, who
once having tasted blood must go on forever—see!"
and he laid his lean hand on the bravo's shoulder, "why
not revenge on the whole sex the wrong done you by
one——"

The captain swung round suddenly and shook off di
Lippo's hand. "Don't touch me," he cried; "at times
like this I am dangerous. What demon put into your
mouth the words you have just used? They have
served your purpose—and she shall die. Count me out
the money, the full hundred—and go."

"It is there;" and di Lippo pointed with his finger
to the purse. "You will find the tale complete—a
hundred crowns—count them at your leisure. *Addio!*
captain. I shall hear good news soon, I trust." Rub-

bing the palms of his hands together, he stepped softly from the room.

Guido Moratti did not hear or answer him. His mind had gone back with a rush for ten years, when the work of a woman had made him sink lower than a beast. Such things happen to men sometimes. He had sunk like a stone thrown into a lake ; he had been destroyed utterly, and it was sufficient to say that he lived now to prey on his fellow-creatures. But he had never thought of the revenge that di Lippo had suggested. Now that he did think of it, he remembered a story told in the old days round the camp fires, when they were hanging on the rear of Charles's retreating army, just before he turned and rent the League at Fornovo. Rodrigo Gonzaga, the Spaniard, had told it of a countryman of his, a native of Toledo, who for a wrong done to him by a girl had devoted himself to the doing to death of women. It was horrible ; and at the time he had refused to believe it. Now he was face to face with the same horror—nay, he had even embraced it. He had lost his soul ; but the price of it was not yet paid in revenge or gold, and, by Heaven ! he would have it. He laughed out as loudly and cheerlessly as on that winter's night when he rode off through the snow ; and laying hands on the purse, tore it open, and the contents rolled out upon the table. " The price of my soul ! " he sneered as he held up a handful of the coins, and let them drop again with a clash on the heap on the table. " It is more than Judas got for his—ha ! ha ! "

CHAPTER III.

SOME few days after his interview with di Lippo, the Captain Guido Moratti rode his horse across the old Roman bridge which at that time spanned the Aulella, and directed his way towards the castle of Pieve, whose outlines rose before him, cresting an eminence about a league from the bridge. The captain was travelling as a person of some quality, the better to carry out a plan he had formed for gaining admission to Pieve, and a lackey rode behind him holding his valise. He had hired horse and man in Florence, and the servant was an honest fellow enough, in complete ignorance of his master's character and profession. Both the captain and his man bore the appearance of long travel, and in truth they had journeyed with a free rein ; and now that a stormy night was setting in, they were not a little anxious to reach their point. The snow was falling in soft flakes, and the landscape was grey with the driving mist, through which the outlines of the castle loomed large and shadowy, more like a fantastic creation in cloudland than the work of human hands. As the captain pulled down the lapels of his cap to ward off the drift which was coming straight in his face, the bright flare of a beacon fire shone from a tower of the castle, and the rays from it stretched in broad orange

bands athwart the rolling mist, which threatened, together with the increasing darkness, to extinguish all
the view that was left, and make the league to Pieve
a road of suffering. With the flash of the fire a weird,
sustained howl came to the travellers in an eerie
cadence ; and as the fearsome call died away, it was
picked up by an answering cry from behind, then another and yet another. There could be no mistaking
these signals ; they meant pressing and immediate
danger.

"Wolves !" shouted Moratti ; and turning to his
knave : " Gallop, Tito !—else our bones will be picked
clean by morning. Gallop ! "

They struck their spurs into the horses ; and the
jaded animals, as if realizing their peril, made a brave
effort, and dashed off at their utmost speed. It was
none too soon, for the wolves, hitherto following in
silence, had given tongue at the sight of the fire; and as
if knowing that the beacon meant safety for their prey,
and that they were like to lose a dinner unless they
hurried, laid themselves on the track of the flying horses
with a hideous chorus of yells. They could not be
seen for the mist ; but they were not far behind. They
were going at too great a pace to howl now ; but an
occasional angry " yap " reached the riders, and reached
the horses too, whose instinct told them what it meant ;
and they needed no further spurring, to make them
strain every muscle to put a distance between themselves and their pursuers. Moratti thoroughly grasped
the situation. He had experienced a similar adventure in
the Pennine Alps, when carrying despatches for Paolo
Orsini, with this difference, that then he had a fresh

horse, and could see where he was going; whereas now, although the distance to Pieve was short, and in ten minutes he might be safe and with a whole skin, yet a false step, a stumble, and nothing short of a miracle could prevent him becoming a living meal to the beasts behind.

He carried, slung by a strap over his shoulder, a light bugle, which he had often found useful before, but never so useful as now. Thrusting his hand under his cloak, he drew it out, and blew a long clear blast; and, to his joy, there came an answer through the storm from the castle. Rescue was near at hand, and faster and faster they flew; but as surely the wolves gained on them, and they could hear the snarling of the leaders as they jostled against and snapped at each other in their haste. Moratti looked over his shoulder. He could see close behind a dark crescent moving towards them with fearful rapidity. He almost gave a groan. It was too horrible to die thus! And he dug his spurs again and again into the heaving flanks of his horse, with the vain hope of increasing its speed. They had now reached the ascent to Pieve. They could see the lights at the windows. In two hundred yards there was safety; when Moratti's horse staggered under him, and he had barely time to free his feet from the stirrups and lean well back in the saddle ere the animal came down with a plunge. Tito went by like a flash, as the captain picked himself up and faced the wolves, sword in hand. There was a steep bank on the side of the road. He made a dash to gain the summit of this; but had hardly reached half-way up when the foremost wolf was upon him, and had rolled down again with a yell, run through the heart. His fellows tore him to shreds, and in a moment began to worry at the struggling horse, whose fore-leg was broken. In a hand-turn the matter was ended, and the wretched beast was no longer visible, all that could be seen being a black swaying mass of bodies, as the pack hustled and fought over the dead animal.

Nevertheless, there were three or four of the wolves who devoted their attention to Moratti, and he met them with the courage of despair. But the odds were too many, and he began to feel that he could not hold out much longer. One huge monster, his shaggy coat icy with the sleet, had pulled him to his knees, and it was only a lucky thrust of the dagger, he held in his left hand, that saved him. He regained his feet only to be dragged down again, and to rise yet once more. He was bleeding and weak, wounded in many places, and the end could not be far off. It was not thus that he had hoped to die ; and he was dying like a worried lynx.

The thought drove him to madness. He was of Siena, and somewhere in his veins, though he did not know it, ran the blood of the Senonian Gauls, and it came out now—he went Berserker, as the old northern pirates were wont to do. Sliding down the bank, he jumped full into the pack, striking at them in a dumb fury. He was hardly human himself now, and he plunged his sword again and again into the heaving mass around him, and felt no pain from the teeth of the wolves as they rent his flesh. A fierce mad joy came upon him. It was a glorious fight after all, and he was dying game. It was a glorious fight, and when he felt a grisly head at his throat, and the weight of his assailant brought him down once more, he flung aside his sword, and grappling his enemy with his hands, tore asunder the huge jaws, and flung the body from him with a yell. Almost at that very instant there was the sharp report of firearms, the rush of hurrying feet, and the blaze of torches. Moratti, half on his knees, was suddenly pulled to his feet by a strong hand, and supported by it he stood, dizzy and faint, bleeding almost everywhere, but safe. The wolves had fled in silence, vanishing like phantoms across the snow; and shot after shot was fired in their direction by the rescue party.

"*Per Bacco!*" said the man who was holding Moratti up; "but it was an affair between the skin and the flesh, signore—steady!" and his arm tightened round the captain. As he did this, a long defiant howl floated back to them through the night, and Guido Moratti knew no more. He seemed to have dropped suddenly into an endless night. He seemed to be flying through space, past countless millions of stars, which, bright themselves, were unable to illumine the abysmal darkness around, and then—there was nothing.

When Moratti came to himself again, he was lying in a bed, in a large room, dimly lighted by a shaded lamp, set on a tall Corinthian pillar of marble. After the first indistinct glance around him, he shut his eyes, and was lost in a dreamy stupor. In a little, he looked again, and saw that the chamber was luxuriously fitted, and that he was not alone, for, kneeling at a *prie-dieu*, under a large picture of a Madonna and Child, was the figure of a woman. Her face was from him; but

ill as he was, Moratti saw that the tight-fitting dress
showed a youthful and perfect figure, and that her head
was covered with an abundance of red-gold hair. The
man was still in the shadowland caused by utter weakness, and for a moment he thought that this was nothing but a vision of fancy ; but he rallied half unconsciously, and looked again ; and then, curiosity
overcoming him, attempted to turn so as to obtain a
better view, and was checked by a twinge of pain, which,
coming suddenly, brought an exclamation to his lips.
In an instant the lady rose, and moving towards him,
bent over the bed. As she did this, their eyes met, and
the fierce though dulled gaze of the bravo saw before
him a face of ideal innocence, of such saintlike purity,
that it might have been a dream of Raffaelle. She
placed a cool hand on his hot forehead, and whispered
softly : " Be still—and drink this—you will sleep."
Turning to a side table, she lifted a silver goblet therefrom, and gave him to drink. The draught was cool
and refreshing, and he gathered strength from it.

" Where am I ? " he asked ; and then, with a sudden
courtesy, " Madonna—pardon me—I thank you."

" Hush ! " she answered, lifting a small hand. " You
are in Pieve, and you have been very ill. But I must
not talk—sleep now, signore."

" I remember now," he said dreamily—" the wolves ;
but it seems so long ago."

She made no reply, but stepped softly out of the
room, and was gone. Moratti would have called out
after her ; but a drowsiness came on him, and closing
his eyes, he slept.

It takes a strong man some time to recover from

wounds inflicted by a wild animal; and when a man has, like Guido Moratti, lived at both ends, it takes longer still, and it was weeks before the captain was out of danger. He never saw his fair visitor again. Her place was taken by a staid and middle-aged nurse, and he was visited two or three times daily by a solemn-looking physician. But although he did not see her whom he longed to see, there was a message both morning and evening from the Count of Pieve and his daughter, hoping the invalid was better—the former regretting that his infirmities prevented his paying a personal visit, and the inquiries of the latter being always accompanied by a bouquet of winter flowers. But strange as it may seem, when he was under the influence of the opiate they gave him nightly, he was certain of the presence of the slight graceful figure of the lady of the *prie-dieu*, as he called her to himself. He saw again the golden-red hair and the sweet eyes, and felt again the touch of the cool hand. He began to think that this bright presence which lit his dreams was but a vision after all, and used to long for the night and the opiate.

At last one fine morning Tito appeared, and began to set out and brush the captain's apparel as if nothing had ever happened. Moratti watched him for a space, and then rising up against his pillows, spoke: " Tito ! "

" Signore ! "

" How is it that you have not been here before ? "

" I was not allowed, Excellency, until to-day—your worship was too ill."

" Then I am better."

" Excellency ! "

There was a silence of some minutes, and the captain
spoke again : "Tito ! "

"Signore ! "

"Have you seen the Count and his daughter ? "

"Excellency ! "

"What are they like ? "

"The Count old, and a cripple. Madonna Felicità,
small, thin, red-haired like my wife Sancia."

Moratti sank down again upon the bed, a satisfied
smile upon his lips. So there was truth in his dreams.
The vision of the night was a reality. He would see her
soon, as soon as he could rise, and he was fast getting
well, very fast. He had gone back many years in his
illness. He had thoughts stirred within him that he
had imagined dead long ago. He was the last man to
day-dream, to build castles in the air ; but as he lay
idly watching Tito, who was evidently very busy clean-
ing something—for he was sitting on a low chair with
his back towards the captain, and his elbow moving
backwards and forwards rapidly—the bravo pictured
himself Guido Moratti as he might have been, a man
able to look all men in the face, making an honourable
way for himself, and worthy the love of a good woman.
The last thought brought before him a fair face and
sweet eyes, and a dainty head crowned with red-gold
hair, and the strong man let his fancy run on with an
uprising of infinite tenderness in his heart. He was
lost in a cloudland of dreams.

"Signore ! "

Tito's harsh voice had pulled down the castle in
Spain, and Tito himself was standing at the bedside
holding a bright and glittering dagger in his hand. But

he had done more than upset his master's dreams. He had, all unwittingly, brought him back in a flash to the hideous reality, for, as a consequence of his long illness, of the weeks of fever and delirium, Moratti had clean forgotten the dreadful object of his coming to Pieve. It all came back to him with a blinding suddenness, and he closed his eyes with a shudder of horror as Tito laid the poniard upon the bed, asking : " Will the signore see if the blade is keen enough ? A touch of the finger will suffice."

CHAPTER IV.

DAYS were yet to pass before Guido Moratti was able to leave his chamber ; but at last the leech who attended him said he might do so with safety ; and later on, the steward of the household brought a courteous invitation from the Count of Pieve to dine with him. As already explained, Moratti had not as yet seen his host ; and since he was well enough to sit up, there were no more dreamy visions of the personal presence of Felicità. He had made many resolutions whilst left to himself, and had determined that as soon as he was able to move he would leave the castle, quit Italy, and make a new name for himself, or die in the German wars. He was old enough to build no great hopes on the future ; but fortune might smile on him, and then—many things might happen. At any rate, he would wipe the slate clean, and there should be no more ugly scores on it.

Not that he was a reformed man ; he was only groping his way back to light. Men do not cast off the past as a snake sheds his skin. He knew that well enough, but he knew, too, that he had seen a faint track back to honour ; and difficult as it was, he had formed a determination to travel by it. He had been so vile, he had sunk so low, that there were moments when a de-

spair came on him ; but with a new country and new
scenes, and the little flame of hope that was warming his
dead soul back to life, there might yet be a chance.
He knew perfectly that he was in love, and when a man
of his age loves, it is for the remainder of his life.
He was aware—none better—that his love was madness, all but an insult, and that it was worse than pre-
sumption to even entertain the thought that he had
inspired any other feeling beyond that of pity in the
heart of Felicità. It is enough to say that he did not
dare to hope in this way ; but he meant to so order his
future life, as to feel that any such sentiment as love
in his heart towards her would not be sacrilege.

He sent back a civil answer to the invitation ; and
a little after eleven, descended the stairway which led
from his chamber to the Count's apartments, looking
very pale and worn, but very handsome. For he was, in
truth, a man whose personal appearance took all eyes.
The apartments of the Count were immediately below
Moratti's own chamber, and on entering, he saw the old
knight himself reclining in a large chair. He was alone,
except for a hound which lay stretched out on the
hearth, its muzzle between its forepaws, and a dining-
table set for three was close to his elbow. Bernabo of
Pieve received his guest with a stately courtesy, asking
pardon for being unable to rise, as he was crippled.
" They clipped my wings at Arx Sismundea, captain—
before your time ; but of a truth I am a glad man to
see you strong again. It was a narrow affair."

" I cannot thank you in words, Count ; you and your
house have placed a debt on me I can never repay."

" Tush, man ! There must be no talk of thanks.

If there are to be any, they are due to the leech, and to Felicità, my daughter. She is all I have left, for my son was killed at Santa Croce."

"I was there, Count."

"And knew him?"

"Alas, no. I was on the side of Spain."

"With the besieged, and he with the League. He was killed on the breach—poor lad."

At this moment a curtain at the side of the room was lifted, and Felicità entered. She greeted Moratti warmly, and with a faint flush on her cheeks, inquired after his health, hoping he was quite strong again.

"So well, Madonna, that I must hurry on my journey to-morrow."

"To-morrow!" Her large eyes opened wide in astonishment, and there was a pain in her look. "Why," she continued, "it will be a fortnight ere you can sit in the saddle again."

"It might have been never, but for you," he answered gravely, and her eyes met his, and fell. At this moment the steward announced that the table was ready; and by the time the repast was ended, Moratti had forgotten his good resolutions for instant departure, and had promised to stay for at least a week, at the urgent intercession of both the Count and his daughter. He knew he was wrong in doing so, and that, whatever happened, it was his duty to go at once; but he hesitated with himself. He would give himself one week of happiness, for it was happiness to be near her, and then —he would go away forever. And she would never know, in her innocence and purity, that Guido Moratti, bravo—he shuddered at the infamous word—loved her better than all the world beside, and that for her sake he had become a new man.

After dinner the Count slept, and, the day being bright, they stepped out into a large balcony and gazed at the view. The balcony, which stretched out from a low window of the dining chamber, terminated on the edge of a precipice which dropped down a clear two hundred feet ; and leaning over the moss-grown battlements, they looked at the white winter landscape before them. Behind rose the tower they had just quitted, and Felicità, turning, pointed to it, saying : " We call this the Torre Dolorosa."

" A sad name, Madonna. May I ask why ? "

" Because all of our house who die in their beds die here."

" And yet you occupy this part of the castle."

" Oh, I do not. My chamber is there—in Count Ligo's Tower ; " and she pointed to the right, where another grey tower rose from the keep. " But my father likes to occupy the Torre Dolorosa himself. He says he is living with his ancestors—to whom he will soon go, as he always adds."

" May the day be far distant."

And she answered " Amen."

After this, they went in, and the talk turned on other matters. The week passed and then another, but at last the day came for Moratti's departure. He had procured another horse. It was indeed a gift which the old Count pressed upon him, and he had accepted it with much reluctance, but much gratitude. In truth, the kindness of these people towards him was unceasing, and Moratti made great strides towards his new self in that week. He was to have started after the mid-day dinner; but with the afternoon he was not gone, and sunset found him on the balcony of the Torre Dolorosa with Felicità by his side.

"You cannot possibly go to-night," she said.

"I will go to-morrow, then," replied Moratti, and she looked away from him.

It was a moment of temptation. Almost did a rush of words come to the captain's lips. He felt as if he must take her in his arms and tell her that he loved her as man never loved woman. It was an effort; but he was getting stronger in will daily, and he crushed down the feeling.

"It is getting chill for you," he said; "we had better go in."

"Tell me," she answered, not heeding his remark, "tell me exactly where you are going?"

"I do not know—perhaps to join Piccolomini in Bohemia—perhaps to join Alva in the Low Countries—wherever a soldier's sword has work to do."

"And you will come back?"

"Perhaps."

"A great man, with a *condotta* of a thousand lances—and forget Pieve."

"As God is my witness—never—but it is chill, Madonna—come in."

When they came in, Bernabo of Pieve was not alone, for standing close to the old man, his back to the fire, and rubbing his hands softly together, was the tall, gaunt figure of the Cavaliere Michele di Lippo.

"A sudden visit, dear cousin," he said, greeting

Felicità, and turning his steel-grey eyes, with a look of cold inquiry in them, on Moratti.

" The Captain Guido Moratti—my cousin, the Cavaliere di Lippo."

" Of Castel Lippo, on the Greve," put in di Lippo.

" I am charmed to make the acquaintance of the Captain Moratti. Do you stay long in Pieve, captain ? "

" I leave to-morrow." Moratti spoke shortly. His blood was boiling, as he looked on the gloomy figure of the cavaliere, who watched him furtively from under his eyelids, the shadow of a sneer on his face. He was almost sick with shame when he thought how he was in di Lippo's hands, how a word from him could brand him with ignominy beyond repair. Some courage, however, came back to him with the thought that, after all, he held cards as well, as for his own sake, di Lippo would probably remain quiet.

" So soon ! " said di Lippo with a curious stress on the word soon, and then added, " That is bad news."

" I have far to go, signore," replied Moratti coldly, and the conversation then changed. It was late when they retired ; and as the captain bent over Felicità's hand, he held it for a moment in his own broad palm, and said : " It is good-bye, lady, for I go before the dawn to-morrow."

She made no answer ; but, with a sudden movement, detached a bunch of winter violets she wore at her neck, and thrusting them in Moratti's hand, turned and fled. The Count was half asleep, and did not notice the passage ; but di Lippo said with his icy sneer : " Excellent—you work like an artist, Moratti."

"I do not understand you;" and turning on his heel, the captain strode off to his room.

An hour or so later, he was seated in a low chair, thinking. His valise lay packed, and all was ready for his early start. He still held the violets in his hand, but his face was dark with boding thoughts. He dreaded going and leaving Felicità to the designs of di Lippo. There would be other means found by di Lippo to carry out his design; and with a groan, the captain rose and began to pace the room. He was on the cross with anxiety. If he went without giving warning of di Lippo's plans, he would still be a sharer in the murder—and the murder of Felicità, for a hair of whose head he was prepared to risk his soul. If, on the other hand, he spoke, he would be lost forever in her eyes. Although it was winter, the room seemed to choke him, and he suddenly flung open the door and, descending the dim stairway, went out into the balcony. It was bright with moonlight, and the night was clear as crystal. He leaned over the battlements and racked his mind as to his course of action. At last he resolved. He would take the risk, and speak out, warn Bernabo of Pieve at all hazards, and would do so at once. He turned hastily, and then stopped, for before him in the moonlight stood the Cavaliere Michele di Lippo.

"I sought you in your chamber, captain," he said in his biting voice, "and not finding you, came here——"

"And how did you know I would be here?"

"Lovers like the moonlight, and you can see the light from her window in Ligo's Tower," said di Lippo, and added sharply : " So you are playing false, Moratti."

The captain made no answer ; there was a singing in his ears, and a sudden and terrible thought was working. His hand was on the hilt of his dagger, a spring, a blow, and di Lippo would be gone. And no one would know. But the cavaliere went on, unheeding his silence.

" You are playing false, Moratti. You are playing for your own hand with my hundred crowns. You think your ship has come home. Fool ! Did you imagine I would allow this ? But I still give you a chance. Either do my business to-night—the way is open—or to-morrow you are laid by the heels as a thief and a bravo. What will your Felicità——"

" Dog—speak her name again, and you die ! " Moratti struck him across the face with his open palm, and Michele di Lippo reeled back a pace, his face as white as snow. It was only a pace, however, for he recovered himself at once, and sprung at Moratti like a wild-cat. The two closed. They spoke no word, and nothing could be heard but their laboured breath as they gripped together. Their daggers were in their hands ; but each man knew this, and had grasped the wrist of the other. Moratti was more powerful ; but his illness had weakened him, and the long lean figure of Michele di Lippo was as strong as a wire rope. Under the quiet moon and the winter stars, they fought, until at last di Lippo was driven to the edge of the parapet, and in the moonlight he saw the meaning in Moratti's set face. With a superhuman effort, he wrenched his hand free, and the next moment his dagger had sunk to the hilt in the captain's side, and Moratti's grasp loosened, but only for an instant. He was mortally wounded, he knew. He was going to die; but it would not be alone. He pressed di Lippo to his breast. He lifted him from his feet, and forced him through an embrasure which yawned behind. Here, on its brink, the two figures swayed for an instant, and then the balcony was empty, and from the deep of the precipice two hundred feet below, there travelled upwards the sullen echo of a dull crash, and all was quiet again.

*   *   *   *   *

When the stars were paling, the long howl of a wolf rang out into the stillness. It reached Felicità in Count Ligo's Tower, and filled her with a nameless terror. " Guard him, dear saints," she prayed ; " shield him from peril, and hold him safe."

THE TREASURE OF SHAGUL

It was past two o'clock, and Aladin, the elephant-driver, had gathered together his usual audience under the shade of the mango tree near the elephant-shed. Aladin was a noted story-teller ; he had a long memory, and an exhaustless fund of anecdote. It was ten years since he had come from Nepaul with Moula Piari, the big she-elephant, and for ten years he had delighted the inhabitants of the canal-settlement at Dadupur with his tales. It was his practice to tell one story daily, never more than one ; and his time for this relaxation was an hour or so after the midday meal, when he would sit on a pile of *sal* logs, under the mango tree, and his small audience, collecting round him in a semi-circle, would wait patiently until the oracle spoke. No one ever attempted to ask him to begin. Once Bullen, the water-carrier, the son of Bishen, after waiting in impatient expectation through ten long minutes of solemn silence, had suggested that it was time for Aladin to commence. At this the old man rose in wrath, and asking the water-carrier if he was his slave, smote him over the ear, and stalked off to the elephant-shed. For three days there was no story-telling, and Bullen, the son of Bishen, had a hard time of it with his fellows. Finally

matters were adjusted ; both Aladin and Bullen were
persuaded by Gunga Din, the tall Burkundaz guard, to
forget the past, and affairs went on in the old way. That
was three years ago, but the lesson had not been forgotten. So although it happened on this April afternoon, that all the elephant-driver's old cronies were
there,—Gunga Dino the Burkundaz, Dulaloo the white-
haired Sikh messenger who had been orderly to Napier
of Magdala, Piroo Ditta the telegraph-clerk, and Gobind
Ram the canal-accountant, with a half-score others—
yet not one of them ventured to disturb the silence of
Aladin, as he sat, gravely stroking his beard, on the
ant-eaten *sal* logs which had mouldered there for so
many years. They were the remains of a wrecked raft
that had come down in a July flood, and having been
rescued from the water, were stacked under the mango
tree for the owner to claim. No owner ever came, but
they had served as food for the white ants, and as a
bench for Aladin, for many a year. The afternoon was
delicious ; a soft breeze was blowing, and the leaves of
the trees tinkled overhead. Above the muffled roar of
the canal, pouring through the open sluices, came the
clear bell-like notes of a blackbird, who piped joyously
to himself from a snag that stood up, jagged and sharp,
out of the clear waters of the Some. To the north the
Khyarda and Kalessar Duns extended in long lines of
yellow, brown, and grey, and above them rose the airy
outlines of the lower Himalayas, while higher still, in
the absolute blue of the sky, towered the white peaks
of the eternal snows. Beeroo, the Sansi, saw the group
under the mango tree as he crossed the canal-bridge,
and hastened towards it. Beeroo was a member of a

criminal tribe, a tribe of nomads who lived by hunting
and stealing, who are to be found in every Indian fair
as acrobats, jugglers, and fortune-tellers, or tramping
painfully through the peninsula with a tame bear or
performing monkeys. In short the Sansis are very
similar to gipsies, if they are not, indeed, the parent
stock from which our own " Egyptians " spring. Beeroo
came up to the sitters, but as he was of low caste, or
rather of no caste, he took up his position a little apart,
leaning on a long knotted bamboo staff, his coal-black
eyes glancing keenly around him. " It is Beeroo," said
Dulaloo the Sikh, and with this greeting lapsed into
silence. Aladin ceased stroking his henna-stained beard,
and looked at the new-comer.

" Ai, Beeroo ! What news ? "

" There is a tiger at Hathni Khoond, and I have
marked him down. Is the Sahib here ? "

" The Sahib sleeps now," replied Aladin ; " it is the
time for his noontide rest. He will awaken at four
o'clock."

" I will see His Honour then," replied Beeroo, " and
there will be a hunt to-morrow."

" Is it a big tiger ? " asked Bullen, the son of Bishen.

" Aho ! " and the Sansi, sliding his hands down the
bamboo staff, sank to a sitting posture.

" When was it the Sahib slew his last tiger ? " asked
Piroo Ditta, the telegraph-clerk.

" Last May, at Mohonagh, near the temple," answered
Aladin ; " I remember well, for the elephant lost a toe-
nail in fording the river-bed—poor beast ! "

" At Mohonagh ! That is where the Shagul Tree is,"
said Gobind Ram.

" True, brother. Hast heard the tale ? "

There was a chorus of " noes," that drowned Gobind
Ram's " yes," and Aladin, taking a long pull at his
water-pipe, began :

" When Raja Sham Chand had ruled in Suket for six
years, he fell into evil ways, and abandoning the shrine
of Mohonagh, where his fathers had worshipped for
generations, set up idols to a hundred and fifty gods.
Prem Chand, the high priest of Mohonagh, cast himself
at the Raja's feet, and expostulated with him in vain,
for Sham Chand only laughed, saying Mohonagh was
old and blind. Then he mocked the priest, and Prem
Chand threw dust on his own head, and departed sore at
heart. So Mohonagh was deserted, and the Raja wasted
his substance among dancing-girls and the false priests
who pandered to him. About this time Sham Chand,
being a fool although a king, put his faith in the
word of the emperor at Delhi, and came down from
the hills to find himself a prisoner. In his despair the
Raja called upon each one of his hundred and fifty gods
to save him, promising half his kingdom if his prayers
were answered ; but there was no reply. At last the
Raja bethought him of the neglected Mohonagh, and
falling on his knees implored the aid of the god, making
him the same promise of half his kingdom, and vowing
that if he were but free, he would put aside his evil ways,
return to the faith of his fathers, and destroy the temples of his false gods. As he prayed he heard a bee
buzzing in his cell, and watching it, saw it creep into
a hollow between two of the bricks in the wall, and then
creep out again, and buzz around the room. Sham
Chand put his hand to the bricks and found they were

loose. He put them back carefully, and waited till night. Under cover of the dark he set to work once more, and removing brick after brick, found that he could make his passage through the wall. This he did and effected his escape. When he came back to Suket he kept his vow, and more than this. Within the walls of the *mandar* of Mohonagh grows a *shagul*, or wild pear tree. On this tree the Raja nailed a hundred and fifty gold mohurs, a coin for each one of the false gods whose idols he destroyed, and decreed 'that every one in Suket who had a prayer answered, should affix a coin or a jewel to the tree. That was a hundred years ago, and now the stem of the Shagul Tree is covered with coins and jewels to the value of *lakhs*. I saw it with my own eyes. This is not all, for when at Mohonagh I heard that the god strikes blind any thief who attempts to steal but a leaf from the tree. *Bus !*—there is no more to tell."

"*Wah ! Wah !*" exclaimed the listeners, and Beeroo put in, "Lakhs of rupees didst thou say, Mahoutjee ? "

"I have said what I have said, O Sansi, and thou hast heard. Hast thou a mind to be struck blind ? "

Beeroo made no answer, and the group shortly afterwards broke up. But Gobind Ram, the canal-accountant, who knew the story of the Shagul Tree, went straight to his quarters. Here he wrote a brief note on a piece of soft yellow paper, and sealed it carefully. Then he drew forth a pigeon from a cage in a corner of the room, and fastening the letter to the bird, freed the pigeon with a toss into the air. The carrier circled slowly thrice above the *neem* trees, and then spreading its strong slate-coloured wings, flew swiftly towards the hills. Gobind Ram watched the speck in the sky until it vanished from sight, then he went in, muttering to himself, " The high priest will know in an hour that Beeroo the Sansi has heard of the Shagul Tree—Ho, Aladin, thou hast too long a beard and too long a tongue," and the subtle Brahmin squatted himself down to smoke.

An hour afterwards, as Aladin was taking the she-elephant to water, he saw a figure going at a long slouching trot along the yellow sandbanks of the Some, making directly towards the north. The old man shaded his eyes with his hands and looked keenly at it ; but his sight was not what it was, and he turned to Mahboob, the elephant-cooly, who would step into his shoes some day, when he died, and asked : " See'st thou that figure on the sandbank there, Mahboob ? "

" It is the Sansi," answered Mahboob.   " Behold ! He limps on the left foot, where the leopard clawed him at Kara Ho. Perchance the Sahib will not hear of the tiger to-day."

" If ever, Mahboob," answered the Mahout ; " would that mine eyes were young again. *Hai !* " and he tapped Moula Piari's bald head with his driving-hook, for her long trunk was reaching out to grasp a bundle of green grass from the head of a grass-cutter, who was bearing in fodder for the Sahib's pony.

Mahboob was not mistaken ; it was Beeroo. When the party broke up, he alone remained apparently absorbed in thought. After a time he took some tobacco from an embroidered pouch hanging at his waist, crushed it in the palm of his hand, and rolled a cone-shaped cigarette with the aid of a leaf, fastening the folds of the leaf together with a small dry stick which he stuck through the cigarette like a hair-pin. At this he sucked, his forehead contracted into a frown, and his bead-like eyes fixed steadily before him. Finally he rose quickly, as one who has made a sudden resolve.

" The tiger can wait for the Sahib," he said to himself ; " but *lakhs* of rupees—they wait also—for me. I will go and worship at Mohonagh. The idol will surely make the convert a gift."

Laughing softly to himself, he stole off with long cat-like steps in the direction of the river. He forded the Some where it was crossed by the telegraph-line, and the water was but breast-deep. Once on the opposite bank, he shook himself like a dog, and breaking into a trot, headed straight for the hills. His way led up a narrow and steep track, hedged in with thorns over which the purple convolvulus twined in a confused network. On either hand were sparse fields of gram and corn, which ran in lozenge shapes up the low hillsides, ending in a tangle of underwood, beyond which rose the solid outlines of the forest. As the sun was setting he came to a long narrow ravine, over which the road crossed. Here he stopped, and instead of keeping to the road, turned abruptly to the right and trotted on. In the darkening woods above him he heard the cry of a panther, and the alarmed jabbering of the monkeys in the trees above their most dreaded enemy. Beeroo marked the spot with a glance as he went on : " I will buy a gun when I come back from Mohonagh," he muttered to himself, " a two-barrelled gun of English make. The Thanadar at Thakot has one for sale, a

birich-lodas ; * and then I will shoot that panther."
Hough ! Hough ! The cry of the animal rang through
the forest again, as if in assent to his thoughts, and
Beeroo continued his way. Just as the sun sank and
darkness was setting in, he saw the wavering glimmer
of a circle of camp-fires and the outlines of figures moving against the light. The flare of the burning wood
discovered also a few low tents, shaped like casks cut in
half lengthwise, and lit up with red the grey fur of a
number of donkeys that were tethered within the radius
of the fires. In a little time he heard the barking of
dogs, and five minutes later was with the tents of his
tribe.

One or two men exchanged brief greetings with him,
and answering them, he stepped up to the centre fire,
where a tall good-looking woman addressed him. " Aho,
Beeroo, is it you ? Is the hunt to be to-morrow ? "

" The Sahib was asleep," answered Beeroo ; " give
me to eat."

The woman brought him food. It was a stew made
of the flesh of a porcupine that had been kept warm
in an earthenware dish, and Beeroo ate heartily of this,
quenching his thirst with a draught of the fiery spirit
made from the blossoms of the *mhowra,* after which he
began to smoke once more, using a small clay pipe
called a *chillum.* His wife, for so the woman was, made
no attempt to converse with him, but left him to the
company of his tobacco and his thoughts. Beeroo sat
moodily puffing blue curls of smoke from his pipe, and
with a black blanket drawn over his shoulders, stared

---

* Breechloader.

steadily into the fire. So he sat for hours, no one disturbing him, sat until the camp had gone to rest, and the wind alone was awake and sighing through the forest. Sagoo, his big white hound, came close to him, and lay by his side, as if to hint that it was time to sleep. Beeroo stroked the lean, muscular flank of the dog, and looked around him. " In a little time," he said to himself, " I will be Beeroo Naik, with a village of my own and wide lands. Beeroo Naik," he repeated softly to himself, with a lingering pride on the title implied in the last word. Then he rolled himself up in his blanket ; Sagoo snuggled beside him, and they slept.

Beeroo awoke long before sunrise. He drank some milk, stole into his tent, and crept out again with a stout canvas haversack in his hands. Into this sack, which contained other things besides, he stuffed some broken meat and bread made of Indian corn, and slung is over his shoulders. Then grasping his staff, he gave a last look around him, and plunged into the jungle. Sagoo would have followed, but Beeroo ordered him back, and the hound with drooping tail and wistful eyes watched the figure of his master until it was lost in the gloom of the trees. Beeroo walked on tirelessly, and by midday was far in the hills. He could go from sunrise to sunset at that long trotting pace of his, rest a little, eat a little, and then keep on till the sun rose again. He was now high up in the hills. The *sal* trees had given place to the screw-pine, silk-cotton and mango were replaced by holm-oak and walnut. In the tangle of the low bushes the dog-rose and wild jasmine bloomed, and the short green of the grass was

spangled with the wood violet, the amaranth, and the
pimpernel. Far below the Jumna hummed down to the
plains in a white lashing flood, and the voice of the
distant river reached him, soft and dreamy, through the
murmur of the pines. As he glanced into the deep of
the valleys, a blue pheasant rose with its whistling call,
and with widespread wings sailed slowly down into the
mist below. The sunlight caught the splendour of his
plumage, and he dropped like a jewel into the pearl
grey of the vapour that clung to the mountain-side.
Beeroo looked at the bird for a moment, and then lifting his gaze, fixed it on a white spot on the summit of
the forest-covered hill to his left. He made out a cone-
like dome, surmounting a square building, built like an
eagle's nest at the edge of the precipice which fell sheer
for a thousand feet to the silver ribbon of the river. It
was the *mandar*, or temple of Mohonagh, and so clear
was the air, that it seemed as if Beeroo had only to
stretch out his staff to touch the white spot before him.
He knew better than that, however, and knew too that
the sun must rise again before he could rest himself
beneath the walls of the temple, and look on the treasure of the shagul.

"*Ram, ram,* Mohonagh ! " he cried, saluting the far-
off shrine in mockery, and then continued his way.
When he had gone thus for another hour or so,
he came upon the traces of a recent encampment.
There was a heap of stale fodder, one or two earthenware
pots were lying about, and the remains of a fire still
smouldered under the lee of a walnut tree. Hard by,
on the opposite side of the track, a huge rock rose
abruptly, and from its scarred side a bubbling spring

plashed musically into a natural basin, and, overflowing
this, ran across the path in a small stream, past the tree
and over the precipice, where it lost itself in a spray
in which a quivering rainbow hung. Here Beeroo
halted, and having broken his fast and slaked his thirst,
proceeded to totally alter his personal appearance.
This he did by the simple process of removing his turban of Turkey red and his warm vest, the only covering
he had for the upper portion of his body. After this he
let down his long straight hair, which he wore coiled in
a knot, to fall freely over his shoulders. Then he
smeared himself all over, head and all, with ashes from
the fire; and when this was done he stood up a grisly
phantom in which no one would have recognised the
Sansi tracker. He hid his sandals and the wearing
apparel he had removed in a secure place in a cleft in
the rocks, and marking the spot carefully, went on—no
longer Beeroo the Sansi, a man of no caste, but a holy
mendicant. In his left hand he held one of the earthen
vessels he had found under the walnut, in his right,
his bamboo staff, and the knapsack hung over his
shoulders. When he had gone thus for about a mile
he heard the melancholy "*Aosh ! Aosh !*" of cattle-
drivers in the hills and the tinkling of bells. Turning
a bluff he came face to face with a small caravan of bul-
locks, returning from the interior, laden with walnuts,
dried apricots, and wool. Each bullock had a bundle of
merchandise slung on either side, and the frontlet of
the leading animal was adorned with strings of blue
beads and shells. The caravan-drivers walked, and as
they urged their beasts along, repeated at intervals their
call, which to European ears would sound more like a

sigh of despair than a cry of encouragement. Beeroo
stood by the side of the road, and, stretching out his
ash-covered hands, held out the vessel for alms. Each
man as he passed dropped a little into it for luck, one a
brown copper, another some dried fruit, a third a handful of parched grain, and Beeroo received these offerings
in a grave silence as became his holy calling. He stayed
thus until the caravan was out of sight; then he collected the few coins and tossed the rest of the contents
of the vessel on to the roadside. He was satisfied that
his disguise was complete, and that he could face the
priests of the temple at Mohonagh without fear of discovery, for the carriers were Bunjarees, members of a
tribe allied to his own, whose lynx-eyes would have discovered a Sansi in a moment unless his disguise was
perfect.

"*Thoba!*" laughed Beeroo to himself as he pressed
on. "Had the Bunjarees only known who I was, I
had heard the whisper of their sticks through the air,
and my back might have been sore; but the blessing of
Mohonagh is upon me," he chuckled.

Beeroo rested that evening in a cave. He rose at
midnight, however, and travelling without a check was
by morning ascending the winding road that led to the
shrine. He was not alone here, for there were a number of pilgrims toiling up the ascent, halting now and
again to take breath, as they wearily climbed the narrow
track set in between the red and brown rocks, and overhung by wild apricot and holm-oak. Among the pilgrims were those who, in expiation of their sins,
wriggled up the height on their faces like snakes, others
who laid themselves flat at every third step, others

again who crawled up painfully on their blistered hands
and knees ; there were women going to thank the god
for the blessing of children, bearded Dogras of the hills,
ash-covered and ochre-robed mendicants, and a fat
mahajun, or money-lender, who had won a lawsuit and
ruined a village. All these were hurrying towards the
shrine, and their hands were full.

Under the arch of the gateway stood Prem Sagar,
the high priest of Mohonagh, and flung grain towards a
countless number of pigeons that fluttered and cooed
around him. " They are the eyes and ears of the temple," he said to himself as he gazed upon them ; " they
warn the shrine of danger, they bring the news of the
world beyond the hills, they are surer than the telegraph
of the Sahibs, for they tell no secrets. Perchance,"
and he looked down on the specks slowly nearing the
gate, " amongst that crowd of fools is Beeroo the Sansi ;
if so the god will welcome him, and there will be another miracle. Purun Chand ! " and he called out to a
subordinate priest who approached him reverently,
" Purun Chand, awaken the god."

Purun Chand placed a conch-horn to his lips, and
blew a long deep-toned call. Its dismal notes were
caught up in the hills and echoed from valley to valley,
until they died away, moaning in the deeps of the forest.
As the call rang out dolefully, the pilgrims ascending
the road fell on their knees, and with one voice cast up
a wailing cry, " Ai, ai, Mohonagh ! " And Beeroo the
Sansi, the man of no caste, whose very presence so
near the temple was an abomination, shouted the
loudest of all.

* * * * *

Half an hour later, Prem Sagar, the high priest, naked to the waist, with his brahminical cord hanging over his left shoulder and a red and white trident painted on his forehead, stood on the stone steps leading up to the shrine, and watched with keen eyes the pilgrims as they came within the temple walls. The devotees took no notice of him, except some of the women who prostrated themselves, while he bowed his head gravely in answer, but said nothing. His lips were muttering prayers in a sing-song tone, but his eyes were tirelessly watching the groups as they came up in files. At last Beeroo appeared, and on his coming to the steps, slightly dragging his left foot, a quick light shone in the high priest's eyes.

"Soh ! It is the holy man !" his thoughts ran on. "Gobind Ram did well to warn me of his limp. There too are the five marks of the leopard's claws, running down the inside of the calf." As Beeroo approached the priest, he imitated the action of a woman before him, and prostrated himself. Prem Sagar pretended not to see him ; but raised his voice to a loud chant, and repeated the mystic words *Om, mane padme, om !* ＊ There was a time when these words caused the heavens to thunder as at the sacred name of Jehovah ; but now the limpid blue of the sky was undisturbed, as the priest called out to the jewel in the lotus, the symbol of the Universal God.

"*Om, mane padme, om !*" repeated Beeroo, and passed into the shrine. He found himself in a room about twenty feet square, the walls and floor blackened

---

[1] "*Om*, the jewel in the lotus, *om !*" The *padma*, or lotus, is the flower from which Brahma sprang.

by age and by the smoke from the cressets which burned
day and night in little niches in the walls. Overhead
the vault of the dome was in inky darkness, and in front
of him, three-headed and four-armed, painted a bright
red, was the grinning idol of Mohonagh. At the feet
of the god were the offerings of the pilgrims, and on
each side of the idol stood an attendant priest holding
a censer, which he swung to and fro, and the fumes
from which, heavy with the odour of the wild jasmine
and the champac, curled slowly up to the blackened
dome. But it was not on the idol, nor on the priests,
nor on the worshippers, that Beeroo's eyes were fixed.
They were bent to the right of the idol, where the trunk
of the Shagul Tree rose from the flooring of the temple
like the body of a huge snake, and, escaping outside
through a cutting in the wall, spread out into branches
and leaves. In fact the temple was built around the
tree, and even through the gloom, Beeroo could see that
the part of the tree within the temple walls was covered
with coins and gems. The coins, old and blackened
with smoke, looked like scales on the snake-like trunk
of the Shagul Tree : the gold and silver of the jewels
were dimmed of their brightness ; but through the
murky scented atmosphere the Sansi saw the dusky
burning red of the ruby, the green glow of the emerald,
the orange flame within the opal, and the countless
lights in the diamond ; and all these came and went like
stars twinkling through the veil of a dark night. The
Sansi almost gasped, such riches as these were beyond
his dreams ; they truly meant *lakhs* of rupees. A single
one of the gems would buy him a village and lands ; if
he could get the whole ! His brain almost reeled at the

thought, and it was with an effort that he steadied himself, and laying his offering at the feet of the god, backed slowly out of the temple.

Between the outer walls and the shrine was a space about a hundred feet square, shaded by a number of walnut trees. Hither the Sansi betook himself, and placing his earthen bowl on the ground, sat down behind it, staring stolidly before him as if trying to lose himself in that abstraction by which the devotee attains to *nirvana.* Some of the pilgrims piously dropped food into the vessel ; but Beeroo took no heed of this, his eyes were fixed on vacancy, and his mind was revolving many things. So hour after hour passed, and Beeroo still sat motionless as a stone. Prem Sagar approached him once and spoke ; but the holy man made no answer, judging it better to pretend to be under a vow of silence, than to betray anything by converse with the Brahmin. The high priest turned away smiling to himself. "Blue-throated Krishna," he murmured, "but the Sansi plays his part well ! I had been deceived myself, had I not been warned by the—god," and he walked to the temple gates, and gazed down into the valley beneath him.

At last the strain of the position he had assumed began to tell upon Beeroo. Tough as he was, he had not had practice in those incredible feats of patient endurance to which the regular *Bairajis,* or holy men, have accustomed themselves. Beeroo would have followed the track of a wounded stag like a jackal for three days ; he would lifted a cow at Jagadri at nightfall, and by morning been in the Mohun Pass ; he would have danced his tame bear at Umritsur at noontide, and when

the moon rose would have been resting at the Taksali
Gate of Lahore ; but to sit without motion for hour
after hour, to sit until his limbs seemed paralyzed and
his blood dead—this was unbearable. At all hazards
this must be ended ; and he suddenly rose, and began to
move up and down, gesticulating wildly. The people
who looked on thought he was mad, and therefore more
holy than ever. They little knew of the method in the
Sansi's madness, and that he was making the frozen
blood circulate once again in his cramped limbs.
When he had done this he came back, ate a little, and
coiling himself up in the dust went to sleep, his sack
under his head.

By sunset most of the pilgrims had departed from the
shrine, leaving only those who, having far to go, determined to camp within the inclosure of the temple walls
for the night. They had brought provisions with them,
and soon fires were sputtering merrily, and little groups
sat around them, enjoying themselves in the subdued
fashion of Indians. The holy man was not forgotten ;
his vessel was soon full of smoking hot cakes of Indian
corn, and one kinder than the others placed a brass
lota of milk beside him. The holy one proved himself
to be very willing to accept these gifts, and doubtless
refreshed by his sleep, ate and drank with a very mun-
dane appetite. While thus engaged, a little child came,
and placing an offering of a string of flowers at his feet,
shyly ran back to his parents. Prem Sagar saw this,
and turning to the same priest who had aroused the idol
in the morning, said : " Purun Chand, while standing at
the temple gates this morning, mine eyes became dim,
and there was a roaring in mine ears. Then I heard

the voice of the idol of Mohonagh, and he said unto
me : ' Five score years have passed to-day since the
days of Sham Chand the king, since the days of the
high priest Prem Chand, since I, Mohonagh, have
spoken. Now to-night is the night of the new moon,
and I, Mohonagh, will work a sign.' Then the darkness
cleared away, and all was as before.   Therefore I say to
thee, Purun Chand, let not the idol be watched to-
night: let the temple gates be kept open that Mohonagh
may enter ; and to-morrow at the dawning we shall
behold his sign."

Purun Chand bowed his obedience to the high priest ;
and then the darkness came, and with it the stars, and
the thin scimitar of the young moon set slantwise in the
sky.   Beeroo was in no hurry ; he had plenty of time to
think out his plan of action, and had resolved to make
his attempt in the small hours of the morning, for
choice, in that still time between night and day, when
all would be asleep, when even if it became necessary
to remove an obstacle from his path, on one would hear
the stroke of the knife or the groan of the victim.   A
little after midnight, then, Beeroo arose to his feet, and
looked cautiously about him.   Everything was very
still ; the camp-fires burned low and there was no sound
except the rustle of the leaves overhead.   The tree beneath which he rested was very near to the temple gates,
and it struck him that they were open.   He crept
softly towards them, and found it was as he thought.
" The blessing of Mohonagh *is* on me," he laughed
lowly to himself as he came back.   He thrust his hand
into his sack, and pulled out a light but strong claw-
hammer, and a knife with a pointed blade keen as a

razor. As he brought them forth they clicked against each other, and in the dead stillness the sharp, metallic sound seemed loud enough to be heard all over the inclosure. Something also disturbed the pigeons on the temple, and there was an uneasy fluttering of wings. The Sansi drew in his breath with a hissing sound. " This will cause a two hours' delay," he said to himself. " I will risk nothing if I can help it." Then he sat him down again and waited.

At last ! He rose once more softly, and crept with long cat-like steps towards the entrance of the shrine. The cressets burning within cast a faint pennon of light out of the pointed archway of the entrance, and as they wavered in the night wind, this banner of fire shook and trembled with an uncertain motion. Beeroo halted in the shadow. He was about to step forward again when he was startled by a strange, shrill chuckling cry that made his very flesh creep. He looked around him in fear, and the elvish laugh came again from amidst the leaves of the walnut trees. The man heaved a sigh of relief ; " Pah ! " he exclaimed in disgust at himself, " it is but a screech-owl." He had to wait a little, however, to steady himself ; and then he boldly pressed forward and through the door of the shrine. There was not a soul within. The glimmering lights cast uncertain shadows around them, and the three heads of the idol faced the Sansi in a stony silence. There was but one eye in the centre of each forehead; but all three of these eyes seemed to lighten, and the thick lips on the three faces to widen in a grin of mockery at the thief. Like all natives of India, Beeroo was superstitious, and a fear he could hardly control fell on him. What if, after all, the

stories of the idol's power were true ? Aladin had not
lied about the Shagul Tree ; why should he lie about the
power of the idol ? Still Mohonagh was not the god of
the Sansis. He would invoke his own gods, deities of
forest and flood, against this three-headed monster.
Then the Shagul Tree was there. He could all but
touch it ; he caught the flash of the winking gems, and
the instincts of the robber, fighting with his fears,
brought back his courage.

"Aho, Mohonagh ! Thy blessing is on me, the
Sansi." He said this loudly in bravado, and was almost
frightened again at the echoes of his own voice in the
vault of the dome. He had spoken with the same feeling
in his heart that makes a timid traveller whistle when
passing a place he dreads. He had spoken to keep his
heart up, and the very sound of his own voice terrified
him. At last the echoes died away and there was
silence in the shrine. Large beads of sweat stood on
the man's forehead. Almost did he feel it in his heart
to flee at once ; but to leave that priceless treasure now !
It could not be. In two strides he was beside the tree.
A wrench of the claw-hammer and a jewelled bracelet
was in his hand ; another wrench and he had secured
another blazing trophy.

"Beeroo ! "

The man looked up in guilty amazement. To his
horror he saw that the three heads of the idol, which
were facing the door when he entered, had moved
round, and were now facing him. The hammer fell
from his hand with a crash, and he stood shivering, a
grey figure with staring eyes and open gasping mouth.

"*Ai*, Mohonagh ! " he said in a choking voice.

" The blessing of Mohonagh is on thee ; " and something that seemed all on fire rose from behind the idol, and laid its hand on Beeroo's face. With a shriek of agony the Sansi rolled on the floor, and twisted and curled there like a snake with a broken back.

When, roused by his cries, the people and the priests awoke and hurried to the temple, they shrank back in terror ; and none dared enter, not even the priests, for from the mouths of the idol three long tongues of flame played, paling the glow of the cressets and throwing its light on the blind and writhing wretch at its feet.

Suddenly a quiet voice spoke at the temple-door, and Prem Sagar the high-priest appeared. " O pilgrims," he said, " be not afraid ! Mohonagh has but protected his treasure, and given us a sign. Said I not he would do this, Purun Chand ? See," he added, as he stepped into the temple, and lifted up the gems from the floor, " this man would have robbed a god ! " And the people, together with the priests, fell on their knees and touched the earth with their foreheads, crying " *Ai, ai,* Mohonagh ! "

Prem Sagar pointed to Beeroo. " Bear him outside the temple-gates and leave him there," he said ; " he is blind and cannot see."

Two or three men volunteered to do this, and they bore him out as Prem Sagar had ordered, and cast him on the roadside without the temple-gates ; and he, to whom day and night were to be henceforth ever the same, lay there moaning in the dust.

Late that morning certain pilgrims returning to their houses found him there, and, being pitiful, offered to guide him back. It is said that the first question he

asked was, "When will it be daylight?" And a
Dogra of the hills answered bluntly, "Fool, thou art
blind"; whereat the Sansi lapsed into a stony silence,
and was led away like a child.

In the tribe of the Sansis, who wander from Tajawala
to Jagadhri where the brass-workers are, and from Jagadhri to Karnal, is a blind madman who bears on his
scarred face the impress of a hand. It is said that he
can cure all diseases at will, for he is the only man living
who has stood face to face with a god.

THE FOOT OF GAUTAMA

The *Gregory Gasper*, or, as the Lascars insisted on calling her, the *Gir Giri Gaspa*, bound from Calcutta to Rangoon and the Straits, had injured her machinery, and was now going, as it were, on one leg, and going very lamely, across the Bay of Bengal. We had got into a dead calm. The sea and the sky fused into each other in the horizon, and the water around us was as molten glass, parting sluggishly before the bows of the ship, instead of dancing back in a creamy foam.

" By Jove ! " said Sladen, as he leaned over the side and watched the lazy brown swell lounge backward from our course, " this *is* a dirty bit of water : that wave should have had a white head to it. I believe we've got into a sea of flat beer."

" We've got to go to Rangoon for hospital, and this is the outwater of the Irawadi," said a passenger from his seat. " We can't be more than sixty miles from the coast, and an Irawadi flood shoots its slime out quite as far as that."

" I prefer to think it's flat ale. It's too hot to go into physical geography, Burgess "; and Sladen, flinging the half-burnt stump of his cheroot overboard, joined us

who sat in torpid silence. The heat was intense. We
had tried every known way to kill time, and failed.

The small excitement of the morning, caused by a
shoal of turtles drifting by solemnly, had passed.
They looked like so many inverted earthen pots in the
water, and we had wasted about fifty of the ship's snider
cartridges on them, until, finally, they floated out of
range and sight, unhurt and safe. Then an Indian
Marine vessel passed us in the offing, and there was a
hot discussion between Sladen and myself whether it was
the *Warren Hastings* or the *Lord Clive.* We appealed
to the captain, who, being a member of the Royal Naval
Reserve, looked with profound scorn on the Indian
Marine. He scarcely deigned to glance at the ship as
he grunted out :

" Oh, it's one of those damned cockroach navy boats :
it's that old tub the *Lord Clive*," and he walked off to
the bridge. Ten minutes afterwards we lost the grey
sides of the old tub in the grey of the sea, and a dark
line of smoke running from east to west was the only
sign of the *Lord Clive,* as she steamed through the dead
calm at fourteen knots an hour. Then we tried nap,
we adventured at loo, and we bluffed at poker. There
was no balm in them, and Sladen twice held a flush
sequence of hearts. Therefore we sat moody and silent,
some of us too sleepy even to smoke.

It was at this moment that the skipper rejoined us,
and behind him came his stout Madrassee butler, with a
tray full of long glasses, in which the ice chinked
pleasantly.

" Drink, boys ! " he said, settling himself in the
special chair reserved for him. " It's the chief's watch,

and I've brought you a particular brew, as you seem
dull and lonesome, so to speak."

It was a particular brew, and we sucked at it lovingly
through the long amber straws.

"Ha!" said the skipper, "I thought that would
stiffen your backbones. Phew! it is hot!" and he
mopped his face with a huge handkerchief.

Sladen burst out: "We've got absolutely on the
hump. Somebody do something to kill time. Can't
some of you fellows tell a story? Any lie will do!
Come, Captain!"

"No, no!" said the skipper. "I'm the senior officer
here, and speak last. Here's Mr. Burgess: he's been in
all sorts of uncanny places, and should be able to tell
us something. I put the call on him—so heave away."

Burgess, the man who had spoken about the outwater
of the Irawadi, leaned back for a moment in his chair,
with half-closed eyes. He was a short, squarely built
man, very sunburnt, with mouth and chin hidden by
the growth of a large moustache and beard. There was
nothing particular in his appearance; yet in following
his calling—that of an orchid-hunter—he had been to
strange places and seen strange things. Sladen, who
knew him well, hinted darkly that he had traversed
unknown tracts of country, had hobnobbed with
cannibals, and held his life in his hands for the past
thirty years.

"You've hit on the very man, Captain," said Sladen.
"Now, Burgess, tell us how you found the snake-orchid,
and sold it to a duchess for a thousand pounds. You
promised to tell me the story one day, you remember?"

"That's too long. I'll tell you a story, however";

and Burgess lifted up his drink, took a pull at it, and,
picking up the straw that leaned back in a helpless manner against the edge of the glass, began twisting it
round his fingers as he spoke.

"All this happened many years ago——"

"When flowers and birds could talk," interrupted the
Boy; and Burgess, turning on 'him, said slowly:
"Flowers and birds can talk *now*. When you are
older you will understand."

The Boy looked down a little abashed, and Burgess
continued: "I am afraid to say how many years ago
I first went to Burma. I was as poor as a rat, and things
had panned out badly for me. Rangoon then was not
the Rangoon of to-day, and the old king Min-Doon Min,
who succeeded to the throne after the war, was still
almost all-powerful. He was not a bad fellow, and
I once did a roaring trade with him at Mandalay:
exchanged fifty packets of coloured candles for fifty
pigeon's-blood rubies. They had a big illumination at
the palace that night, and I only narrowly escaped being
made a member of the cabinet. I, however, got the
right of travelling through his majesty's dominions,
wherever and whenever I pleased; but the chief queen
made it a condition that I should supply no more
coloured candles. She preferred the rubies; and I
fancy old Min-Doon Min must have had a bad time of
it, for the queen was as remarkable for her thrift as for
her tongue. She was as close as that"—Burgess held
up a square brown fist before us, and, as he did so, I
noticed the white line of a scar running across it, below
the knuckles, from thumb to little finger. He caught
my eye resting on it, and laughingly said: "It's a seal

of the kind friends I have in Kinnabalu. But to resume, as the story-books say. All this about Min-Doon is a ' divarsion,' and I'll go back to the point when I found myself first at Rangoon, with all my wardrobe on my back, and a two-dollar bill in my pocket. After drifting about for some time, I got employment in a rice-shipping firm, and set myself to work to learn the language. In about a year I could speak it well, and, having got promotion in the firm, felt myself on the high road to fortune. It was hard work : the boss knew the value of every penny he spent, and took every ounce he could out of his men."

" Bosses are cut out of the same pattern even now," murmured the Boy. " The breed don't seem to improve."

Burgess took no notice of the interruption, but went on : " I was finally placed in charge of some work at Syriam ; and a little misfortune happened—my overman died. It was rather a job to get another. Men were not easily picked up in those days. But at last I unearthed one, or rather he unearthed himself. He hailed from the States, and described himself as a Kentucky man—the real ' half-horse, half-alligator ' breed. I asked no questions, but set him to work, and reported to the boss, who said ' All right.' The new man seemed to be a gem : he turned up regularly, stayed till all hours, and never spared himself. He was a great lanky fellow, with dark hair, and eyes so palely grey that they seemed almost white. They gave him an odd appearance ; but, as good looks were not a qualification in our business, it did not matter much what he was like. He had been a miner, and had also been to sea, and knew how to obey an order at the double. One day he suddenly looked up from his table—we sat in the same room—and asked if I had heard of treasure ever being buried in or near old pagodas.

" ' Every one hears such stories,' I answered ; ' but why do you ask ? '

" ' Wal,' he went on, in his slow drawl, ' I've bin readin' ez haow a Portugee called Brito, or some sich name, did a little bit of piracy in these hyar parts, until his games were stopped by the local Jedge Lynch. They ran a stick through him, as the Burmese do now to a dried duck.'

" ' What's that got to do with buried treasure ? '

" ' You air smart ! This Brito, before his luck petered out, had a pow'ful soothin' time of it with the junks an' pagodas, and poongyies, as they call their clergy. Guess he didn't lay round hyar for nuthin', an' if all I've heard be true, vermilion isn't the name for the paint he put on the squint-eyes.

" ' But——'

" He put up his hand. ' So long. I'm thinkin' that, ef I'd a smart pard—one who saveyed their lingo —we might strike a lead of luck.'

" I was always a bit of a roving character, and fond of a little adventure, so that the conversation interested me ; still, however, I objected, more with a desire to see how much Stevens, as he called himself, knew than anything else.

" ' See thar,' he said, pulling out a map from his drawer and unrolling it on the table. ' See thar ! This is where Brito and his crowd were,' and he laid a long forefinger on the mouths of the Irawadi. ' When

they bested him, the Burmese got little or nuthin' back.
I want a pard—one who knows the lingo, an' is a white
man. You set me up when I'd struck bed rock ; an' I
says to myself, Wal, this 'ere *is* a white man. Ef ever
Hake Stevens gets a pile, it's to be halves. The pile's
thar—will you jine ? '

"He stood up, and put his hand on my shoulder.
It really wasn't good enough. Stevens had simply
got hold of a very ordinary legend after all, and I
laughed back, ' You'll make more out of a rice-boom,
Stevens, some day, than ever you will out of Brito's
treasure.' He rolled up the map and put it back into
his drawer.

" ' I've done the squar' thing by you, pard,' he said.
' No one can deny ez I haven't done the squar' by you.'

" ' Of course,' I answered, and turned to my duties.
From that time, however, Stevens seemed to be able to
think of nothing but his imaginary treasure. Some
days afterwards he did not come to work, and the following day we got an ill-spelt letter, resigning his post,
and asking that the money due to him should be sent to
a certain address. We paid up, and got a Chinaman in
his place."

" In a short time the Chinaman will be doing every-
body's work in Burma," said Sladen. " Hand over the
baccy, please, Captain."

The skipper flung Sladen a black rubber tobacco
pouch, and Burgess, in this interlude, finished his glass.

" I clean forgot all about Stevens, when one evening,
as I was sitting in my rooms over a pipe, my servant told
me some one wished to see me. I told the man to admit
him, and Stevens came in. He seemed fairly well off ;

but was, if possible, a trifle thinner than when I last saw
him. He shook me by the hand, disjointed himself like
a fishing-rod, and sank into a chair.

"'Wal, pard, will you jine?'

"'Still at the old game, Stevens?   No, I don't think
I'll join on a fool's search like that.'

"'Fool's search, you call it. Very wal, let it be
naow; but I want you to come with me this evening
to an entertainment. It's a sort of swarrey; but I guess
ez we'll be the only guests.'

"'Have a whiskey first?'

"'I guess ez haow a wet won't hurt,' and he poured
himself out a glass from the bottle—we weren't up to
decanters in Burma then.

" I thought I might as well go, and, having made up
my mind, we were walking down the street in the next
ten minutes. Rangoon was not laid out in squares as it
is now, with each street numbered, so that losing your
way is an impossibility. Well as I knew the place, I
found that Hake Stevens was aware of short cuts and
by-lanes which I had never seen before. We entered
the Chinese quarter. It was a feast-day for John, and
the street was alight with paper lanterns : dragons, ser-
pents, globes, and tortoises swung to and fro in all
manner of colours. Here a green dragon went open-
mouthed at a yellow serpent, there an amber tortoise
swung in a circle of crimson-and-blue globes. We
passed a joss house, where there was an illuminated
inscription to the effect that enlightenment finds its way
even amongst the outer barbarians, and, turning to the
left, much where Twenty-Seven Street is now—a fire
wiped out all that part of Rangoon years ago—went up

a gully, and finally stopped before a small shop. Sitting in a cane chair in the doorway was a short man, so enormously stout that he was almost globular. 'Is he in?' asked Stevens, in English; and the man, with his teeth closed on the stem of the opium pipe he smoked, answered 'Yess,' or rather hissed the words between his lips. We passed by him with some little difficulty, for he made no effort to move, and, ascending a rickety staircase, entered a small room, dimly lighted by a cheap kerosene lamp. In one corner of the room an old man was seated. He rose as we entered, and saluted us.

"'This is the host,' and Stevens waved his hand in introduction. 'But he knows only about six words of English, and I know nothing of his derned lip, so you see my new pard an' I cayn't very well exchange confidences.'

"I confess to a feeling of utter disappointment when I saw what we had come to; but there was no use in saying anything. 'Who is he? How did you get to know him?' I asked Stevens. He closed an eyebrow over one of his white-grey eyes with a portentous wink.

"'That, pard, is one of the secrets of the past. We hev the future before us.'

"I never could quite make Stevens out. He spoke the most obtrusive Yankee; yet with turns of expression which at times induced me to think he was playing a part.

"'Very well,' I laughed, 'I don't want to look back; but may I ask what is the entertainment this gentleman has provided for us?'

"'Wal,' replied Stevens, 'he's just one of their medi-

cine-men : goes off to sleep, and then tells you all about
everything. I'm goin' to lay round for him to tell us
where Brito's pile is. Spirit-rappin' does strange things
in my country, an' I don't see ez how this old cuss
moutn't be of help.'

"The old tack again !—I resigned myself to fate.
There is no use in going into preliminaries. Stevens
stated what he wanted, and I explained fully and clearly
what was required. We then paid our fee, which the
old gentleman wrapped up for security in a corner of
the saffron sash he wore round his head, and told us to
sit down before him. Then he stripped himself to the
waist—there wasn't much to remove—and spread a
square of white cloth on the floor ; on this he placed a
mirror, brought the light close to the mirror, and then
settled himself cross-legged before his arrangement of
mirror and light.

"' Listen ! ' he said in Burmese. ' I have given my
word, and will show you what you want ; but you must
not speak, and you must follow my directions im-
plicitly.'

"I translated to Stevens, who willingly agreed.

"' Now shut your eyes.'

"We did so, and I felt his hands passing over my
face. Then something cold touched my forehead,
leaving a sensation much like that caused by a menthol
crystal. A moment later a subtle odour filled the room
—an odour indescribably sweet and heavy, the effect of
which on me was to make me feel giddy.

"' Open your eyes !'

"I almost started, for the words were spoken in the
purest English. We obeyed, and found the room full

of a pale blue vapour. The lamp had gone out ; but the mirror was instinct with light, and threw a halo around it, showing the dim outline of the sorcerer crouched low down with his face between his hands.

" ' Look ! '

" The voice seemed to come from all parts of the room at once, and Stevens' hand clutched on to my shoulder, the fingers gripping in like a vice. We bent over the glass, and saw reflected in it, not our own faces, but a wide creek, overhung by forest on each side, and a row of six colossal images of Buddha, or Gautamas as they are called, lining one of the banks. Whilst we looked on this silent scene, a boat with a couple of native oarsmen came round the elbow of the creek. In the stern sat a man in an old-fashioned dress, with a cuirass on ; and as the boat grounded lightly near the figure of the largest Gautama, he leaped actively to land, holding up from the ground a long, basket-hilted rapier. The two men followed, bearing with them an iron-bound chest, and laid it at the feet of the biggest Gautama ; then returning to the boat, they brought picks therefrom, and began to dig, the man with the rapier standing over them, resting on the hilt of his sword. They dug away under the foot of the idol, and finally concluded they had gone far enough. The chief examined their work, and some words passed. We saw the lips moving, but heard nothing. The box was buried· carefully, and the stones and earth put back, so as to remove all traces of the hiding-place of the treasure. Some further directions were given, and one of the two natives stooped as if to throw some brushwood over the spot. The next moment the rapier passed through his

body. He twisted himself double, and rolled over dead.
The other turned to flee, but there was a flash, a small
curl of blue and grey smoke, and he fell forward on his
face into the water and sank. The cavalier, still
holding the pistol in his hand, went up to the first man.
There was no doubt he was dead; so the Don put back
his pistol, wiped his sword carefully with a handful
of grass, and returned it to its scabbard; then he
dragged the body to the creek and flung it in. After
that he gave a last look at the foot of the Gautama, and,
jumping into the boat, began to paddle himself away.

"'Dead men tell no tales.' The words seemed to
burst from Stevens. Instantly there was a blinding
flash, and when we recovered ourselves the room was as
before. The cloth and mirror had gone, and the old
sorcerer was seated on his stool in the corner of the
room, the lamp burning dimly beside him.

"'You spoke,' he said. 'I can do no more.'

"I looked at Stevens reproachfully, and he understood. His face was very pale, and his lips blue with
excitement. After a little he recovered himself, and
said, with a shake of eagerness in his voice :

"' Cayn't this old cuss start fresh, an' give us another
run ?'

"' I can do nothing,' replied the man to my inquiry.
'You must go now.'

"We turned to depart, and when we got into the
street Stevens said to me : 'I'll see you home. I'm
afraid I busted the show.'

"' I'm afraid you have ; but it's no use crying over
spilt milk.'

"Stevens made no answer, and we walked back to

my rooms without saying a word. At the door he left
me abruptly, refusing all offers to come in. Once in my
rooms, I tried to think out the matter, but gave it up
and went to bed. Sleep wouldn't come, so I lay awake
the whole night, picturing to myself over and over again
the grim scene I had seen enacted in the mirror. Towards morning I dropped into a troubled sleep, and
awoke rather late. I got out of bed thinking that the
events of the past night were, after all, nothing more
than a dream ; but it all came back to me. When I
went down to breakfast I found Stevens waiting for
me, and he pressed me earnestly to join him in a search
for the place we had seen in the looking-glass. I was
in an irritable mood. ' Great Scott ! ' I said, ' can't
you see that all this is only a conjurer's trick ? How
many thousand Gautamas are there in Burma ? Are
you going to dig them all up ? '

   " ' Some men don't know their luck, pard,' he said,
as he left me ; and, although I thought of him sometimes, I never heard anything more of him for a long
time.

   " A run of bad luck came now, and the boss suspended
payment—went bung, in fact—and I was thrown on my
beam ends. I had something in the stocking, though ;
and it was about this time that my thoughts kept turning continually towards the orchid trade. It first struck
me in this way : A friend of mine had written from
home, pointing out that a demand had arisen for orchids ; and the small supply I sent was sold on such
favourable terms that I was seriously considering a
larger venture. I thought the matter over, and one
evening after dinner determined to give it a final con-

sideration. So I lit my pipe, and strolled out towards
the jetties—a favourite walk of mine. It was bright
moonlight ; and I walked up and down the planking,
more and more resolved at every turn I took to decide
upon the orchid business.

"At one end of the jetty there was a crane that
stretched out its arm in a how-de-do sort of manner to
the river below it. I walked up to it with idle curiosity,
and when I came close, saw the figure of a European,
apparently fast asleep, near the carriage of the crane.
A common 'drunk' or a loafer, I thought to myself—
when the figure rose to a sitting posture, and, as the
moonlight shone on its face, I could not make a
mistake.

"'Stevens !' I said.

"'Wal, pard ?' and Hake Stevens, without another
word, rose up and stood before me.

"I saw at a glance that he was in rags, and that about
the third of one stockingless foot was protruding in an
easy manner from his boot ; the other boot seemed more
or less wearable. Stevens had a habit of walking with a
lurch to his left—heeling over to port, as it were—which
accounted for the fact I observed.

"'Why,' I said, putting my hand on his shoulder,
'how has it come to this ? Why didn't you come to
me ?'

"'Have you got a smoke ?' he asked.

"For answer I handed him my baccy pouch, and he
loaded an old pipe.

"'Light-o !'

"I struck a vesta, and handed it to him. By the
flare of it I could see him very white and starved.

" ' Now,' I added, ' you come straight home with me.'

" ' Guess ez haow I was making tracks thar, when I broke down, an' had to heave to. I hev found it this time. See hyar.'

" ' First come home with me, and then you can tell me all about it. I won't hear a word till you've had something to eat and a rest.'

" It was only a few minutes' walk to my rooms ; but I had to half carry Stevens there. Those were the days when cabs were unknown, remember. As soon as we arrived, I told my boy to raise supper ; and in the meantime Stevens had a stiff whiskey, a bath, and changed into some of my things. He looked a figure of fun as he came out, with about a yard of lean leg and leaner arm sticking out of the things I'd given him. But, Lord ! you should have seen him wolf the cold meat and pickles ! When he'd done, I was for just marching him straight to bed. But, no : he was determined to tell me his story ; so I let him run his course.

" ' Pard,' he said, ' when I busted the caboodle that night, an' left you, I said to myself : " Hake Stevens, you chowder-headed clam, you jest make this level ; you've done an all-fired foolish thing, an' now you've got ter eat yer leek." The next mornin' I gave you another try, but you wouldn't rise to it ; so I went off an' took a passage to Henzada. It was all in the low countries that Brito was, an' I dctermined to work the thing in squars—work every inch of it, ef it took me a hundred years, until I found thet creek with the images. I got to Henzada in a rice boat ; then I pulled out my map, marked my squars, an' set to work. I bought a paddle canoe, an' blazed every creek I went up. I made

up my mind ez I should work down'erds from Henzada,
ez thet was the furthest point old Brito struck.   I
calc'lated thet ef he was hard pressed, an' the Burmee
squint-eyes were gettin' the jamb on him, he would lay
fur to hide his greenbacks ez far from his usual
bars ez possible.   Wal, I worked those creeks up an'
down, night an' day, gettin' what I could out of the
villagers on payment, an' when the dollars ran out, got
it without payment.   Snakes !   How the squitters fed
on me !   An' I was a'most so starved thet, ef I could
on'y hev managed it, I'd hev fed on them like a fish,
an' got some of myself back agen.   Wal, it woke snakes
when they found I swooped down on their cokynut
plantations, and one thing and another ; but a freeborn
American ain't goin' fur to starve when these hyar
yeller Burmans gits their bellies full.   The local sheriff
and his posse turned out, an' thar was a vigilance com-
mittee behind every tree.   Shootin' was not in my line,
unless forced to ; so I skedaddled, an' they after me.   It
was a tight race, an' I was so weak I felt I could hardly
hold out ; so I thought I'd better take to land.   I
shot the canoe under some branches, an', to my surprise,
found they overhung an' concealed a small passage,
hardly wide enough for two canoes abreast.   Up this
I went : it was easier goin' than walkin' through the
thorns.   After about four hours of shovin' through slime,
it widened out ; an' then, turnin' a great clump of bamboos, I swung round to my right—an' what do you think
I saw ? '

" He stretched his hand out to me, and the grey of his
eyes seemed absolutely to whiten.

" ' Ez I live, I saw the six big images all in a row,

each one bigger than the other ; an' they war smilin'
across the creek, as they smiled when Brito buried his
treasure thar, an' God knows how many years before.
I ran the boat ashore, jumped off, an' patted the big
idol's knee—couldn't reach further up ; an' then I came
back to find you. The gold lies thar, pard, an' we are
made men : it's thar, I say. Come back with me ;
share an' share alike—hands on it.'

"His voice cracked as he brought his story to this
abrupt close ; and I said nothing, but shook his outstretched hand.

"'When can we start ?' he asked.

"'You must pull yourself together a bit, Stevens,
before we do anything of the kind.'

"Then I told him briefly how I was a free man, and
able to go where I listed ; and that, as I could combine
my first essay in orchid-hunting with the search for
Brito's treasure, I didn't care how soon I went. But
it could not be until Stevens was better able to travel,
as the rains were coming on, and further exposure might
mean death to him.

"'And now,' I said, 'you'd better turn in and have
a snooze. I'm a bit sleepy myself.'

"With that he got up and shambled off to bed. The
next morning he was in a high fever, and it was some
time before he was right again. At length he said he
was once more fit ' to fight his weight in wild cats.' He
wasn't by any means that : he was still weak, and not
able to face any great hardship ; but enforced idleness
was sending the man mad, and I thought we'd better
make a start. I did not mean to go in for any
particular roughing it. It was only subsequently that

I learned what sort of music an orchid-hunter has to face."

Burgess stopped for a moment, and pointed his finger at the Boy, who lay flat on his back, sound asleep, with his lower jaw open.

" If you're feeling like that, I'll reel up."

" Go ahead," said the skipper : " if you've done nothing else you've quieted that young limb for the present, and we owe you a vote of thanks for that."

" Go on, Burgess," said Sladen : " you've burnt your ships now, and can't go back."

The man laughed—a pleasant, low laugh, that was good to hear.

" Very well—I'll go on. I totted up my savings, and found I could fairly risk the venture. We made arrangements to go to Henzada first, and the passage was done in a big rice boat : there was no flotilla company in those days. We simply crawled to our destination, and I was pretty sick of the journey. It nearly drove Stevens mad, however ; he fretted and fumed until I almost thought he'd be ill again. Whenever we could stop, we did ; and I collected as many orchids as I could. Heavens ! the rubbish I picked up in those days ! Stevens did nothing but swear at the *serang* and pore over the notes in his pocket-book. He got into a way of repeating the notes in his book aloud. ' Third turnin' to the right, first to the left, three big jack trees, and then the passage.' He was learning his notes by heart, he said, in case anything happened.

" When we reached Henzada, a difficulty arose which we should have foreseen. Stevens was recognised, and his late visit only too well remembered. The result was trouble ; but the Myook—there was only a Myook there in those days—was open to argument, backed up with palm oil, and Stevens was let off with a fine. Of course I paid, and was correspondingly sorry for myself ; but we'd gone too far now to recede. We bought a boat—or rather I did—hired a couple of men to help, and started. Stevens had selected some good picks at Rangoon, and these formed a not unimportant item of our outfit. In three days we reached a big creek.

" ' It was hyar that I cut from those Injuns on the war-path,' said Stevens, ' and we cayn't be mor'n a mile from the gully—we should be there by nightfall.'

" It was noonday, almost as hot as it is now, and I was snoozing comfortably, when I heard Stevens shout :

" ' Hyar we are, pard—wake up ! '

" The boat swung lightly round, and shot under the overhanging branches of a large jack tree as he spoke, and I had to stoop very low to save my head. Stevens was trembling with excitement.

" ' In thar,' he called out—' tell them to steer in thar, an' then right ahead.' He pointed to a small opening, about three feet wide, up which a long straight cut of water extended. We got the boat in with some little trouble, and then slipped along easily. The cut was as straight as a canal, overhung on each side with a heavy undergrowth. As we went deeper into the forest this undergrowth became less, and finally almost ceased. Every yard of our advance took us amongst trees which grew more gigantic as we went on. Some of the trees were splendid, going up fifty or sixty feet before throwing out a single branch ; and the bamboos—I never saw such bamboos. As we continued our course it be-

came darker and darker, until we entered the blackest
bit of forest I ever saw. We could hear the drip of the
dew from leaf to leaf. The few rays of sunlight that
straggled in fell in level bars on the green of the leaves,
shadowing the dim outlines of the long colonnades of
tree trunks, and occasionally lighting up the splendour
of some rare orchid in full bloom. A hundred times
I wanted to stop and collect specimens, but Stevens
would not hear of it.

"'No, no, old pard ! let's get on. We'll come back
hyar in our steam yacht, an' you can then root away for
etarnity. We're on the right trail, an' in ten hours—
my God ! I cayn't think ez how your mind can turn to
roots now.'

" I was a little surprised myself ; but the love of these
flowers was in me, and not all the gold in Asia could stop
that. In this way we travelled for about four hours ; and
then towards evening a broad band of daylight spread
suddenly before us, and, almost before I was aware of it,
we were out of the long, snake-like cutting, and, turning
a magnificent clump of bamboos, came upon a wide
stretch of water.

"' There they air !' said Stevens.

" There they were—six huge statues—standing in a
row on the edge of the inland lake, each colossal image
larger than the other, all with their faces set towards
the west. It was almost sunset, and the sky was aflame
with colour, which was reflected back by the water, over
which the Gautamas looked in serene peace. There
was not a sound except the soft murmuring of the breeze
amongst the tree tops. As I live, it was the place we had
seen in the mirror, and for a moment that tragedy of

the past came before me in all its clearness—and I was in dreamland.

"'Wal, pard! Struck ile at last.'

"The sound of Stevens' voice came to me as from a far distance. In the sunlit haze before me I saw the Don paddling his boat away, his long black moustaches lifted with the snarling laugh he had laughed, when he hid his treasure so that no man could tell.

"The boat grounded softly, and Stevens shook me by the shoulder.

"'Wake up, old hoss!—wake up!'

"I pulled myself together and looked at my companion. His face was full of a strange excitement, and as for myself, I felt as if I could hardly speak. As a matter of fact, we wasted no time in words ; but took off our coats and set to work. Our small crew lent a willing hand. It was under the left foot of the biggest Buddha we dug, and in about half an hour made a hole big enough for a man to stand in over his waist.

"'Guess he must have burrowed down far,' said Stevens, 'or we've missed the spot.' Even as he spoke his pick struck with a sharp clang against something.

"'Iron against iron,' yelled Stevens, as he swung his pick round like a madman. He worked so furiously that it was impossible to get near him ; but finally he stopped, and said very calmly :

"'Thar's the pile, pard.'

"We shook hands, and then, with the aid of the men, lifted out the box. It was exceedingly heavy. When we got it out there was some difficulty in opening it, but a revolver cartridge and the pick solved the matter. As the lid went up, we saw before our eyes a pile of gold, jewellery and precious stones. Hake Stevens ran his fingers through them lovingly, and then lay down on the ground, laughing and crying. Then he got up again, and plunged his arms up to the elbows into the winking mass—and his eyes were as the eyes of a madman. I put my hand into the box and pulled out a fistful of gems. Stevens grasped me by the wrist, and then loosed his hold at once.

"'Oh God! oh God!'

"'Why, what is the matter, Stevens? Look at these beauties!' and I held out my hand to him. He looked back at me in a strange sort of way, and said, in a husky voice:

"'Keep that lot, pard. Don't let them be mixed with the others. See! I will take what I can hold, too, and we will divide the rest.' He put his hand amongst the jewels and drew it back with a shudder. 'They're hot as hell,' he said.

"I thought the best thing to do was not to notice his strange manner.

"'Keep them to cool,' I said, flinging what I had with me into the box, and shutting the lid, 'and come and have some dinner. I'm famished.'

"'Do you think these fellows are all right?' Stevens said, apparently trying to pull himself together, as he indicated the crew with a glance.

"'We ought to be a match for twice the number; but we'll keep a look out.'

"We went to dinner in the boat, carrying our box with us. Our crew lit a fire near one of the idols, and cooked their food, whilst we ate our very simple meal. The sun had gone down, and the moon was fighting with a heavy mass of clouds that had sprung up apparently from nowhere, and were gathering in mountainous piles overhead. The low rumbling of distant thunder came to our ears.

"'Looks like rain. Jehoshaphat !—it is rain.'

"A distant moaning sound that gradually increased in volume was audible, the tree tops bent and swayed, the placid surface of the lagoon was beaten into a white foam, and the storm came. We heard a yell from the boatmen on the bank. The next moment we were torn from our moorings, and went swinging down the creek in pitchy darkness. Overhead and around all hell was loose. The paddles were swept away, and we spun round in a roaring wind, in a din of the elements, and a darkness like unto what was before God said, 'Let there be light.' I shouted to Stevens, but could not hear my own voice. Suddenly there came a deafening crash, and a chain of fire hung round the heavens. I saw Stevens crouching in the boat, with his face resting on the box, and his arms clasped around it. 'By the Lord !' he was gibbering and mowing to himself—even above the storm I heard his shrill cry—'the idols, the idols ! they're laffin' at us.' I turned my head as he spoke : the blackness was again lit up, and I saw by it the calm, smiling faces of the Buddhas. All their eyes were fixed on us, and in that strange and terrible light the stony smiles on their faces broadened in devilish mockery. The rain came down in sheets ; and the continual and ceaseless flashes of lightning flared on the angry yellow water around us, and made the rain seem as if there were millions of strands of fine silver and gold wires hanging from the blackness above.

It was all I could do to keep myself in the canoe. At
each flash I looked at Stevens, and saw him in the same
posture, crouching low, like a cat. Then he began to
sing, in a shrill voice, that worked its way, as a bradawl
through wood, past all the noise of the elements. And
now the whole heavens were bright with a pale light
that was given back by the hissing water around. The
raindrops sparkled like gems, and hit almost with the
force of hailstones. Stevens rose with a scream, and
stood in the boat.

"'Sit down, for God's sake!' I called out.

"'I'm holding them with my life—the diamonds,
the jewels!' he yelled with a horrid laugh, and shook
his fist at something. I followed his movements; and
there, riding in the storm, was a small canoe, paddled by
a man in the dress of old days. He was smiling at
Stevens as, with long easy sweeps of his paddle, he came
closer and closer.

"'Shoot him!' yelled Stevens, as he pulled out his
revolver and fired once, twice, and then flung it with all
his might at the vision. In the effort he overbalanced
the boat, and all I can remember is that I was swimming for dear life, and being borne down with frightful rapidity through that awful light. I saw something, which might have been Hake Stevens, struggling
for a moment on the water; but, Stevens or not, it sank
again almost immediately, and some one laughed too as
this happened.

"And I think," said Burgess, "that's about all. I
never saw Hake Stevens again, and I don't want ever to
see Brito's jewels any more."

"How did you get out?"

"By absolute luck. I don't very well remember now ; and——By Jove ! here comes the breeze."

Even as he spoke, a cool puff of wind fanned us into life.

THE DEVIL'S MANUSCRIPT

CHAPTER I.

THE BLACK PACKET.

" M. DE BAC ? De Bac ? I do not know the name."

" Gentleman says he knows you, sir, and has called on urgent business."

There was no answer, and John Brown, the ruined publisher, looked about him in a dazed manner. He knew he was ruined ; to-morrow the world would know it also, and then—beggary stared him in the face, and infamy too. For this the world would not care. Brown was not a great man in " the trade," and his name in the *Gazette* would not attract notice ; but his name, as he stood in the felon's dock, and the ugly history a cross-examination might disclose would probably arouse a fleeting interest, and then the world would go on with a pitiless shrug of its shoulders. What does it matter to the moving wave of humanity if one little drop of spray from its crest is blown into nothing by the wind ? Not a jot. But it was a terrible business for the drop of spray, otherwise John Brown, publisher. He was at his best not a good-looking man, rather mean-looking

than otherwise, with a thin, angular face, eyes as shifty
as a jackal's, and shoulders shaped like a champagne-
bottle. As the shadow of coming ruin darkened over
him, he seemed to shrink and look meaner than ever.
He had almost forgotten the presence of his clerk. He
could think of nothing but the morrow, when Simmonds' voice again broke the stillness.

" Shall I say you will see him, sir ? "

The question cut sharply into the silence, and
brought Brown to himself. He had half a mind to say
" No." In the face of the coming to-morrow, business,
urgent or otherwise, was nothing to him. Yet, after all,
there could be no harm done in receiving the man. It
would, at any rate, be a distraction, and, lifting his
head, Brown answered :

" Yes, I will see him, Simmonds."

Simmonds went out, closing the green baize door behind him. There was a delay of a moment, and M. De
Bac entered—a tall, thin figure, bearing an oblong par-
cel, packed in shiny, black paper, and sealed with flame-
coloured wax.

" Good-day, Mr. Brown ; " and M. De Bac, who, for
all his foreign name, spoke perfect English, extended his
hand.

Brown rose, put his own cold fingers into the warm
grasp of his visitor, and offered him a seat.

" With your permission, Mr. Brown, I will take this
other chair. It is nearer the fire. I am accustomed to
warm climates, as you doubtless perceive ; " and De Bac,
suiting his action to his words, placed his packet on the
table, and began to slowly rub his long, lean fingers
together. The publisher glanced at him with some

curiosity. M. De Bac was as dark as an Italian, with clear, resolute features, and a moustache, curled at the ends, thick enough to hide the sarcastic curve of his thin lips. He was strongly if sparely built, and his fiery black eyes met Brown's gaze with a look that ran through him like a needle.

"You do not appear to recognise me, Mr. Brown?" —De Bac's voice was very quiet and deep-toned.

"I have not the honour——" began the publisher; but his visitor interrupted him.

"You mistake. We are quite old friends; and in time will always be very near each other. I have a minute or two to spare"—he glanced at a repeater—"and will prove to you that I know you. You are John Brown, that very religious young man of Battersea, who, twelve years ago, behaved like a blackguard to a girl at Homerton, and sent her to——but no matter. You attracted my attention then; but, unfortunately, I had no time to devote to you. Subsequently, you effected a pretty little swindle—don't be angry, Mr. Brown—it *was* very clever. Then you started in business on your own account, and married. Things went well with you; you know the art of getting at a low price, and selling at a high one. You are a born 'sweater.' Pardon the word. You know how to keep men down like beasts, and go up yourself. In doing this, you did me yeoman's service, although you are even now not aware of this. You had one fault, you have it still, and had you not been a gambler you might have been a rich man. Speculation is a bad thing, Brown—I mean gambling speculation."

Brown was an Englishman, and it goes without

saying that he had courage. But there was something
in De Bac's manner, some strange power in the steady
stare of those black eyes, that held him to his seat as
if pinned there.

As De Bac stopped, however, Brown's anger gave
him strength. Every word that was said was true, and
stung like the lash of a whip. He rose white with
anger.

"Sir!" he began with quivering lips, and made a
step forwards. Then he stopped. It was as if the
sombre fire in De Bac's gaze withered his strength. An
invisible hand seemed to drag him back into his seat
and hold him there.

"You are hasty, Mr. Brown;" and De Bac's even
voice continued: "you are really very rash. I was
about to tell you a little more of your history, to tell
you you are ruined, and to-morrow every one in London
—it is the world for you, Brown—will know you are a
beggar, and many will know you are a cheat."

The publisher swore bitterly under his breath.

"You see, Mr. Brown," continued his strange visitor,
"I know all about you, and you will be surprised, perhaps, to hear that you deserve help from me. You are
too useful to let drift. I have therefore come to save
you."

"Save me?"

"Yes. By means of this manuscript here," he
pointed to the packet, "which you are going to publish."

Brown now realized that he was dealing with a
lunatic. He tried to stretch out his arm to touch the
bell on the table; but found that he had no power to

do so. He made an attempt to shout to Simmonds; but
his tongue moved inaudibly in his mouth. He seemed
only to have the faculty of following De Bac's words,
and of answering them. He gasped out :

"It is impossible ! "

" My friend "—and De Bac smiled mirthlessly—
" you will publish that manuscript. I will pay. The
profits will be yours. It will make your name, and you
will be rich. You will even be able to build a church."

" Rich ! " Brown's voice was very bitter. " M.
De Bac, you said rightly. I am a ruined man. Even if
you were to pay for the publication of that manuscript
I could not do it now. It is too late. There are other
houses. Go to them."

" But not other John Browns. You are peculiarly
adapted for my purpose. Enough of this ! I know
what business is, and I have many things to attend to.
You are a small man, Mr. Brown, and it will take little
to remove your difficulties. See ! Here are a thousand pounds. They will free you from your present
troubles," and De Bac tossed a pocket-book on the table
before Brown. " I do not want a receipt," he went
on. " I will call to-morrow for your final answer, and
to settle details. If you need it I will give you more
money. This hour—twelve—will suit me. *Adieu !* "
He was gone like a flash, and Brown looked around in
blank amazement. He was as if suddenly aroused from
a dream. He could hardly believe the evidence of his
senses, although he could see the black packet, and the
neat leather pocket-book with the initials " L. De B."
let in in silver on the outside. He rang his bell
violently, and Simmonds appeared.

"Has M. De Bac gone ? "

"I don't know, sir. He didn't pass out through the door."

"There is no other way. You must have been asleep."

"Indeed I was not, sir."

Brown felt a chill as of cold fingers running down his backbone, but pulled himself together with an effort. "It does not matter, Simmonds. You may go."

Simmonds went out scratching his head. "How the demon did he get out ? " he asked himself. "Must have been sleeping after all. The guv'nor seems a bit dotty to-day. It's the smash coming—sure."

He wrote a letter or two, and then taking his hat, sallied forth to an aërated bread-shop for his cheap and wholesome lunch, for Simmonds was a saving young man, engaged to a young lady living out Camden Town way. Simmonds perfectly understood the state of affairs, and was not a little anxious about matters, for the mother of his *fiancée,* a widow who let lodgings, had only agreed to his engagement after much persuasion ; and if he had to announce the fact that, instead of "thirty bob a week," as he put it, his income was nothing at all, there would be an end of everything.

"M'ria's all right," he said to his friend Wilkes, in trustful confidence as they sat over their lunch ; "but that old torpedo "—by which name he designated his mother-in-law-elect—"she'll raise Cain if there's a smash-up."

In the meantime, John Brown tore open the pocket-book with shaking hands, and, with a crisp rustling, a number of new bank-notes fell out, and lay in a

heap before him. He counted them one by one. They
totalled to a thousand pounds exactly. He was a small
man. M. De Bac had said so truly, if a little rudely,
and the money was more than enough to stave off ruin.
De Bac had said, too, that if needed he would give him
more, and then Brown fell to trembling all over. He
was like a man snatched from the very jaws of death.
At Battersea he wore a blue ribbon ; but now he went
to a cabinet, filled a glass with raw brandy, and drained
it at a gulp. In a minute or so the generous cordial
warmed his chilled blood, and picking up the notes,
he counted them again, and thrust them into his breast-
pocket. After this he paced the room up and down
in a feverish manner, longing for the morrow when he
could settle up the most urgent demands against him.
Then, on a sudden, a thought struck him. It was
almost as if it had been whispered in his ear. Why
trouble at all about matters ? He had a clear thousand
with him, and in an hour he could be out of the
country ! He hesitated, but prudence prevailed.
Extradition laws stretched everywhere ; and there was
another thing—that extraordinary madman, De Bac,
had promised more money on the morrow. After all,
it was better to stay.

As he made this resolve his eyes fell on the black
packet on the table. The peculiar colour of the seals
attracted his attention. He bent over them, and saw
that the wax bore an impress of a V-shaped shield, within which was set a trident. He noticed also that
the packet was tied with a silver thread. His curiosity
was excited. He sat down, snipped the threads
with a penknife, tore off the black paper covering,

flung it into the fire, and saw before him a bulky
manuscript exquisitely written on very fine paper.
A closer examination showed that they were a
number of short stories.   Now Brown was in no
mood to read ; but the title of the first tale caught his
eye, and the writing was so legible that he had glanced
over half a dozen lines before he was aware of the fact.
Those first half-dozen lines were sufficient to make him
read the page, and when he had read the page the publisher felt he was before the work of a genius.

He was unable to stop now ; and, with his head resting between his hands, he read on tirelessly. Simmonds
came in once or twice and left papers on the table, but
his master took no notice of him. Brown forgot all
about his lunch, and turning over page after page read
as if spellbound. He was a business man, and was
certain the book would sell in thousands. He read as
one inspired to look into the author's thoughts and see
his design. Short as the stories were, they were Titanic
fragments, and every one of them taught a hideous lesson of corruption. Some of them cloaked in a religious
garb, breathed a spirit of pitiless ferocity ; others were
rich with the sensuous odours of an Eastern garden ;
others, again, were as the tender green of moss hiding
the treacherous deeps of a quicksand ; and all of them
bore the hall-mark of genius. They moved the man
sitting there to tears, they shook him with laughter,
they seemed to rock his very soul asleep ; but through
it all he saw, as the mariner views the beacon fire on a
rocky coast, the deadly plan of the writer. There was
money in them—thousands—and all was to be his.
Brown's sluggish blood was running to flame, a strange

strength glowed in his face, and an uncontrollable admiration for De Bac's evil power filled him. The book, when published, might corrupt generations yet unborn ; but that was nothing to Brown. It meant thousands for him, and an eternal fame to De Bac. He did not grudge the writer the fame as long as he kept the thousands.

"By Heaven!" and he brought his fist down on the table with a crash, "the man may be a lunatic ; but he is the greatest genius the world ever saw—or he is the devil incarnate."

And somebody laughed softly in the room.

The publisher looked up with a start, and saw Simmonds standing before him.

"Did you laugh, Simmonds ? "

"No, sir!" replied the clerk with a surprised look.

"Who laughed then ? "

"There is no one here but ourselves, sir—and I didn't laugh."

"Did you hear nothing ? "

"Nothing, sir."

"Strange !" and Brown began to feel chill again.

"What time is it ?" he asked with an effort.

"It is half-past six, sir."

"So late as that ? You may go, Simmonds. Leave me the keys. I will be here for some time. Goodevening."

"Mad as a coot," muttered Simmonds to himself ; "must break the news to M'ria to-night. Oh, Lor' !" and his eyes were very wet as he went out into the Strand, and got into a blue omnibus.

When he was gone, Brown turned to the fire, poker

in hand. To his surprise he saw that the black paper
was still there, burning red hot, and the wax of the
seals was still intact—the seals themselves shining like
orange glow-lights. He beat at the paper with the
poker ; but instead of crumbling to ashes it yielded
passively to the stroke, and came back to its original
shape. Then a fury came on Brown. He raked at the
fire, threw more coals over the paper, and blew at the
flames with his bellows until they roared up the chimney ; but still the coppery glare of the packet-cover
never turned to the grey of ashes. Finally, he could
endure it no longer, and, putting the manuscript into
the safe, turned off the electric light, and stole out of
his office like a thief.

CHAPTER II.

WHEN Beggarman, Bowles & Co., of Providence Passage, Lombard Street, called at eleven o'clock on the morning following De Bac's visit, their representative was not a little surprised to find the firm's bills met in hard cash, and Simmonds paid him with a radiant face. When the affair was settled, the clerk leaned back in his chair, saying half-aloud to himself, "By George! I am glad after all M'ria did not keep our appointment in the Camden Road last night." Then his face began to darken. "Wonder where she could have been, though?" his thoughts ran on; "half sorry I introduced her to Wilkes last Sunday at Victoria Park. Wilkes ain't half the man I am though," and he tried to look at himself in the window-pane, "but he has two pound ten a week—Lord! There's the guv'nor ringing." He hurried into Brown's room, received a brief order, and was about to go back when the publisher spoke again.

"Simmonds!"

"Sir."

"If M. De Bac calls, show him in at once."

"Sir," and the clerk went out.

Left to himself, Brown tried to go on with the manuscript; but was not able to do so. He was impatient for the coming of De Bac, and kept watching the hands of the clock as they slowly travelled towards twelve. When he came to the office in the morning Brown had looked with a nervous fear in the fireplace, half expecting to find the black paper still there ; and it was a considerable relief to his mind to find it was not. He could do nothing, not even open the envelopes of the letters that lay on his table. He made an effort to find occupation in the morning's paper. It was full of some absurd correspondence on a trivial subject, and he wondered at the thousands of fools who could waste time in writing and in reading yards of print on the theme of " Whether women should wear neckties." The ticking of the clock irritated him. He flung the paper aside, just as the door opened and Simmonds came in. For a moment Brown thought he had come to announce De Bac's arrival ; but no—Simmonds simply placed a square envelope on the table before Brown.

" Pass-book from Bransom's, sir, just come in ; " and he went out.

Brown took it up mechanically, and opened the envelope. A type-written letter fell out with the pass-book. He ran his eyes over it with astonishment. It was briefly to inform him that M. De Bac had paid into Brown's account yesterday afternoon the sum of five thousand pounds, and that, adjusting overdrafts, the balance at his credit was four thousand seven hundred and twenty pounds thirteen shillings and three pence. Brown rubbed his eyes. Then he hurriedly glanced at the pass-book. The figures tallied—there was no error, no mistake. He pricked himself with his penknife to see if he was awake, and finally shouted to Simmonds :

" Read this letter aloud to me, Simmonds," he said.

Simmonds' eyes opened, but he did as he was bidden, and there was no mistake about the account.

" Anything else, sir ? " asked Simmonds when he had finished.

" No—nothing," and Brown was once more alone. He sat staring at the figures before him in silence, almost mesmerizing himself with the intentness of his gaze.

" My God ! " he burst out at last, in absolute wonder.

" Who is your God, Brown ? " answered a deep voice.

" I—I—M. De Bac ! How did you come ? "

" I did not drop down the chimney," said De Bac with a grin ; " your clerk announced me in the ordinary way, but you were so absorbed you did not hear. So I took the liberty of sitting in this chair, and awaiting your return to earthly matters. You were dreaming, Brown—by the way, who *is* your God ? " he repeated with a low laugh.

" I—I do not understand, sir."

" Possibly not, possibly not. I wouldn't bother about the matter. Ah ! I see Bransom's have sent you your pass-book ! Sit down, Brown. I hate to see a man fidgeting about—I paid in that amount yesterday on a second thought. It is enough—eh ? "

Brown's jackal eyes contracted. Perhaps he could get more out of De Bac ? But a look at the strong impassive face before him frightened him.

" More than enough, sir," he stammered ; and then, with a rush, " I am grateful—anything I can do for you ? "

" Oh ! I know, I know, Brown—by the way, you do not object to smoke ? "

" Certainly not. I do not smoke myself."

" In Battersea, eh ? " And De Bac pulling out a
silver cheroot case held it out to Brown. But the publisher declined.

" Money wouldn't buy a smoke like that in England,"
remarked De Bac, " but as you will. I wouldn't smoke
if I were you. Such abstinence looks respectable and
means nothing." He put a cigar between his lips, and
pointed his forefinger at the end. To Brown's amazement an orange-flame licked out from under the finger-
nail, and vanished like a flash of lightning ; but the
cigar was alight, and its fragrant odour filled the room.
It reached even Simmonds, who sniffed at it like a buck
scenting the morning air. " By George ! " he exclaimed in wonder, " what baccy ! "

M. De Bac settled himself comfortably in his chair,
and spoke with the cigar between his teeth. " Now
you have recovered a little from your surprise, Brown,
I may as well tell you that I never carry matches.
This little scientific discovery I have made is very convenient, is it not ? "

" I have never seen anything like it."

" There are a good many things you have not seen,
Brown—but to work. Take a pencil and paper and
note down what I say. You can tell me when I have
done if you agree or not."

Brown did as he was told, and De Bac spoke slowly
and carefully.

" The money I have given you is absolutely your own
on the following terms. You will publish the manuscript I left with you, enlarge your business, and work
as you have hitherto worked—as a ' sweater.' You may

speculate as much as you like. You will not lose. You
need not avoid the publication of religious books, but
you must never give in charity secretly. I do not object to a big cheque for a public object, and your name
in all the papers. It will be well for you to hound
down the vicious. Never give them a chance to recover
themselves. You will be a legislator. Strongly up-
hold all those measures which, under a moral cloak,
will do harm to mankind. I do not mention them. I
do not seek to hamper you with detailed instructions.
Work on these general lines, and you will do what I
want. A word more. It will be advisable whenever
you have a chance to call public attention to a great evil
which is also a vice. Thousands who have never heard
of it before will hear of it then—and human nature is
very frail. You have noted all this down?"

"I have. You are a strange man, M. De Bac."

M. De Bac frowned, and Brown began to tremble.

"I do not permit you to make observations about me,
Mr. Brown."

"I beg your pardon, sir."

"Do not do so again. Will you agree to all this?
I promise you unexampled prosperity for ten years. At
the end of that time I shall want you elsewhere. And
you must agree to take a journey with me."

"A long one, sir?" Brown's voice was just a shade
satirical.

M. De Bac smiled oddly. "No—in your case I
promise a quick passage. These are all the conditions
I attach to my gift of six thousand pounds to you."

Brown's amazement did not blind him to the fact of
the advantage he had, as he thought, over his visitor.

The six thousand pounds were already his, and he had given no promise. With a sudden boldness he spoke out.

" And if I decline ? "

" You will return me my money, and my book, and I will go elsewhere."

" The manuscript, yes—but if I refuse to give back the money ? "

" Ha ! ha ! ha ! " M. De Bac's mirthless laugh chilled Brown to the bone. " Very good, Brown—but you won't refuse. Sign that like a good fellow," and he flung a piece of paper towards Brown, who saw that it was a promissory note, drawn up in his name, agreeing to pay M. De Bac the sum of six thousand pounds on demand.

" I shall do no such thing," said Brown stoutly.

M. De Bac made no answer, but calmly touched the bell. In a half-minute Simmonds appeared.

" Be good enough to witness Mr. Brown's signature to that document," said De Bac to him, and then fixed his gaze on Brown. There was a moment of hesitation, and then—the publisher signed his name, and Simmonds did likewise as a witness. When the latter had gone, De Bac carefully put the paper by in a letter-case he drew from his vest pocket.

" Your scientific people would call this an exhibition of odic force, Brown—eh ? "

Brown made no answer. He was shaking in every limb, and great pearls of sweat rolled down his forehead.

" You see, Brown," continued De Bac, " after all you are a free agent. Either agree to my terms and keep the money, or say you will not, pay me back, receive your note-of-hand, and I go elsewhere with my book. Come—time is precious."

" And from Brown's lips there hissed a low " I agree."

" Then that is settled," and De Bac rose from his chair. " There is a little thing more—stretch out your arm like a good fellow—the right arm."

Brown did so ; and De Bac placed his forefinger on his wrist, just between what palmists call " the lines of life." The touch was as that of a red-hot iron, and with a quick cry Brown drew back his hand and looked at it. On his wrist was a small red trident, as cleanly marked as if it had been tattooed into the skin. The pain was but momentary ; and, as he looked at the mark, he heard De Bac say, " Adieu once more, Brown. I will find my way out—don't trouble to rise." Brown heard him wish Simmonds an affable " Good-day," and he was gone.

CHAPTER III.

"THE MARK OF THE BEAST."

IT was early in the spring that Brown published
"The Yellow Dragon"—as the collection of tales left
with him by De Bac was called—and the success of the
book surpassed his wildest expectations. It became the
rage. There were the strangest rumours afloat as to
its authorship, for no one knew De Bac, and the name
of the writer was supposed to be an assumed one. It
was written by a clergyman; it was penned by a school-
girl; it had employed the leisure of a distinguished
statesman during his retirement; it was the work of
an ex-crowned head. These, and such-like statements,
were poured forth one day to be contradicted the next.
Wherever the book was noticed it was either with the
most extravagant praise or the bitterest rancour. But
friend and foe were alike united on one thing—that of
ascribing to its unknown author a princely genius. The
greatest of the reviews, after pouring on "The Yellow
Dragon" the vials of its wrath, concluded with these
words of unwilling praise: "There is not a sentence
of this book which should ever have been written, still
less published; but we do not hesitate to say that, having been written and given to the world, there is hardly
a line of this terrible work which will not become im-
mortal—to the misery of mankind."

Be this as it may, the book sold in tens of thousands, and Brown's fortune was assured. In ten years a man may do many things ; but during the ten years that followed the publication of " The Yellow Dragon," Brown did so many things that he astonished " the city," and it takes not a little to do that. It was not alone the marvellous growth of his business—although that advanced by leaps and bounds until it over-shadowed all others—it was his wonderful luck on the Stock Exchange. Whatever he touched turned to gold. He was looked upon as the Napoleon of finance. His connection with " The Yellow Dragon " was forgotten when his connection with the yellow sovereign was re-membered. He had a palace in Berkshire ; another huge pile owned by him overlooked Hyde Park. He was a county member and a cabinet-minister. He had refused a peerage and built a church. Could ambition want more ? He had clean forgotten De Bac. From him he had heard no word, received no sign, and he looked upon him as dead. At first, when his eyes fell on the red trident on his wrist, he was wont to shudder all over ; but as years went on he became accustomed to the mark, and thought no more of it than if it had been a mole. In personal appearance he was but little changed, except that his hair was thin and grey, and there was a bald patch on the top of his head. His wife had died four years ago, and he was now contemplating another marriage—a marriage that would ally him with a family dating from the Confessor.

Such was John Brown, when we meet him again ten years after De Bac's visit, seated at a large writing-table in his luxurious office. A clerk standing beside him was cutting open the envelopes of the morning's post, and placing the letters one by one before his master. It is our friend Simmonds—still a young man, but bent and old beyond his years, and still on "thirty bob" a week. And the history of Simmonds will show how Brown carried out De Bac's instructions.

When "The Yellow Dragon" came out and business began to expand, Simmonds, having increased work, was ambitious enough to expect a rise in his salary, and addressed his chief on the subject. He was put off with a promise, and on the strength of that promise Simmonds, being no wiser than many of his fellows, married M'ria; and husband and wife managed to exist somehow with the help of the mother-in-law. Then the mother-in-law died, and there was only the bare thirty shillings a week on which to live, to dress, to pay Simmonds' way daily to the city and back, and to feed more than two mouths—for Simmonds was amongst the blessed who have their quivers full. Still the expected increase of pay did not come. Other men came into the business and passed over Simmonds. Brown said they had special qualifications. They had; and John Brown knew Simmonds better than he knew himself. The other men were paid for doing things Simmonds could not have done to save his life; but he was more than useful in his way. A hundred times it was in the mind of the wretched clerk to resign his post and seek to better himself elsewhere. But he had given hostages to fortune. There was M'ria and her children, and M'ria set her face resolutely against risk. They had no reserve upon which to fall back, and it was an option between partial and total starvation. So "Sim," as

M'ria called him, held on and battled with the wolf at the door, the wolf gaining ground inch by inch. Then illness came, and debt, and then—temptation. " Sim " fell, as many a better man than he has fallen.

Brown found it out, and saw his opportunity to behave generously, and make his generosity pay. He got a written confession of his guilt from Simmonds, and retained him in his service forever on thirty shillings a week. And Simmonds' life became such as made him envy the lot of a Russian serf, of a Siberian exile, of a negro in the old days of the sugar plantations. He became a slave, a living machine who ground out his daily hours of work ; he became mean and sordid in soul, as one does become when hope is extinct. Such was Simmonds as he cut open the envelopes of Brown's letters, and the great man, reading them quickly, endorsed them with terse remarks in blue pencil, for subsequent disposal by his secretary. A sudden exclamation from the clerk, and Brown looked up.

" What is it ? " he asked sharply.

" Only this, sir," and Simmonds held before Brown's eyes a jet black envelope ; and as he gazed at it, his mind travelled back ten years, to that day when he stood on the brink of public infamy and ruin, and De Bac had saved him. For a moment everything faded before Brown's eyes, and he saw himself in a dingy room, with the gaunt figure of the author of " The Yellow Dragon," and the maker of his fortune, before him.

" Shall I open it, sir ? " Simmonds' voice reached him as from a far distance, and Brown roused himself with an effort.

"No," he said, "give it to me, and go for the present."

When the bent figure of the clerk had passed out of the room, Brown looked at the envelope carefully. It bore a penny stamp and the impress of the postmark was not legible. The superscription was in white ink, and it was addressed to Mr. John Brown. The "Mr." on the letter irritated Brown, for he was now The Right Hon'ble John Brown, and was punctilious on that score. He was so annoyed that at first he thought of casting the letter unopened into the waste-paper basket beside him, but changed his mind, and tore open the cover. A note-card discovered itself. The contents were brief and to the point :

"*Get ready to start. I will call for you at the close of the day. L. De B.*"

For a moment Brown was puzzled, then the remembrance of his old compact with De Bac came to him. He fairly laughed. To think that he, The Right Hon'ble John Brown, the richest man in England, and one of the most powerful, should be written to like that ! Ordered to go somewhere he did not even know ! Addressed like a servant ! The cool insolence of the note amused Brown first, and then he became enraged. He tore the note into fragments and cast it from him. "Curse the madman," he said aloud, "I'll give him in charge if he annoys me." A sudden twinge in his right wrist made him hurriedly look at the spot. There was a broad pink circle, as large as a florin, around the mark of the trident, and it smarted and burned as the sting of a wasp. He ran to a basin of water and dipped his arm in to the elbow ; but the pain became intolerable, and, finally, ordering his carriage, he drove home. That evening there was a great civic banquet in the city, and amongst the guests was The Right Hon'ble John Brown.

All through the afternoon he had been in agony with his wrist, but towards evening the pain ceased as suddenly as it had come on, and Brown attended the banquet, a little pale and shaken, but still himself. On Brown's right hand sat the Bishop of Browboro', on his left a most distinguished scientist, and amongst the crowd of waiters was Simmonds, who had hired himself out for the evening to earn an extra shilling or so to eke out his miserable subsistence. The man of science had just returned from Mount Atlas, whither he had gone to observe the transit of Mercury, and had come back full of stories of witchcraft. He led the conversation in that direction, and very soon the Bishop, Brown, and himself were engaged in the discussion of *diablerie*. The Bishop was a learned and a saintly man, and was a " believer " ; the scientist was puzzled by what he had seen, and Brown openly scoffed.

" Look here ! " and pulling back his cuff, he showed the red mark on his wrist to his companions, " if I .were to tell you how that came here, you would say the devil himself marked me."

" I confess I am curious," said the scientist ; and the Bishop fixed an inquiring gaze upon Brown. Simmonds was standing behind, and unconsciously drew near. Then the man, omitting many things, told the history of the mark on his wrist. He left out much, but he told enough to make the scientist edge his chair a little further from him, and a look of grave compas-

sion, not untinged with scorn, to come into the eyes of
the Bishop. As Brown came to the end of his story he
became unnaturally excited, he raised his voice, and,
with a sudden gesture, held his wrist close to the
Bishop's face. " There ! " he said, " I suppose you
would say the devil did that ? "

And as the Bishop looked, a voice seemed to breathe
in his ear : " *And he caused all . . . to receive a mark*
in their right hand, or in their foreheads." It was as if
his soul was speaking to him and urging him to say the
words aloud. He did not ; but with a pale face gently
put aside Brown's hand. " I do not know, Mr. Brown
—but I think you are called upon for a speech."

It was so ; and, after a moment's hesitation, Brown
rose. He was a fluent speaker, and the occasion was
one with which he was peculiarly qualified to deal. He
began well ; but as he went on those who looked upon
him saw that he was ghastly pale, and that the veins
stood out on his high forehead in blue cords. As he
spoke he made some allusion to those men who have
risen to eminence from an obscure position. He spoke
of himself as one of these, and then began to tell the
story of " The Devil's Manuscript," as he called it, with
a mocking look at the Bishop. As he went on he completely lost command over himself, and the story of the
manuscript became the story of his life. He concealed
nothing, he passed over nothing. He laid all his sordid
past before his hearers with a vivid force. His listeners were astonished into silence ; perhaps curiosity kept
them still. But, as the long tale of infamy went on,
some, in pity for the man, and believing him struck
mad, tried to stop him, but in vain. He came at last

to the incident of the letter, and told how De Bac was
to call for him to-night. " The Bishop of Browboro',"
he said with a jarring laugh, " thought De Bac was the
fiend himself," but he (Brown) knew better ; he—he
stopped, and, with a half-inarticulate cry, began to back
slowly from the table, his eyes fixed on the entrance to
the room. And now a strange thing happened. There
was not a man in the room who had the power to move
or to speak ; they were as if frozen to their seats ; as
if struck into stone. Some were able to follow Brown's
glance, but could see nothing. All were able to see
that in Brown's face was an awful fear, and that he was
trying to escape from a horrible presence which was
moving slowly towards him, and which was visible to
himself alone. Inch by inch Brown gave way, until he
at last reached the wall, and stood with his back to it,
with his arms spread out, in the position of one crucified. His face was marble white, and a dreadful terror
and a pitiful appeal shone in his eyes. His blue lips
were parted as of one in the dolors of death.

The silence was profound.

There were strong men there ; men who had faced
and overcome dangers, who had held their lives in their
hands, who had struggled against desperate odds and
won ; but there was not a man who did not now feel
weak, powerless, helpless as a child before that invisible,
advancing terror that Brown alone could see. They
could move no hand to aid, lift no voice to pray. All
they could do was to wait in that dreadful silence and
to watch. Time itself seemed to stop. It was as if
the stillness had lasted for hours.

Suddenly Brown's face, so white before, flushed a

crimson purple, and with a terrible cry he fell forwards on the polished woodwork of the floor.

As he fell it seemed as if the weight which held all still was on the moment removed, and they were free. With scared faces they gathered around the fallen man and raised him. He was quite dead ; but on his forehead, where there was no mark before, was the impress of a red trident.

A man, evidently one of the waiters, who had forced his way into the group, laid his finger on the mark and looked up at the Bishop. There was an unholy exultation in his face as he met the priest's eyes, and said :

" He's marked twice—*curse him !* "

UNDER THE ACHILLES

O Charity ! thy mystery
Doth cover many things.

" Now, don't break hup the 'appy 'ome ! "

" Move those wite mice o' yourn hon, then, 'stead o' sittin' like a hitalian monkey hon a bloomin' barrel horgan."

A hansom had backed into a green Atlas in Piccadilly Circus, at the point where Regent Street and Piccadilly meet. From his height of vantage the omnibus driver threw a sarcasm at the cabman, and Jehu, instead of attending to business, lifted his head to fling back an answer. The sorrel in the hansom likewise lifted his head, stood on his hind legs, and then, plunging sideways on to the pavement, locked the wheels of the two conveyances together, completely stopping the roadway. It was not a good time for a thing of this kind to happen. It was Piccadilly Circus, just after the big furnaces of the theatres had let out their red-hot contents. The molten stream was hissing through the streets, boiling in the throbbing Circus. Such a crowd was there, too, as no city besides may show ; but London need not plume itself on this. Here, in that hour, when the past of one day was becoming the present of

217

another, assembled together the good and the bad. The
honest father of a family, with a pure wife or daughter
on his arm, jostled the soiled dove in her jewelled
shame. Here were gathered the men whose lives by
daylight were white, those who trod the primrose path,
and the workers of the nation ; gilded infamy, tawdry
sin, joy and sorrow, shame and innocence, vice blacker
than night, more hideous than despair. Above blazed
the electric stars of the Monico and the Criterion. A
stream of fire marked Coventry Street. To the right
the lamp glare terminated abruptly in Waterloo
Place, leaving the moon and the lonely Park together. From all the great arteries, through Shaftes-
bury Avenue, through Coventry Street, through the
Haymarket, the toilers of the night beat up to the
roaring Circus, and it was full. I, a derelict of
humanity, was there. In the crowd that fought and
elbowed its way for room—it was a crowd all elbows—
I was the first to reach the hansom. There were two
occupants : a man who lay back with a scared face, and
a woman who laughed as she attempted to step out. It
was as daylight, and the rush of an awful recollection
came to me—God help me ! It was my wife ! My
hand stretched out to aid fell to my side ; but, as I
staggered back, the brute in the hansom plunged yet
more violently than before. There was an alarmed cry,
a swaying motion, and the cab turned over slowly, like
a foundering ship. I could not control myself. I
sprang forward, and lifting the woman from the cab
placed her on the pavement. There was a bit of a cheer,
and before I knew it she thrust her purse into my hand.

" Take this, man, and——"

I waited to hear no more ; a sudden frightened look came into her eyes, and I turned and fled up Piccadilly. Some fool cried " Stop thief ! " Some other one took up the cry. In a moment every one was running. I ran with the crowd, my hand still clenched tightly on the purse, which seemed to burn into it. It was too well dressed a crowd to run far. Opposite Hatchett's it tired, and public attention was engaged by an altercation, which ended in a fight, between a bicyclist and a policeman. I had sense enough left to pull up and slacken my pace to a fast walk. I went straight on. It did not matter to me where I went. If I had the pluck I should have killed myself long ago. It takes a lot of pluck to kill one's self. Five years had gone since Mary passed out of my life. Five years ! It was six years ago that I, Richard Manning of the Bengal Cavalry, had cut for hearts, and turned up—the deuce ! What right had I to blame her ? Whose fault was it ? I asked this question aloud to myself, and a wretch selling matches answered :

" Most your hown, guv'nor : buy a box o' matches to warm yer bones with a smoke—honly a penny ! "

I looked up with a start. I was opposite the Naval and Military. Once I belonged there. The very thought made me mad again, and I cursed aloud in the bitterness of my heart.

" Drunk as a fly," remarked the match-seller to the public at large, indicating me with a handful of match-boxes.

Opposite Apsley House I was alone. All the big crowd on the pavement had died away, only the street seemed full of flashing lights.

Surely some one called Dick ? I stopped, but for a
second only. I must be getting out of my mind, I
thought, as I hurried on again. A few steps brought
me to Hyde Park Corner. A few more brought me close
to the foot of the Achilles, and, without knowing what
I was doing, I sank into a seat. One must rest somewhere, and I was dead beat. The long shadow of the
statue fell over me, clothing me in darkness. It fell
beyond too, on to the walk, and the huge black silhouette stretched even unto the trees. A portion of
my seat was in moonlight, and the muffled rumble of
carriage wheels reached my ears from the road in front.
It might have been fancy ; but I saw a dark figure glide
past the moonlit road into the shadow behind me.
Some poor wretch—some pariah of the streets as lost
as I. I wonder if any of the three-volume novelists
ever felt the sensation of being absolutely stone broke.
Nothing but these words " stone broke " can describe
it. I am not going to try and paint a picture of my
condition. I was stone broke, and Mary—the very air
was full of Marys !

Mechanically I opened the purse I still held in my
hand, and looked at its contents. I don't know why I
did this. I remember once shooting a stag, and when
I came up to it, I found the poor beast in its mortal
agony trying to nibble the heather—it was nibbling the
heather. And here I was, wounded to death, looking
at the contents of a Russian leather purse with idle
curiosity. It was heavy with gold—her gold—Mary's.
Damn her ! she ruined my life. I flung the purse from
me, and it made a black arc in the moonlight, ere it fell
with a little clash beyond. I saw the gold as it rolled

on the gravel walk in red splashes of light. Ruined my
life ? Did Mary do this ? The old, old story—" the
woman gave me and I did eat." Of course Mary ruined
my life. Had I anything to do with the wreck of hers ?
If so, I had committed worse than murder—I had killed
a soul. I put my hot head between my hands and tried
to think it out ; I would think it all out to-night, and
give my verdict for or against myself. If against me,
then I knew how to die at last. It would not be as at
that other time, when my courage failed me. The bitterness of death was already past. I would go over
what had been, balance each little grain, measure forth
each atom, and the end would be—the end.

It needed no effort. The past came up of itself before me. Five years of soldiering in Afghanistan, the
heights of Cherasiab, the march to Candahar, a medal,
a clasp, a mention in dispatches. This was good. Then
came that staff appointment at Simla, and the down-
ward path. Life was so easy, so pleasant. I was always
gregarious, fond of my fellow-creatures, easy-going ;
and as each day passed I slipped down lower and lower.
There were other deeps to come, of which I then knew
not. A lot of conscience was rubbed out of me by that
time. Mrs. Cantilivre must answer for that. There
again : the blame on the woman ! But when a society
belle makes up her mind to form a man, she takes a
lot of the nap off the fine feelings. I tried to pull up
once or twice, but the effort was beyond me. I drifted
back again. Things that were formerly looked upon
by me as luxuries became necessaries ; I developed a
taste for gambling, and got into debt. Pace of this
kind could not last long. There came a day when I

got ill, and then came furlough. A long spell of leave,
with a load of debt on my shoulders ; but my creditors
were, to do them justice, very patient. The voyage
gave me plenty of opportunity to reflect, and the folly
of the past came before me vividly. I would bury the
past, have done with Myra Cantilivre, and start afresh.
England again ! Words cannot describe the feelings
that stirred me when I saw the Eddystone, with the big
waves lashing about it. Arriving on Sunday, I had to
spend the afternoon in Plymouth, and saw Drake looking out over the sea. All the old fire was warming back
in my heart. There was time to mend all yet : when I
got back I meant to win the cherry ribbon and bronze
star—no more flirtation under the deodars for me—I
would soldier again.

A few months later I met Mary, and in a month she
had promised to be my wife. I can see her yet as she
stood before me with downcast head, and the pink flush
on her cheek. She lifted her eyes to mine, and the look
in them was my answer. A few months afterwards we
were married, and almost immediately sailed for India.
I give my word that I meant all that a man should mean
for his wife. ⸱ But one cannot live in the world and look
on things in the same light as an innocent woman. I
had buried all the past, as I thought, forever. Myra
Cantilivre was dead to me, but she had done her work.
It was an effort to me always to live in the pure air of
Mary's thoughts, and one day I said something on board
the steamer that jarred on my wife. It was a come-
down from cloudland, and was the first little rift within
the lute. I pulled myself up, however, and smoothed it
over. Then the scheme which I worked out took its

birth in my mind. If there was to be any happiness in our future life, Mary must either come down to my level or I must go up to hers. I had tried and failed. There was nothing for it but to bring her down. This fine sensitiveness of hers necessitated my having to play the hypocrite forever. Then again I did not like to unveil myself. Every man likes to be a hero to his wife. I suppose she finds him out, however, sooner or later. Perhaps it would be better to let Mary find out gradually. It would in effect be carrying out my programme in the best possible way. Now, I had hitherto concealed from Mary the fact that I was in debt ; but something happened at Simla, soon after we reached there, that necessitated her knowing this. There was another little difference. It was not, Mary said, the matter of the debt, but the fact of my concealing it, that hurt her. She brought up in minute detail little plans of mine, sketched without consideration of the bonds of my creditors, and put them in such a manner that it appeared as if I had told untruths to her regarding myself. The confession has to be made : they were practically untruths ; but a man during his courtship, and the first weeks of his married life, has often to say things which would not bear scrutiny. My wife showed she had a retentive memory, and, for a girl, a very clear and incisive way of putting things. The storm passed over at last, and then Mary set herself to put my disordered affairs to rights. Debts had to be paid, and rigid economy was the order of the day ; but coming back to Simla meant coming back to the old things. I tried to second Mary's efforts to the best of my ability ; but I felt I couldn't last long. I met Mrs. Cantilivre

one evening at Viceregal Lodge. She received me like
an old friend, and begged to be introduced to Mary.
She made only one reference to what had been :

" And so, Dick, the past is all forgotten ? "

" It is good to forget, Mrs. Cantilivre ; and I am
now hedged in with all kinds of fortifications."

I looked towards Mary, where she stood talking to
Redvers of the Sikhs—I always hated Redvers, and
never saw what women admired in him.

Myra laughed at my speech—it was an odd little
laugh, and I did not like it.

" Who makes her dresses ? " she asked. " And now
give me your arm and take me to your wife."

I should not have done it, I know I should not, but
my hand was forced. If I had had the moral courage
I should have got out of it somehow. It was just that
want of moral courage that broke me. This is something like a verdict against myself, but it is worth while
setting forth the whole indictment. I began to tire of
Mary's rigid rules of honesty and strict economy. She
tied me down too much. I should have been allowed a
run now and again. The short of it was that I began
to break out of bounds, and in a few months was leading my old life once again. There was this difference,
however—that formerly I had nothing to fear, whereas
now it was necessary to conceal things. I flattered myself that I was still her idol. I should have known she
had long ago perceived that the idol was of the earth,
earthy. I had occasionally to resort to falsehood, and
was almost as invariably discovered. I had not a sufficiently good memory to be a complete liar. The shame
of it was knowing I was discovered ; but Mary never

threw it up to my face. She set herself to her duty
loyally, though day by day I could see the despair eating its way through her. I had taken to gambling
again, and as usual had bad luck and lost heavily. This
necessitated my having to borrow some more money,
which I arranged to pay back by instalments ; and then
I had to tell my wife that, owing to an alteration in the
scales of pay, my income was so much the less. I upbraided the rules of the service, and on this occasion
Mary believed me. I resolved to gamble no more. About
this time my wife got ill, and when she recovered there
was a small Mary in the house. During her illness
things were so upset that I was compelled to frequent my
club more than ever. To add to the worry to which I was
subjected, the child got ill, and really seemed very ill
indeed. All this involved expenditure which I did
not know how to meet, and in despair one evening I
turned to the cards again. It was the only thing to do.
It was absurd to lose all I had lost, for the want of a
little pluck to pull it back again.

One evening I had just cut into a table when a note
was put into my hands. It was from my wife, asking
me to come home at once, as the child seemed very ill.
It was rather hard luck being dragged home ; and I
could do nothing. So I dropped a note back to Mary to
say she had better send for the doctor, and that I would
come as soon as possible. I meant to go immediately
after one rubber. I won. It would have been a sin
to have turned on my luck, and I played on until the
small hours of the morning, and for once was fortu-
nate. I rode back in high spirits. Near my gate some
one galloped past me ; I thought I recognised Brasing-

ham's (the doctor's) nag, but wasn't quite sure. At any rate, if it was, Mary had taken my advice. I rode in softly and entered the house. A dim light was burning in the sitting-room ; beyond it was the baby's room. I lifted the curtain and entered. As I came in my wife's ayah rose and salaamed, then stole softly out. I cannot tell why, but I felt I was in the presence of death. Mary was kneeling by the little bed, and in it lay our child, very quiet and still. I stepped up to my wife and put my hand on her shoulder. She looked up at me with a silent reproach in her eyes. " Wife," I said, " give me one chance more "; and without a word she came to me and lay sobbing on my heart.

We went away after that for about a month ; and I think that month was a more restful one than any we had spent since the first weeks of our marriage. By the end of it, however, I was weary of the new life. I must have been mad, but I longed to get again to the old excitements. I told Mary that when we came back she should go out as much as possible—that the distraction of society would be good for her. She agreed passively. We went out a great deal after that ; and somehow my wife discovered the falsehood I had told her about the reduction in my income. She did not upbraid me, but she let me understand she knew, with a quiet contempt that stung me to the quick. From this moment she changed. Whilst formerly I had to urge her to mix in society, she now appeared to seek it with an eagerness that a little surprised me. Redvers was always with her. At any rate this made things more comfortable for me in one way, for I could more openly go my own path.

I renewed my acquaintance with Mrs. Cantilivre. She always said the right thing, and she understood men—at any rate she understood me. If Mrs. Cantilivre had been my wife I would have been a success in life. Bit by bit all my old feelings for her awoke again, and then the crash came. It was the night of the Cavalry Ball. I asked Myra Cantilivre for a dance ; but she preferred to sit it out. I cannot tell how it happened, but ten minutes after I was at her feet, telling her I loved her more than my life—talking like a madman and a fool.

She bent down and kissed my forehead. " Poor boy ! " she said ; and as I looked up I saw Mary on Redvers' arm not six feet from us. I rose, and Myra Cantilivre leaned back in her chair and put up the big plumes of her fan to her face. Mary turned away without a word, and walked down the passage with her companion.

I followed, but dared not speak to her. Old Cramley, the Deputy Quartermaster General, buttonholed me. He was a senior officer, and I submitted. Half an hour later, when I escaped, my wife was gone. I reached home at last. Mary was there, in a dark grey walking dress, a small bag in her hand. I met her in the hall, and she stepped aside as if my touch would pollute her.

" Mary," I said, " I can explain all."

" I want no explanation : let me pass, please."

She went out into the night.

In two days all Simla knew of it, and in six months I was a ruined man.

There is no help for it—the verdict is against me ; and yet for five years I have been through the fire, and

I am strong now—there would be no blacksliding if another chance were given to me. Regrets ! There is no use regretting—ten times would I give my life to live over the past again. " Mary, my dear, I have killed you : may God forgive me ! "

Some one stepped out of the shadow into the moonlight as I raised my head with the bitter cry on my lips.

" Dick ! "

" Mary ! "

And we had met once more.

THE MADNESS OF SHERE BAHADUR

THE mahout's small son, engaged with an equally small friend in the pleasant occupation of stringing into garlands the thick yellow and white champac blossoms that strewed the ground under the broad-leaved tree near the lentena hedge, was startled by an angry trumpet, and looked in the direction of Shere Bahadur.

"He is *must*," said one to the other, in an awe-struck whisper, and then, a sudden terror seizing them, they bounded silently and swiftly like little brown apes into a gap in the hedge and vanished.

There were ten thousand evil desires hissing in Shere Bahadur's heart as he swayed to and fro under the huge peepul tree to which he was chained. Indignity upon indignity had been heaped upon him. It was a mere accident that Aladin, the mahout who had attended him for twenty years, was dead. How on earth was Shere Bahadur to know that his skull was so thin? He had merely tapped it with his trunk in a moment of petulance, and the head of Aladin had crackled in like the shell of an egg. Shere Bahadur was reduced to the ranks. For weeks he had to carry the fodder supply of the Maharaj's stables, like an ordinary beast of burden and a low-caste slave ; a fool to boot had been put to attend on him. It was not to be borne. Shere Bahadur clanked his chains angrily, and ever and anon flung wisps of straw, twigs, and dust on his broad back and mottled forehead. He, a Kemeriah of Kemeriahs, to be treated thus ! He was no longer the stately beast that bore the yellow and silver howdah of the Maharaj Adhiraj in solemn procession, who put aside with a gentle sweep of his trunk the children who crowded the narrow streets of Kalesar. No, it was different now. He was a felon and an outcast, bound like a thief. Something had given way in his brain, and Shere Bahadur was mad. The flies hovered on the sore part over his left ear, where the long peak of the driving-iron had burrowed in, and, with a trumpet of rage, the elephant blew a cloud of dust into the air and strained himself backwards.

Click ! click ! The cast-iron links of the big chain that bound him snapped, and Shere Bahadur was free. He cautiously moved his pillar-like legs backwards and forwards to satisfy himself of the fact, and then, with the broad fans of his ears spread out, stood for a moment still as a stone. High up amongst the leaves the green pigeons whistled softly to each other, and a grey squirrel was engaged in hot dispute with a blue jay over treasure-trove, found in a hollow of one of the long branches that, python-like, twined and twisted over-head. Far away, rose tier upon tier of purple hills, and beyond them a white line of snow-capped peaks stood out against the sapphire of the sky. Hathni Khund was there, the deep pool of the Jumna, where thirty years before Shere Bahadur had splashed and swam.

It was there that he fought and defeated the hoary
tusker of the herd, the one-tusked giant who had bullied
and tyrannized over his tribe for time beyond Shere
Bahadur's memory.

Perhaps a thought of that big fight stirred him, perhaps the breeze brought him the sweet scent of the
young grass in the glens. At any rate, with a quick,
impatient flap of his ears, Shere Bahadur turned and
faced the hills. As he did so his twinkling red eyes
caught sight of the Kalesar state troops on their parade
ground, barely a quarter of a mile from where he stood.
The fat little Maharaj was there, standing near the
saluting point. Close to him was the Vizier, with the
court, and, last but not least, a knowing little fox-terrier
dug up the earth with his forepaws, scattering it about
regardless of the august presence.

The Maharaj was proud of his troops. He had raised
them himself in an outburst of loyalty, the day after a
birthday gazette in which His Highness Sri Ranabir
Pertab Sing, Maharaj Adhiraj of Kalesar, had been admitted a companion of an exalted order. The Star of
India glittered on the podgy little prince. He was
dreaming of a glorious day when he, he himself, would
lead the victorious levy through the Khyber, first in the
field against the Russ, when a murmur that swelled to
a cry of fear rose from the ranks, and the troops melted
away before their king. Rifles and accoutrements were
flung aside ; there was a wild stampede, and the gor-
geously attired colonel, putting spurs to his horse, mingled with the dust and was lost to view. The Maharaj stormed in his native tongue, and then burst into
English oaths. He had a very pretty vocabulary, for had

he not been brought up under the tender care of the
Sirkar ? He turned in his fury towards the Vizier,
but was only in time to see the snowy robes of that
high functionary disappearing into a culvert, and the
confused mob of his court running helter-skelter across
the sward. But yet another object caught the prince's
eye, and chilled him with horror. It was the vast bulk
of Shere Bahadur moving rapidly and noiselessly
towards him. Sri Ranabir was a Rajpoot of the bluest
blood, and his heart was big : but this awful sight, this
swift, silent advance of hideous death, paralyzed him
with fear. Already the long shadow of the elephant
had moved near his feet, already he seemed impaled
on those cruel white tusks, when there was a snapping
bark, and the fox-terrier flew at Shere Bahadur and
danced round him in a tempest of rage. The elephant
turned, and made a savage dash at the dog, who skipped
nimbly between his legs and renewed the assault in the
rear. But this moment of reprieve roused His Highness. The prince became a man, and the Maharaj
turned and fled, darting like a star across the soft green.
Shere Bahadur saw the flash of the jewelled aigrette,
the sheen of the order, and, giving up the dog, curled
his trunk and started in pursuit. It was a desperate
race. The Maharaj was out of training, but the time
he made was wonderful, and the diamond buckles on
his shoes formed a streak of light as he fled. But, fast
as he ran, the race would have ended in a few seconds
if it were not for Bully, the little white fox-terrier.
Bully thoroughly grasped the situation, and acted accordingly. He ran round the elephant, now skipping
between his legs, the next moment snapping at him be-

hind—and Bully had a remarkably fine set of teeth.
The Maharaj sighted a small hut, the door of which
stood invitingly open. It was a poor hut made of
grass and sticks, but it seemed a royal palace to him.
" Holy Gunputty ! " he gasped. " If I could——"
But it was no time to waste words. Already the snake-
like trunk of his enemy was stretched out to fold round
him, when with a desperate spurt he reached the door,
and dashed in. But Shere Bahadur was not to be
denied. He stood for a moment, and then, putting forward his forefoot, staved in the side of the frail shelter
and brought down the house. Sri Ranabir hopped out
like a rat, and it was well for him that in the cloud of
dust and thatch flying about he was unobserved, for
Shere Bahadur, now careless of Bully's assaults and certain of his man, was diligently searching the *débris*.
But he found nothing save a brass vessel, which he
savagely flung at the dog. Then he carefully stamped
on the hut, and reduced everything to chaos. In the
meantime Sri Ranabir, unconscious that the pursuit had
ceased, ran on as if he was wound up like a clock, ran
until his foot slipped, and the Maharaj Adhiraj rolled
into the soft bed of a nullah, and lay there with his eyes
closed, utterly beaten, and careless whether the death
he had striven so hard to avoid came or not. Then
there was a buzzing in his ears and everything became a
blank.

*　　*　　*　　*　　*

" Blessed be the prophet ! He liveth." And the
Vizier helped his fallen master to rise, aided by the
Heir Apparent, in whose heart, however, there were

thoughts far different from those which found expression on the lips of the Nawab Juggun Jung, prime minister of Kalesar. The sympathetic, if somewhat excited, court crowded round their king, and a little in the distance was the whole population of Kalesar, armed with every conceivable weapon, and keeping up their courage by beating on tom-toms, blowing horns, and shouting until the confusion of sound was indescribable.

" Come back to the palace, my lord.   They will drive the evil one out of him." And the Vizier waved his hand in the direction of the crowd, and pointed to where in the distance Shere Bahadur was making slowly and steadily for the hills.   But the Maharaj Adhiraj would do no such thing.   " Ryful lao ! " he roared in his vernacular ; " Gimme my gun ! " he shrieked in English. There was no refusing ; a double-barrelled gun was thrust in his hands, he scrambled on the back of the first horse he saw, and, followed by his cheering subjects and the whole court, dashed after the elephant.

" Mirror of the Universe, destroy him not," advised the Vizier who rode at the prince's bridle-hand.   " The beast is worth eight thousand rupees, and cannot be replaced.   The treasury is almost empty, and we will want him when the Lat Saheb comes."   The Maharaj was prudent if he was brave, and the empty treasury was a strong argument.   Besides, they were getting rather close to Shere Bahadur and outpacing the faithful people.   But he gave in slowly.   " What is to be done ? " he asked, taking a pull at the reins.

" The people will drive him back," replied the Vizier, " and we will chain him up securely.   He is but *must*, and in a month or so all will pass away."

Shere Bahadur had now reached an open plain, where he stopped, and turning round, faced his pursuers.

" Go on, brave men ! " shouted the Vizier. " A thousand rupees to him who links the first chain on that Shaitan, Drive him back ! Drive him back ! "

There is the courage of numbers, and this the people of India possess. They gradually formed a semi-circle round Shere Bahadur, cutting off his retreat to the hills, and attempted by shouts and the beating of tom-toms to drive him forwards. But they kept at a safe distance, and the elephant remained unmoved.

" Prick him forwards," roared the Vizier. " Are none of ye men ? Behold ! the Light of the Universe watches your deeds ! A *must* elephant—*pah !* What is it but an animal ? "

" By your lordship's favour," answered a voice, " he is not *must*, only angry—there is no stream from his eye. Nevertheless, I will drive him to the lines, for I am but dust of the earth, and a thousand rupees will make me a king." Then a red-turbaned man stepped out of the throng. It was the low-caste cooly who had been put to attend to the elephant on Aladin's death. He was armed with a short spear, and he crept up to the beast on his hands and knees, and then, rising, dug the weapon into the elephant's haunch. Shere Bahadur rapped his trunk on the ground, gave a short quick trumpet, and, swinging round, made for the man. He did this in a slow, deliberate manner, and actually allowed him to gain the crowd. Then he flung up his head with a screech and dashed forward.

Crack ! crack ! went both barrels of Sri Ranabir's

gun, and two bullets whistled harmlessly through the air. The panic-striken mob turned and fled, bearing the struggling prince in the press. The elephant was, however, too quick, and, to his horror, Sri Ranabir saw that he had charged home. Then Sri Ranabir also saw something that he never forgot. Not a soul did the elephant harm, but with a dogged persistence followed the red turban. Some bolder than the rest struck at him with their tulwars, some tried to stab him with their spears, and one or two matchlocks were fired at him, but to no purpose. Through the crowd he steered straight for his prey, and the crowd itself gave back before him in a sea of frightened faces. At last the man himself seemed to realize Shere Bahadur's object, and it dawned like an inspiration on the rest. They made a road for the elephant, and he separated his quarry from the crowd. At last ! He ran him down on a ploughed field and stood over the wretch. The man lay partly on his side, looking up at his enemy, and he put up his hand weakly and rested it against the foreleg of the elephant, who stood motionless above him. So still was he that a wild thought of escape must have gone through the wretch's mind, and with the resource born of imminent peril he gathered himself together inch by inch, and made a rush for freedom. With an easy sweep of his trunk Shere Bahadur brought him back into his former position, and then—the devil came out, and a groan went up from the crowd, for Shere Bahadur had dropped on his knees, and a moment after rose and kicked something, a mangled, shapeless something, backwards and forwards between his feet.

" Let him be," said the Vizier, laying a restraining

hand on Sri Ranabir. "What has he killed but
refuse? The Shaitan will go out of him now."

When he had done the deed Shere Bahadur moved a
few yards further and began to cast clods of earth over
himself. Then it was seen that a small figure, with a
driving-hook in its little brown hand, was making
directly for the elephant.

"Come back, you little fool!" shouted Sri Ranabir.
But the boy made no answer, and running lightly forward, stood before Shere Bahadur. He placed the
tinsel-covered cap he wore at the beast's feet, and held
up his hands in supplication. The crowd stood breath-
less; they could hear nothing, but the child was evidently speaking. They saw Shere Bahadur glare
viciously at the boy as his trunk drooped forward in a
straight line. The lad again spoke, and the elephant
snorted doubtfully. Then there was no mistaking the
shrill treble "Lift!" Shere Bahadur held out his
trunk in an unwilling manner. The boy seized hold
of it as high as he could reach, placed his bare feet on
the curl, and murmured something. A moment after
he was seated on the elephant's neck, and lifting the
driving-iron, waved it in the air.

"Hai!" he screamed as he drove it on to the right
spot, the sore part over the left ear. "Hai! Base-
born thief, back to your lines!"

And the huge bulk of Shere Bahadur turned slowly
round and shambled off to the peepul tree like a lamb.

"By the trunk of Gunputty! I will make that lad a
havildar, and the thousand rupees shall be his," swore
the Maharaj.

"Pillar of the earth!" advised the Vizier, "let this

unworthy one speak. It is Futteh Din, the dead
Aladin's son. Give him five rupees, and *let him be
mahout.*"

*   *   *   *   *

When I last saw Shere Bahadur he was passing
solemnly under the old archway of the "Gate of the
Hundred Winds" at Kalesar. The Maharaj Adhiraj
was seated in the howdah, with his excellency the
Nawab Juggun Jung by his side. On the driving-seat
was Futteh Din, gorgeous in cloth of gold, and they
were on their way to the funeral-pyre of the Heir Apparent, who had died suddenly from a surfeit of cream.

As they passed under the archway a sweetmeat-seller
rose and bowed to the prince, and Shere Bahadur,
stretching out his trunk, helped himself to a pound or
so of Turkish Delight.

"Such," said the sweetmeat-seller to himself ruefully,
as he gazed after the retreating procession, "such are
the ways of kings."

REGINE'S APE

Ir is a May morning in the north of India—such a
morning as comes when the hot wind has been blowing
for three weeks, and has shrivelled everything before
it, like tea-leaves under the fan of a drying engine.
The Grand Trunk Road, a long line of grey dotted in
with dust-covered *kikur* trees, stretches for three hundred miles to the frontier, and to the right and left of
it, beginning at the village of the Well of Lehna
Singh, which lies but a quoit-cast from the roadside, spreads a plain, dry, arid, and parched—
agape with thirst—the seams running along its brown
surface like open lips panting for rain, the cool
rain which will not come yet, although, at times,
the distant rumble of thunder is heard, and dark
clouds pile up in the horizon, only to melt away
into nothing. The tall *sirpat* grass has been cut, and
its pruned stalks, stiff as the bristles on a hair-brush,
extend in regular patches of yellow, spiky scrub, with
bands of mottled brown and grey earth between them.
Here and again it would seem there are scattered pools,
for the eyes, running over the landscape, shrink back
from a sudden flash, as of water reflecting the fierce
light of the sun. It is not so, however, for, except what

the groaning Persian wheels drag up from the deep wells, there is never a drop of water for man, for beast, or for field. Those gleaming stretches from which the pained eyes turn are nothing more than the bare earth, covered with a saline efflorescence, soft and silver white, as if it were dry and powdered foam. It is yet early, and the light is not so dazzling as to prevent the eye resting on the patchwork of the plain, studded here and there with clumps of trees, that mark a well and the hamlet that has grown up around it. To found a village here it is only necessary to dig a well, and behold! mud huts spring up like fungi, and a hamlet has come into being. Right across the plain is a dark line of *kikur* and *seesum* trees. That is where the dry bed of the Deg torrents lies. Only let it rain, and the Deg will come down, an angry yellow flood, alive with catfish, and bubble its way to the wide but not less yellow bosom of the Ravi. Beyond the dry bed of the torrent, and towards the east, are a number of sand dunes covered with the soda plant, and looking like ant-hills in the distance. In the east itself the sun looms through a red haze, and against this ruddy, semi-opaque mist, a dust-devil rises in a spiral column, and opening out at the top, like an expanding smoke wreath, spreads sullenly against the sky line. On a morning such as this, two men are beating for a boar in a large patch of *sirpat* grass. One man is at each end of the grass field, and between them are twenty or thirty *Sansis*, a criminal tribe, who make excellent beaters whatever their other faults may be. With the man to the right of the field we have little concern. It is with the man to the left that this story deals. As he sits his fretting Arab, and

the sunlight falls on his features, it would need but a
glance to tell he was a soldier. The careful ob-
server might, however, discover in that glance that
there was something wrong about the good-looking face.
The eyes were too close together, the bow of the mouth
both weak and cruel, although the chin below it was
firm enough. If the grey helmet he wore were removed,
it would have been seen that the head was small and
somewhat conical in shape, the head of a Carib rather
than that of an European. As he slowly advanced his
horse along the edge of the field, keeping in line with
the beaters, it was evident that he was in a high state
of excitement, and the shaft of his spear was shivering
in his hand.

Whirr ! whirr ! A couple of black partridge rise
from the grass and sail away till they look like cock-
chafers in the distance. Then there is a scramble, a
hare dashes out, and scurries madly across the plain, his
long ears laid flat on his back, and his big eyes almost
starting out of his head with fright. The beaters yell
at this, and the Arab plunges forward ; but the rider,
who is growing pale with excitement, holds him in, and
he dances along sideways in a white sweat—both horse
and man all nerves. Two mangy jackals slink out of
the grass, give a sly look around, and then lope along
in the direction taken by the hare. It will be bad for
puss if they come across him. As yet not a sign of the
boar, and the Arab is almost pulling Sangster's arms off.
He looks across at his friend, and sees him well to the
right, on his solemn-looking black, and he catches sight
of a pale blue curl of smoke from Wilkinson's pipe.

"By George !" he muttered, "only think of

smoking now ! Steady——" He might as well have
tried to stop an engine. There is a chorus of yells,
shrieks, and howls from the beaters, a sudden waving of
crackling grass, the plunge of a heavy body, and in a
hand-turn an old boar breaks cover, and, with one savage
look about him, heads at a tremendous pace for the Deg.
The Arab has seen it, and lets himself out like a buck,
and then all is forgotten except the fierce excitement
of the chase. Sangster can hear the drumming of the
black's hoofs behind him, and fast as he goes Wilkinson
draws alongside, his teeth still clenched over the stem
of his pipe. The boar is well to the front, a brown spot
bobbing up and down, racing for his life, as he means to
fight for it when the time comes. He is not afraid,
his little red eyes are aflame with wrath, and as he goes
he grinds his tusks till the yellow foam flies off them on
to his brindled sides. He is not in the least afraid,
and he fully intends, at the proper time, to adjust matters
with one or both his pursuers. It is his way to run
first and fight afterwards—that is, providing the enemy
can run him to a standstill. If not—well, the fight
must be deferred to another day, and in the meantime
it is capital going, except over that ravine-scarred
portion of the plain called the " Gridiron," where, at
any rate, the advantage will lie with him.

Side by side the two men race. Wilkinson knows
perfectly well that when the time comes he can draw
away from the Arab, which, with all its speed and pluck,
is no match for a fifteen-hand Waler. He is calculating
on gaining " first spear " with a sudden rush ; but has
missed out of this calculation the consequences of an
accident. In the middle of the " Gridiron," the Waler

makes a false step between two grass-crowned hum-
mocks, and Sangster is left alone with the boar, whilst
Wilkinson, with a sore heart, crawls out of a water-cut,
and, after many an ineffectual effort, succeeds in catch-
ing his horse and following the chase, now almost out
of sight.

In the meantime the boar has all but reached the
Deg, and safety lies there. Could he only gain one of
the hundred ravines that cobweb the plain, a quarter
mile or so from the dry bed of the torrent, he would
yet live to run, and maybe fight, on another day. He
strains every nerve to effect this object, and Sangster,
seeing this, calls on his horse, and the Arab, answering
gallantly, brings him almost up to the boar with a rush.
Sangster can see the foam on the boar's jowl, flecked
with bright spots of red ; blood-marks from the hunted
animal's lips, wounded by the sharp tushes as he ground
them together in his wrath ; already has he reached out
his arm to deliver the spear, when, quick as lightning,
the boar jinks to the right, and, dashing down a deep
and narrow ravine, is lost to view. Sangster saw the
bristles on his back as the beast vanished, and the speed
of his horse bore him almost to the edge of the steep
bank of the Deg before he could stop and turn him.
When Sangster came back to the point where he had
lost the boar he realized that it was useless to make any
attempt to find the animal. In a hasty look round he
had given when Wilkinson came to grief he had seen
that the accident to his friend was not serious, and he
now resolved to cross the Deg by an old bridge known
as " Shah Doula's Pool," and make his way back to the
beaters along the " soft " that bordered the metalling of

the Grand Trunk Road.   It would be shady there, and
he was parched with thirst, and very much out of
temper.   Failure in anything made this nervous man
extraordinarily irritable, and he was in a mood to pick
a quarrel on the slightest provocation.

Sangster reached the bridge in this frame of mind,
and as he crossed it came upon a curious scene.   Under
the shade of a *peepul*, whose heart-shaped leaves shel-
tered him from the sun, sat a devotee staring fixedly into space with his lustreless eyes.   Beyond a cloth around
his waist he had no clothing, his body was smeared
with ashes, and on his ash-covered forehead was drawn
a trident in red ochre.   His hair, which was of great
length, and had been bleached by exposure from black to
a russet brown, fell over his thin shoulders in a long
matted mane.   Sitting there, he was, up to this point,
like any one of the hundred wandering mendicants a
man might meet in a week's march in India ; but here
the resemblance ceased, for this man was of those who,
in the fulfilment of a vow, was prepared to inflict upon
himself and to endure any torture.   He sat cross-legged,
and what at first Sangster thought was the dry and
blasted bough of a stunted *kikur* tree behind the man
he saw, at a second glance, was nothing less than the
devotee's arm, which he had held out at a right angle
to his body, until it had stiffened immovably in that
position, and had shrunk until it seemed that the
cracked skin alone covered the bone.   How long the
arm had been held to reach this condition no one can
say.   But it was long enough for the nails to have
grown through the palm of the clenched hand, over
which they curled and drooped like tendrils.   The

ascetic's gourd lay before him, into which some pious
passer-by had dropped a handful of parched rice, and
behind him gambolled a grey monkey, an entellus or
lungoor, who gibbered and mowed at Sangster as he rode
up, but made no attempt to retreat—evidently he was
tame, and used to people.

Although Sangster had nearly seven years of service,
he knew nothing about the East ; his knowledge of
its peoples and their characters expressed itself in two
words, brief and strong. He knew nothing and cared
less for the complex laws, the mystic philosophy, the
immemorial civilization of the great empire which he,
in his small way, was helping to hold for England.
He fortunately represented only a small class of the
servants of the Queen, that class who hold the native
to be a brute, a little, if at all, better than the grey ape
who leered over the devotee's shoulder at the Arab and
his rider. Sangster, however, knew something of the
language, and some devil prompted him to rein in, and
imperiously ask the sitting figure if the boar had gone
that way. He might as well have asked the ape, for
that figure, seated there in the dust, with its rigid arm
stretched out, and dull look staring into vacancy, would
have been oblivious if a hundred boars had passed
before it, and was so lost in abstraction that it
was even unconscious of the presence of the fiery
champing horse and equally impatient man, who
were right in front of its unwinking eyes.   Of
course there was no answer, and Sangster angrily
repeated the question, lowering the point of his spear
as he did so, and slightly pricking the man below
him.   What came into the little brain of the ape

it is hard to say ; but it was an instinct that told him his master was in danger, and with a dog-like fidelity he resolved to defend him. Springing forward the beast grasped the shaft of the lance, and, with chattering teeth, pushed it violently on one side. All the little temper Sangster had left went to shreds ; with an oath he drew back his arm, the spear-head flashed, and the next moment passed clean through the shrieking animal, and was out again, no longer bright but dripping red. With a pitiful moan the poor brute almost flung itself into the devotee's lap, and died there, its arms clasped around the lean waist of its master. All this happened so suddenly, so quickly, that Sangster had barely time to think of what he had done ; but, as he raised his red spear, a horror came on him, so human was the cry of the dying ape, so like a child did it lie in its death-agony. He would have turned away and ridden off, but a power he could not control kept him there, and for a space there was a silence, broken only by the drip from the spear-head, and the soft whistle of a *huryal* or green pigeon from the shade of the leaves overhead.

The ascetic gently put aside the dead ape, and rose, a grey phantom, to his feet. So large was his head, so small his body, and so long the withered bird-like legs that supported him, that he appeared to be some uncanny creature of another world. He was overcome with a terrible excitement, his breast heaved, his lips moved with a hissing sound, and he unconsciously tried to shake his rigid right arm at the destroyer. Then his voice came, shrill and fierce, with a note of unending pain in it, and he dropped out slowly, and with a deadly hate in each word : " *Cursed be the hand that wrought this deed !*

Cursed be thou above thy fellows ! May Durga dog thee through life, and let thy life itself end in blood ! Now go !"

Without a word Sangster turned to the left, and galloped along the banks of the Deg. At any other time he could have found it in his heart to laugh at the curse of the mad ascetic, for so he thought the man to be ; but the limp body of the dead ape was before him, and its pitiful cry was ringing in his ears. As he rode on he caught a glimpse of his dull spear-point. It was only the blood of an animal after all ; but he flung the lance away with a jerk of his arm, and it fell softly into the broad-leaved *dakh* shrubs and lay there, long and yellow in the sunlight. He pressed on madly ; the white line of the Grand Trunk Road was now close, and he could make out a gigantic figure on a gigantic horse. It was Wilkinson ; but how huge he looked ! Sangster's head seemed bursting, and there was a drumming in his ears. Somehow he managed to keep his seat, and at last heard Wilkinson's cool voice.

" Got the pig, old man ? Good God !——" For Sangster, with a flushed red face, slid from his saddle, and lay senseless in the white burning dust.

In a moment Wilkinson had sprung to earth and was bending over his friend.

" Sunstroke, by Jove ! Must get him back at once."

*　　*　　*　　*　　*

One does not recover from sunstroke in a little, and in most cases it leaves a permanent mark behind it. Sangster was no exception to the rule. For weeks he lay between life and death. There were times when he tottered on the brink of that dark precipice, down which we must all go sooner or later ; but he rallied at last. Finally he was well enough to travel, and the sick man came home. He had never mentioned to a soul what he had done at Shah Doula's Pool. If he had spoken of it during his illness, it was doubtless set down to the ravings of delirium. When at length he recovered his senses, he could only recall what had happened to him in a vague manner. But he was no longer his own cheery, somewhat noisy self. He was listless, moody, and apathetic. Over his mind there seemed to brood a shadow that would take to itself neither form nor substance, and against which he could not battle. The doctors said the long sea-voyage home would set him right in this respect. They were wrong, and day after day the man lay stretched on his cane deck-chair, or paced up and down in sullen silence, exchanging no word with his fellow-passengers. At last they reached Plymouth, and although it was seven years since he had left England, he never even glanced out of the windows as the train bore him to his Berkshire home. He arrived at last and was made much over. Kind hands tended him, and loving hearts were there to anticipate his slightest whim. It was impossible to resist this, and in a little time the clouds seemed to roll away from his mind, and he was once more gay and bright. One warm sunny day, as he was lying in a hammock under the shade of a sycamore, hardly conscious that he was awake, and yet knowing he was not asleep, his mind seemed to slip back of its own accord into the past. In an instant the soft

turf, the mellow green trees, the restful English landscape faded away. A wind that was as hot as a furnace
blast beat upon him. All around was a dreary waste,
and above, the sky was a cloudless, burning blue. He
was once again holding in his fiery Arab, and listening
to the curse hissing out from the lips of the devotee.
He almost heard the blood dropping from his spear on
to the grey dust below his horse's hoofs, and from the
heart-shaped *peepul* leaves—it was no longer a sycamore he was beneath—the whistle of the green pigeon
came to him soft and low. A strange terror seized him.
He sprang out of the hammock. He had not been
asleep. It was broad daylight, and yet he could have
sworn that for the moment time had rolled backwards,
and that he was eight thousand miles away from the
square, red brick parsonage, in the firwoods of Berkshire. And then he began to understand.

He went into the house his old brooding self, and in
a week, finding life there insupportable, ran up to town.
Here he took chambers close to his club, and plunged
into dissipation. He was not naturally a man given
that way, and he did not take to it kindly. But he
held his course and broke the remains of his health,
and wasted his substance in a vain effort to shake off
the weight from his soul. But it was useless, and now
a weariness of life fell upon him, and something seemed
to be ever whispered in his ear to end all. The temptation came upon him one evening with an almost
irresistible force. He was to dine out that evening,
and had just finished dressing when his eye fell on a
small plated Derringer that lay on the table before him.
He took it up and held it in his hand. But a little

touch on the trigger, and there would be an end of all things. It was so easy. Only a little touch! He placed the round muzzle to his temple, and stood thus for a second. He could hear the ticking of his watch, he could feel the pulse in his temple throbbing against the cold steel of the pistol, he could feel his very heart beating. His whole past rose up before him. He closed his eyes, set his teeth, his finger was on the trigger, when he heard a low laugh, a mocking laugh of triumph, that, soft as it was, seemed to vibrate through the room. Sangster's hand dropped to his side, and he looked round with a scared face. At the time this occurred he was standing at his dressing-table, and the only light was that from two candles, one on each side of the glass. The bedroom was separated from the sitting-room by a folding door, overhung by a heavy crimson curtain, and this part of the room was in semi-darkness. As Sangster turned his white face to the curtain he saw nothing, although the laugh was still ringing in his ears ; but, as he looked, a pale blue mist rose before the curtain ; a mist that seemed instinct with light, and in it floated the body of the devotee, the rigid arm extended towards him and a smile of infernal malice on the withered lips. For a moment Sangster stood as if spell-bound—a cold sweat on his forehead. Then, for he was no coward, he nerved himself, and advanced towards the vision. As he stepped up, mist and figure faded into nothing, and he was alone. But he could bear to be so no longer, and thrusting the pistol into the breast pocket of his coat, hurried outside. Once in the street, he hailed a hansom and was driven to his destination.

During his stay in town he had sought every class of society, and chance had thrown him in the way of Madame Régine. Who she was is not material to this story, but she was the one person he had met who could for the moment make Sangster forget his gloom.

In her way, too, Régine was attracted by this man, so grave and silent, yet who was able to speak of things and scenes she had never heard of, and who looked so different from the other men she came across in her literary and artistic circle.

Of late, with a perversity which cannot be accounted for, he had avoided seeing her, and she was more than glad he was coming that night; and as for him, he almost had it in his heart to thank God he was to see Régine that evening.

Madame knew how to select her guests. There were but half a dozen people, and it was very gay. At first Sangster could not shake off his depression, but as the wine went round and the wit sparkled he pulled himself together, and in a half-hour had forgotten what had happened before he came to the house. They were late that evening ; but the time came to go at last. Sangster, however, lingered—the latest of all to say good-bye.

As he went up to her she put aside his hand with a smile.

" I have not seen you for ages. You might stay for another ten minutes and talk to me."

" I shall be delighted."

" That is nice of you—and I will show you a present I have had from India. You can smoke if you like."

"I suppose it is little things like this that you do that make you so charming a hostess."

"Thank you," she laughed, a pink flush in her cheeks, "and now wait a moment and I will give you a surprise."

And Sangster heard the same sneering laugh that he had heard in his rooms. It came from nowhere ; but it chilled him to ice, and the answer in his lips died to nothing. He alone heard it, loud as it was, for Madame looked for a moment at him as she spoke and then there was a swish of trailing garments, and she was gone. A little time passed, and Sangster thought he would smoke. In an absent manner he put his hand in his breast pocket and pulled out—not his cigarette case, but the pistol. He smiled grimly to himself as he held it in his hand.

"Might as well do it here as anywhere else," he muttered.

On the instant he felt two soft furry arms round his neck, and something sprang lightly to his shoulders. He gave a quick cry and looked up to meet the grinning face of an entellus monkey leering into his eyes.

"My God !" he gasped, and the sharp report of the Derringer cut into Régine's peal of laughter, and changed its note to a scream of horror. When the police came she was bending over the body of the madman, laughing in shrill hysterics, and the ape gibbered at them from his seat on the high back of a chair.

A SHADOW OF THE PAST

THE sunbirds, hovering and twittering over the *neem* trees, signalled to me the approach of the coming hot weather. The sky was a steel grey, and over the horizon of the wide plain before my bungalow, on which the short grass was already dry and crisp, hung a curtain of pale brown dust. Here and there on the expanse of faded green were small herds of lean kine, and, almost on the edge of the road bordering the plain, a line of water-buffaloes sluggishly headed for a shallow pool about a mile or so westward, where they would wallow till the sun went down, and then be driven home with unwilling steps to their byres. The herd bull came last of all, and on his back sat a little naked boy, a pellet bow in his hand, and a cotton bag full of mud pellets slung over his shoulder. He was singing in a high-pitched tuneless voice, and his song seemed to enrage the " brain-fever " bird in the mango tree, where he had hidden silent since the dawn. The bird objected in a shrill crescendo of ringing notes that brought the pellet bow into play, and then there was a whistle of grey-brown wings as he flew to a safer spot, and a silence broken only by the monotonous *tink, tink, tink* of the little green barbet or coppersmith. There were times, when fever held me in its grip, that the maddening iteration of its cry was almost unbearable, and to this day I nurse a hatred to that little green-coated and red-throated plague—of a truth " the coppersmith hath done me much evil." I stood in my veranda watching the retreating figure of the Judge, as he drove away full of a project of spending a month in Burma—an enterprise he had been vainly tempting me to share ; but I had other fish to fry : my way was westwards, not eastwards, and besides I had slaved for six long years in Burma, and knew it far too well. One glance at the Judge as he turned the elbow of the road, and was lost to view behind the siris trees, one look at the thirsty plain, and the shivering heat haze, through which glinted, now and again, the distant spear-heads of a squadron of Bengal Lancers trotting slowly back to their barracks, and I turned in to my study. I had determined to devote the day to the destruction of old papers, and set about my task in earnest. There was one drawer in particular that had not been touched for three years. I had forgotten what it contained, and opened it slowly, thinking it was possibly an Augean Stable ; but nothing met my eyes except a small packet of papers. Yet with that one look came back to me the memory of a life's tragedy. The papers should have been destroyed long ago, and now—I hesitated no longer, but tore them up into the smallest fragments, glad to be rid, as I thought, of the miserable record of a man's folly, of his crime, and of his shame.

But an awakened memory is not easily set at rest, and, in the stillness of that Indian day, the whole thing returned with an insistent force, dead voices spoke to me once more, and bitter regrets hummed of the past, the past that can never be retrodden—and then there arose out of the shadows in vivid distinctness the memory of that supreme moment when John Mazarion cast his soul to hell. It all came back like a picture : that lonely Himalayan mountain side, the black pines, the silent eternal snows, Mazarion with his pale white face, and Rani with her laughing eyes. An eagle screamed above us, I remember, and with a hissing of wings dropped over the abyss into the blue mists that clung to the mountain side.

John Mazarion and I had been friends at school, and we met again as young men with a common interest in our lives, for we had both adopted an Indian career. Mazarion had gone into the Indian Marine, and I— I wanted in those days to build empires as did Clive and Hastings, and so I sought honour in another service, and got sent to Burma for my pains and—the empires have yet to be built. There was yet another interest between John and myself, and that was Nelly. Being young men we did as young men do, and both fell in love ; but unfortunately we both fell in love with the same woman, and Nelly took Mazarion. It was a bitter thing for me then ; but now that I have come to an age when I can argue with myself, I can see it was but natural. John was a big handsome man with fair hair and limpid blue eyes, and Nelly—well, a man does not care to write about the woman he loves ; she was Nelly and that is enough. Though I never spoke of it, I fancy Nelly must have known I loved her, for in that tender womanly way which good women alone

have she gave me strength to endure, and for her sake
I wished Mazarion good luck, and sailed for the East.
John followed in a few weeks, and I understood
they were to be married in three years, when Mazarion
got his step—a long engagement ; but the purse of an
Indian officer is mostly a lean one, and Nelly's people
were not rich. Well, as I said before, I began my
Eastern career in Burma, and Mazarion's duties led him
to the Bay of Bengal and to the Burman waters. We
never met for close on four years ; but occasionally I
came to Rangoon, the capital of Burma, and there I
heard much of him, and always in connection with some
story of stupid folly. The best of men would shrink
from daylight being thrown on all their actions ; but
what would have been wrong in any man's case became
doubly so, and doubly dishonourable, in the case of John
Mazarion—at least I thought and think so, for Nelly's
face used to rise before me with a look of patient
waiting in the sweet eyes.

At last we met in the club at Rangoon and lunched
together.   He incidentally let out that he had got
his step in promotion nearly a year ago, and went
on to answer the unspoken question in my look.

" Nelly will have to wait a year or so more, I'm afraid
—I'm deuced hard up. But I suppose you're in the same
street.   Come and have a smoke."

I was not in the same street ; but I went and had a
smoke. We talked of many things, and when I left
I knew that John had slipped down, but how far down
I was yet to know. Before I left the club I accepted
an invitation to supper with him in his rooms ; he had
received a port appointment, and was for the present

stationed in Rangoon. I went to that supper. There were two or three others there, and a lady—God save the mark !—who did the honours of the house. I could have struck Mazarion where he sat brazening the whole thing out ; but I held myself in somehow and saw it through. I was the first to go, and Mazarion followed me to the door—shame was not quite dead in him. " Look here, old man," he said, you're off home, I know, and will see Nelly. You needn't—and—you know what I mean—" holding out his hand.

I drew back. " Yes, I know what you mean, and I will keep silent. But I would to God I hadn't accepted your cursed hospitality ! "

And I turned and walked down the stairway, leaving him on the landing, white with rage. In a month from that day I was in England, and a week later I had seen Nelly. I well remember it was with a beating heart that I came to the door of the suburban villa with the May tree in bloom near the gate, and in a minute or so was in the little drawing-room I knew so well. In the place of honour was a large photograph of Mazarion in his naval uniform, and near it was a vase with a votive offering of fresh flowers. I felt who had placed them there, and swore bitterly under my breath. Then the door opened and Nelly came in with outstretched hands.

" I'm so glad to see you, Mr. Thring, after all these years."

" And it seems to me as if I had never been away. I shook off the East with the first grey sky I saw."

Then we sat and talked, but I carefully avoided the subject of Mazarion, and now and again parried a leading question because I did not know what to say, and felt miserable when I saw the eager light in Nelly's eyes fade into a look of disappointment. Finally Mrs. Carstairs, Nelly's mother, came in, and it was a relief, for I had to go over my experiences again. But I struck on the rocks at last when Mrs. Carstairs said : " Well, I suppose you are lucky in getting back in four years—though that does seem such a long time."

" Yes, I suppose I am, Mrs. Carstairs. There are men who have been away ten years and more, and whose prospects of seeing home again are still far."

I thought I heard the faintest echo of a sigh, and grew hot all over. My hand shook so that I could hear the teacup I held rattle on the saucer. I was a tactless fool.

" How hard ! " said Mrs. Carstairs, " and there is poor John still out there, waiting for his step. I wonder when he will get it and be able to come home."

I looked at Nelly. Her eyes were ablaze and her cheeks flushed, and the words " waiting for his step " rang in my ears. Mazarion had got his step a year ago —he had told me so himself. I could say nothing.

" I suppose you have seen John," Mrs. Carstairs went on. " You and he used to be such friends. When did you last meet ? "

" About six weeks ago, in Rangoon ; he was looking very well."

" I am so glad. We—that is, Nelly has not heard for nearly two months, and when he last wrote he said he was very busy, and likely to go on a long cruise."

Now I knew Mazarion had held that port appointment for nearly six months, and would hold it for a year or so to come without any likelihood of going on a cruise, and I of course knew that he was lying—lying to the dear heart that loved him so well. To this day I know not whether I did right or wrong in holding my tongue, in saying nothing, and when I left them I left them still in that fool's paradise of trust and love and hope. I saw them once again before I left. I could not go back without one more look at Nelly. As I said good-bye she timidly slipped a small packet into my hands, and I promised it would reach John Mazarion in safety.

On the voyage back I thought of many things, and reproached myself for having parted with Mazarion as I had. For her sake I should have made some effort to pull him right, and as it were I had simply kicked him down a step lower, for I had made him feel his infamy, and that is not the way to help a man to recover his own self-respect. I had been hasty—for the moment my temper had got the better of me—with the usual result. And so I determined not to send him Nelly's gift, but, on reaching Rangoon, to deliver the packet with my own hands.

I found him in his office on the river face, and, as I expected, there was a coldness and constraint in his manner. Our eyes met—his still with anger in them—and then he dropped his look.

"I have brought this," I said, "from Miss Carstairs. I promised it should reach you safely."

He took the packet from me in silence, but I saw his hands shake and the crow's-feet gather about his eyes. He fumbled with the seals, then let the packet drop on the table, and looked at me again as I blurted out: "I have said nothing—not a word."

"I do not understand, sir."

"John Mazarion," I cut in, "you are still to her what you have ever been. Man! you know not what you are throwing away. See here, John! You are my oldest friend, and I can't let you go like this. Pull up and turn round; give yourself a chance. If—if money is wanted—well, I've saved a bit——"

He simply leaned back in his chair and laughed. And such a laugh! There was not a ring of mirth in it—a tuneless, mocking laugh such as might come from the throat of a devil. Then he stopped and looked at me, the hard lines still in the corners of his mouth and round his eyes.

"Thring, you're a meddlesome fool! Take my advice and let each man stir his own porridge. I want no interference and none of your damned advice. I mean to live my own life."

"It isn't of you alone I am thinking."

He fairly shook with rage. "Go!" he burst out. "Go! I hate the sight of you, with your lips full of talk about duty and self-respect and honour. Go!"

I left the man, but for all his violence I felt that his anger was really against himself, and that my words had gone home.

A year, two years passed. Three times in this interval I had heard from Nelly, and on each occasion the letter was not so much for me as to obtain news of Mazarion. She was still watching and waiting—wasting the treasures of her heart as many another woman has done on men as worthless as Mazarion. And I—I was powerless to help her for whom I would have given my life. Twice I had answered to say that I had

no news to give ; but on the third occasion it was on
the heels of her letter that news reached me. It came
from the commander of a river steamer who dined with
me in my lonely district house on the banks of the
Irawadi.

"The man has practically gone to the devil," said
Jarman in his blunt outspoken way ; "he got a touch
of the sun about a year ago."

"I never heard of that."

"I'm not surprised at that ; it's a wonder you hear
anything in this doggone hole. Well, when Mazarion
came round again the pace was faster than ever. I
can't help thinking that his brain never really righted
itself ; but he acted like a fool, and a madman, and a
blackguard combined—with the usual result."

"You don't mean to say he's broken !"

"About as good as broke. Government is long-
suffering, but in common decency they couldn't over-
look the things Mazarion did. They've given him a
chance, however. He's had six months' sick leave to
settle his affairs, and he's cleared off to some hill station
or other in India."

So it had come to this. And late that night I took the
bull by the horns and wrote to Mrs. Carstairs, telling
her exactly how things were, and in the morning my
heart failed me and I tore up that letter and wrote another one to Nelly, in which all that I said of Mazarion
was that he had gone on leave to the Indian hills ; and
this letter I posted.

I little knew how near the time was when I should
go myself. My tour of service in Burma was coming
to an end, and that end was hastened by the rice-

swamps of Henzada. A medical certificate did the rest, and within the month I was ordered to India, and, best of good luck, to a Himalayan station. In a fortnight I was out of Burma—in India—in the Himalayas.

How I enjoyed that journey from the plains ! How strength seemed to come back by leaps and bounds as we rushed through the belt of forest that girdled the mountains, past savannahs of waving yellow tiger-grass, through purple-blossomed ironwood and lilac jerrol, through stretches of bamboo jungle in every shade of colour, with their graceful tufts of culms a hundred feet and more from the ground, through giant sal and toon woods whose sombre foliage was lightened by the orange petals of the palas, and the blazing crimson bloom of the wax-like flowers of the silk cotton ! Higher still, and the tropical forest is now but a hazy green sea that quivers uneasily below. Now the hedge-rows are bright with dog-roses, and the shade is the shade of oak and birch and maple. In the long restful arcades of the forest, by the edges of the trickling mountain springs, the sward is gay with amaranth and marguerite, the pimpernel winks its blue eyes from beneath its shelter of tender green, and a hundred other nameless woodland flowers spangle the glades. Higher still and the whole wonder of the Himalayas is around me, one rolling mass of green, purple, and azure mountains, with a horizon of snow-clad peaks standing white and pure against the perfect blue of the sky.

There was a window at the club which used to be my favourite seat, for it commanded a matchless view, and it was here that I used to sit and positively drink in strength with every puff of fresh, pure air that came in past the roses clustering on the trelliswork outside. A friend joined me—one who like myself had escaped to the hills after wrecking his health in a Burman swamp. He had known Mazarion, and somehow the conversation turned upon him, and Paget asked me to step with him into the hall. Once there he pointed to a small board which I had noticed before, but never had the curiosity to examine. On that board was posted the name of John Mazarion as a defaulter.

"He has gone under utterly," said Paget as we regained our seats, "for this is not all that has happened."

"Could anything be worse?"

"Well, I rather think so. Do you know the man has flung away all shame and has gone to live like a beastly Bhootea—a hill man—a savage on the mountain side?"

"What!"

Why, every one knows it here. It happened about three months ago—just after that affair," and he indicated the board in the hall with a turn of his hand.

"The man must be mad."

"Not he; only he hasn't pluck enough to blow his brains out. He's not alone either, but has taken a wife —a Bhootea woman. They're not far off from here— over there on that spur," and he pointed to a wooded arm of the mountains that stood out above a grey rolling mist.

"My God!" and I put my head between my hands. "The cad! the worthless brute!" I burst out. "See here, Paget: perhaps you're wrong—perhaps this story isn't true?"

Paget carefully dusted a speck from his coat-sleeve.

"I know what you're thinking of, Thring. That girl
at home. I heard something about the affair. I used to
feel inclined to kick him when I saw her picture in his
rooms at Rangoon beside that of the other one—you
know whom I mean.   Yes, it's all true, and you can go
and see if you like.   The Boothea girl is called Rani ;
she's devilish pretty.   It's the 'squalid savage' business,
you know ; but the man is a moral hog—damn him ! "

Saying this, Paget, who was a good fellow after his
kind, lit another cigar, and nodding his head in farewell
went off to the billiard-room, and I sat still—thinking,
thinking, with fury and shame in my heart. At last
I could endure it no longer, and then suddenly rose
and walked to my rooms—I lived in the club. I was
hardly conscious of what I did, but I remember ordering
my pony, and then my eyes fell on a case containing
a small pair of dainty revolvers.   I took them mechanically from their velvet-lined beds, loaded them carefully, and slipped them in a courier-bag.   Then I
mounted the pony and rode off to find Mazarion. The
road was longer than I thought ; but it seemed as if
some instinct guided me—some power, I know not what,
was over me, and led my steps straight to my goal.

It is curious how in moments like this unimportant
and trivial incidents impress themselves on the mind.
I remember tying the pony to a white rhododendron,
and that in so doing I dropped my cigar. It was the
only one I had, and it lay smouldering before me,
crosswise on the petals of one of the huge lemon-scented
flowers that had fallen from the tree. I kicked it
from me, and then went onwards on foot. In about
half an hour I came to a little tableland of greensward,

which hung over a grey abyss. Huge black pines rose stiffly on the rocks that beetled over the level turf, and to the edge of the rocks there clung, like a wasp's nest, a wretched hut, with a thin blue smoke rising from between the rafters of its moss-grown roof.

It was touching sunset, and the west was a blaze of crimson and gold. The face of the pine-covered crag towering above me was in black shadow; but the mellow light was bright on the green turf at my feet. It cast a ruddy glow over the withered trunk of a huge fallen pine that lay athwart the open, and then fell in long rainbow-hued shafts on the uneasy mists that filled the valley, and stole up the mountain side in soft-rolling billows of purple, of grey, and of silver-white. The pine trunk was not ten paces from me, and walking up to it I took out the pistols from the courier-bag and placed them on the rough bark, and from their resting-place the polished barrels glinted brightly in the evening light. I knew I was near my man, and if ever there was an excuse for doing what I meant to do, I had that defence. As I stood there, one hand on the tree trunk and still as a stone, a red tragopan crept out from the yellow-berried bramble at the edge of the steep. For a moment we looked at one another, and then he dropped his blue-wattled head an was off like a flash, and at the same instant there was a scream and a rush of wings, as a homing eagle dropped like a falling stone over the pines, and whizzing past me was lost to view. I walked to the edge of the precipice over which he had flown to his eyrie on the face of the cliffs below; I could see nothing but that heaving swell of billows, and now some one laughed—a sweet, melodious laugh like the tinkling of a silver bell. I turned sharply, and Rani stood before me. It could be none other than she. Bhootea, savage, Mongol—whatever she was, she was of those whom God had dowered with beauty, and she stood before me a lithe, supple elf of the woods. The rounded outlines of her form were clear through the single garment she wore, clasped by an embroidered zone at the waist, and holding forth a pitcher with a shapely arm, she offered me some spring water to drink. I shook my head, and she laughed again like the song of a bird, and asked in English, speaking slowly :

" You want—my—man ? "

Before I could answer, the door of the hut opened and Mazarion and I had met again.

" You—you ! " and he paled beneath his sunburnt cheeks.

" Even I." And we stared at each other, my temples throbbing and my hands clenched. He was dressed as a native of the hills, in a long loose gabardine, with a cloth wound round his waist. His fair hair hung in an unkempt tangle to his neck, and he had a beard of many weeks' growth. All the beauty had gone from his face, and sin had set the mark of the beast on him ; he had become a savage ; he had gone back five thousand years, to the time when his cave-dwelling ancestors hunted the aurochs and the sabre-toothed tiger. There was that in our gaze which stilled the laughter in Rani's eyes, and she crept closer to him, standing as if to cover him. His head drooped slowly forwards, and the fingers of his hands opened and shut ; he was fighting something within himself.

" Send the woman away," I said. " You know why I

have come," and I pointed to the pistols on the fallen
tree trunk.

Rani saw the gesture. Her glance shifted uneasily
from one to the other of us, and then rested on the
weapons, and now, trembling with an unknown fear,
she clung to her man.

" Send her away. You hear." My own voice came
to me as from a far distance.

He put her aside gently, where she stood shivering in
every limb, and came forwards a step.

" I cannot," he said thickly, and speaking with an
effort ; " I cannot—not with you——"

" I will force you to." I spoke calmly enough, but
there was a red mist before my eyes and a drumming in
my ears. Fool that I was to think that God would give
His vengeance to my hands ! And then I struck
him where he stood, struck him twice across the face,
and with a cry like that of a mad beast he was on
me.

We were both strong men, and he was fighting for
his life ; but I—I had the strength of ten then ; all the
pent-up rage of years was roaring within me, and there
was a pitiless hate in my heart. I would kill him like
the unclean thing he was should be killed. With all
my force I struck him again and again, and I felt as if
something crashed under the blow. We fell together
and rose again, and with a mighty effort I flung him
from me. He staggered to his feet, his face white and
bleeding, his blue lips hissing curses. He was then
facing me, his back but a yard from the edge of the
abyss, against which the mists were beating like a grey
sea. He read the meaning in my look, and made one

last struggle, one last rush for safety, but I hit him fair
on the forehead, and he threw up his arms with a gasp,
staggered back a pace, and was gone. Far below there
sounded something like a dull thud and a cry, and then
all was still. Nelly was avenged.

It was all over. I could see nothing as I peered into
the mist before me, and then I was brought to myself by
the sound of sudden sobbing, and there was Rani
stretched on the grass and plucking at the turf like a
mad thing. She was a woman after all, and, poor, wild
waif of the jungles, hers was no sin and no wrong. But
her sobs and the agony on her face brought on a sudden
revulsion and a horror at my deed. It was as sudden,
as swift, as the tumult of passions which had driven
me to kill the man, and now the blackness of night
had settled on my soul. I made no attempt at speech
with the woman, but silently took up the pistols, gave
one last shivering glance at the deep and at the pros-
trate figure of Rani, and then fled through the forest,
my one thought to put miles between me and my deed.
By the time I had found the pony and mounted him
I was able to reflect a little, and it was with a guilty
start that I realized there was a witness, and—and—
But the place was a lonely one. And Rani—would her
word count against mine ? Never ! And then I laughed
shrilly and galloped on.

I reached the club just in time to dress for dinner.
Strange ! I could not bear the thought of being alone—
I who had lived for a year at a time a solitary. I
dressed in haste, and as I came out my servant handed
me my letters—the English mail had just come in, he
said. I would have flung them from me, but that the

first letter in my hand was in Mrs. Carstairs' writing. With a vague presentiment of evil I opened and read. Nelly was ill, Nelly was dying. Some fool had told her of John Mazarion, and had killed her as surely as with the stroke of a knife. As I read, the lines blurred one into the other, and something seemed to give way in my brain. I rose and staggered as one drunken, and then—and then, strong man as I was, I fainted and remember no more.

It was a long illness. I do not know what the doctors called it ; but they pulled me through, as they thought. It was another thing, however, that cured me. I remember how, when my brain first righted itself, the awful memory of Mazarion's end came back again and sat over me like a dreadful vampire. Each whispered word of the nurses in attendance on me, each noise I heard, seemed to presage the announcement that my guilt was known. One day I asked the nurse whether I had been delirious, and what I had said.

She flushed a little. She was a good woman, and an untruth was hateful to her. Then she fenced :

" Oh, one always says strange things in delirium ; but you're getting quite strong now, and Captain Paget is coming to see you to-day. It was he who found you insensible, and he has been as good as any ten of us——"

" Paget—Paget found me ? "

She put her finger to her lips and a cool hand on my eyes, and I seemed to fall asleep.

How long I slept I cannot quite say, but I became conscious of whispering voices in the room.

" There's no doubt about it, and it's his only chance,

I think. Just give him the news quietly when he awakes. Yes, he may have a glass of port before."

I lay still, but trembling under my covers. It had come at last. Oh, the shame of it ! the sin of it !—I a common murderer. It was too much, and I tried to start up, but fell back weakly, and saw Paget sitting by the bed, smiling kindly at me.

"Not yet, old man—in a day or so. Take this port, will you ?"

I drank it with an effort ; but it warmed me and gave me strength.

"You're to be shipped home in a few days—lucky beggar ! Wouldn't mind getting ill myself if I could get leave."

I smiled in spite of myself.

"That's right. Feeling better, I see. We had another interesting patient also, but he cleared out a week or so ago from hospital. It was that fellow Mazarion. Remember him ?"

"Mazarion !"

"Yes. Fell over the edge of a precipice and on to a ledge of rock. Got his fall broken somehow by the branches of a tree, and the wild raspberry bushes, or he'd have been in Kingdom Come—eh ? What ?"

"Thank God !" I felt a load lifted from my heart, the shadows had passed from my soul. I lay back, my eyes closed and a peace upon me. And then I prayed for the first time in many a long day, and whilst I prayed I fell once more asleep. There came to me in that sleep a dream of Nelly—of Nelly robed in white with a glory around her, and she smiled and beckoned me to come.

Well, I was once more in England, and because she wished it I was allowed to see Nelly. She lay on her cushions very pale and white, but for the red spot on each cheek, and an unnatural brightness of the eyes. I knew it was a matter of time, and all that we could do was to wait and hope.

It came at last, one dreary evening, when the lamps were burning dimly in the streets through the ceaseless, insistent drizzle. I cannot linger over this or my heart would break. We stood by her, sad and silent, waiting for the end. It was not long in coming. She had been as it were asleep, when suddenly she awoke and her voice was strong with the strength of death. She called to me :

" Mr. Thring, you know that story about John. Is —is it true ? "

Oh, the chattering ape who had killed her ! Her mother's eyes met mine ; but I could see nothing but Nelly—Nelly looking at me with a wistful entreaty. I could not ; right or wrong, I could not.

" It is not true, dear. He will come back to you."

" Say that again."

" He will come back to you, Nelly."

" He must follow," and she closed her eyes with a sweet smile on her lips.

Then my dear's hand went out to clasp mine in thanks, and I held the chill fingers in my grasp.

" Mother—kiss me. John—you will come," and she was gone.

*   *   *   *   *

I had stolen out of the house, leaving them with their

dead. As I closed the gate, and stepped on to the pavement a ragged figure came out of the mist and, standing beside the lamp-post, looked towards the house and the drawn blinds. The light fell on the wasted form and haggard features. I could not mistake ; it was John Mazarion.

I went up to him and touched him on the shoulder. He started back and stared at me vacuously.

" She lies there dead," I said.

" Dead ! "

" Ay, dead. She died with your name on her lips."

He looked at me stupidly. Then something like a sob burst from him, and with bowed head and shambling steps he turned, and crossing the road went from my life.

THE END.